Like the Ladies  It was not
large, no more ower that
shimmered in it f. Its heart
was a burning g glass and
matrix, fire and

"I'm ready," she said steadily.

His nod became a bow. His hands rose. He gathered the light of that place and spun it before her, until she looked down on the orb of the world.

Averil traced the lines of magic across the living earth, straight lines of leys and curving lines of the power of life and spirit that every living thing fed on—and, woven throughout, the wildness that was never far from the surface of any living place. Westward between the cold sea and the mountains, it was strongest; it sang to her, luring her away from the strait-ened path of order and discipline.

She wrenched her mind away before the wildness consumed it. There was nothing here that she had not seen before; such living maps as these were commonplace in the acolytes' schoolroom. This was larger, that was all, and more intricately wrought. It was a work of art in its own right.

Then it changed. Maybe Bernardin had altered the spell, or maybe this was part of its magic. The land turned to glass. Great shapes moved beneath, a slow shifting of coils and a gleam of scales.

She shuddered, but she had no power to escape from the vi-sion. It changed again, to what at first she thought must be an invasion of ants. Then she realized they were men—armies.

They spread like a stain of blood, welling up from the heart of Lys, where a city lay athwart its river: golden Lutèce with its sixty towers and its royal chapel that rivaled the Ladies' chapel on the Isle in its power and glory. Now there was a canker in its heart.

The Serpent and the Rose

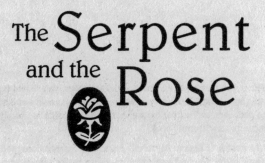

KATHLEEN BRYAN

A TOM DOHERTY ASSOCIATES BOOK
NEW YORK

This is a work of fiction. All of the characters, organizations, and events portrayed in this novel are either products of the author's imagination or are used fictitiously.

THE SERPENT AND THE ROSE

Map by Jackie Aher

A Tor Book
Published by Tom Doherty Associates, LLC
175 Fifth Avenue
New York, NY 10010

www.tor.com

Tor® is a registered trademark of Tom Doherty Associates, LLC.

ISBN-13: 978-0-7653-5174-6
ISBN-10: 0-7653-5174-9

First Edition: March 2007
First Mass Market Edition: February 2008

Printed in the United States of America

0 9 8 7 6 5 4 3 2 1

*For the Duc de Berry and
the artists of the Sainte-Chapelle,
without whom this book could not exist*

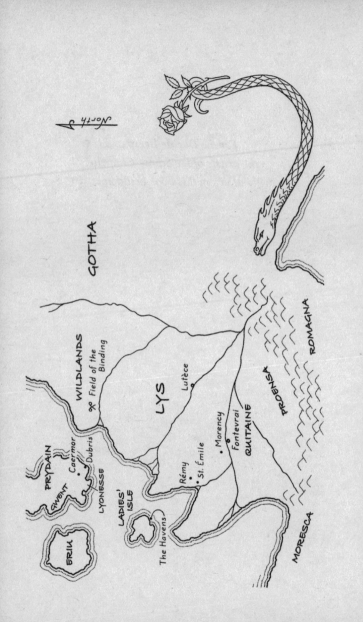

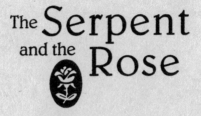

The Serpent and the Rose

PRELUDE

The chapel was made of light. Its walls were white stone, translucent, drinking sunlight by day and the moon's light by night. Its floor was a pavement of mosaics, shimmering tesserae of glass and gold and precious stones. But its brilliance—its glory—filled every window: shards of jeweled glass that ascended from floor to vaulted ceiling in a fabric of living light.

The light sang. It was an eerie song, almost too high to hear, like the shiver of crystal. To Averil it was perfectly clear, although no one else seemed aware of it.

She could hear it even through the chanting of sweet high voices, Ladies of the Isle and their acolytes singing the morning office. She knew the words by heart. They were so familiar that all the meaning was gone from them, subsumed into the place and the light and magic that pervaded it.

The music poured out of her, with no part of her mind on it. Her eyes were dazzled with light.

From where she sat in the choir, the dark carved wood of the screen had the weight of earth beneath the soaring beauty of the enchanted glass. The image there was as familiar as the words of the office, but something in the morning light made it all new.

A tree grew out of emerald-green grass, with twisted trunk and gnarled branches. Apples grew on the branches, red and gold and green. The sky was supernally blue.

Only slowly, if one rested one's eyes on the glass and let them slip from focus, did the subtler image come clear. In the twisted trunk and knotted branches was a shimmering shape, a coil of scales winding upward through the tree. High up, almost to the rayed gold of the sun, the shadow of the tree's top resolved itself into a serpent's head. Its fanged jaws gripped the silver apple of the moon.

Averil shivered. It was part of her instruction to find and study every work of magic or the maker's art on this island, but this disturbed her in more ways than she could easily understand.

The morning office ended. Ladies and acolytes left the chapel in procession, a line of white robes and grey.

Averil stayed where she was. There were glances—she felt them brushing past her—but meditation between sacred offices was permitted.

She did not know if she would call it that. She rose from her stall in the choir and walked slowly toward the altar. It was banked with spring flowers; their fragrance washed over her.

All her senses were heightened, so that the flowers' sweetness was as sharp as pain. She raised her eyes above the altar. Under the glowing wheel of the rose window, the great triptych told its tale in shards of light. On the right hand, twelve Knights stood armed with sword and spear and shield, and on each shield was a blood-red rose. On the left hand, twelve Ladies stood robed in white, in each right hand a white rose, and in each left hand a staff of power.

In the center was the great rite and sacrifice, the Young God locked in battle with the Serpent. Red blood and black streamed from a thousand wounds. Grey coils writhed around golden armor. White fangs gleamed, dripping blue-green venom. The Young God stabbed with a broken sword. The Serpent struck at the vulnerable throat.

Its eye was gold, the exact color of the Young God's armor. It rolled toward Averil.

She gasped. Her knees ached: she had fallen to the floor.

The spell was broken. The Serpent was neither alive nor free. It was only glass in the window above her, colored and painted and sealed with magic.

She could still feel that awareness on her. The shock was not that it was evil beyond evil, chaos incarnate—but that it was not. It was old, yes—ancient. But there was deep wisdom in it, and a subtle humor.

She wrenched her mind away from thoughts so blasphemous they made her stomach heave. That was the Serpent's evil: lies and temptation. She was an acolyte of the Isle of Glass, heir to the Twelve Ladies who had guarded the Young God and bound the Serpent in its agelong prison, descendant by blood of the First Paladin, the blessed Longinus, whose spear had pierced the Serpent and made it vulnerable to the Young God's stroke. She should resist every temptation.

That was easier said than done. She turned her back resolutely on the chapel that had become so suddenly and strangely perilous.

1

The hayrick exploded in a swirl of straw and dust and squawking chickens. The yard dogs yelped and fled with their tails between their legs; the bull bellowed in his pen.

Gereint stood in the middle of the whirlwind, eye to eye with a shape as insubstantial as it was powerful. He had an impression of wings and fangs and eyes—a hundred eyes, each different from the next, and all fixed on him. Studying him. Reducing him to absolute insignificance.

God knew, he was used to that. "My apologies," he said as politely as he knew how. "I didn't mean to disturb you."

The whirlwind plucked at his hair with unexpectedly gentle fingers, running them through it, then tugging on the tail of his shirt. It seemed more amused than not. When he bowed, it rippled in what might have been laughter. Then it scattered, dividing into a hundred tiny breezes. They danced through the barnyard and set the remains of the hayrick to spinning before, with a sigh, they fluttered to the ground.

"Gereint."

His mother's voice was quiet. That was much more disturbing than a full-throated bellow. He turned slowly, shedding bits of hay. "I was only trying to—"

"Don't say it," she said.

But he had to. Not that she would ever understand, but he never stopped trying. "I was going to feed the cows, and I thought, you know, if the hay could move itself, how much more time I'd have to milk them. I didn't mean to—"

"You never do," said Enid.

A great anger was rising in him. It was years old and miles

deep, and he had been throttling it down for as long as he could remember. He dared not let it loose. It was bad enough that he had scattered a month's worth of hay all over creation.

A very small part of it escaped him. Words, that was all they were. Nothing else. "If you would let me learn how to control this thing—if you would just acknowledge that I have it—"

It was no use. Her face had shut down, just as it always did. "Now you have the yard to rake as well as the cows to milk and feed. Salvage what hay you can. It can go for bedding if it's too far gone for anything better."

"Mother," he said. He knew it was futile, but if he did not say it, the top of his head was going to fly off. "Mother, for once in your life, please listen. It's happening more often, and it's getting worse. You can't just keep on ignoring it."

"Rake," she said. "Feed. Milk." Then she was gone, back to hitching up the wagon. It was market day, and she had a stall to tend.

The thing inside Gereint was so strong he could barely see. There was a buzzing in his ears and a drumming in his skull. He prayed he could keep it from bursting loose.

It helped to focus on raking and feeding and milking. If Enid had been there, she would have pointed to that as proof that she was right. He could control the thing inside—the magic.

She refused to say the word. He said it aloud with his cheek pressed to the brown cow's side. "Magic. Magic, magic, magic. I am so full of magic I don't know what to do. And she won't— even—admit that I have it."

The cow lowed in protest. He had milked her dry. He rubbed her forehead in apology, swung the full bucket onto the milk cart and went on to the next.

AFTER THE COWS were milked, there was plowing to do in the lower field. Gereint very deliberately thought of nothing but keeping the mule straight in the furrow and making that furrow as straight and deep as it should be.

He noticed rather distantly that the early morning sun had

faded and a chill wind had begun to blow. It was still spring, after all, and the weather could be treacherous. When the first drops of rain fell, they stung, as if the heart of each was sleet.

He had half the field plowed. He pondered another furrow, but the northern horizon was blue-black. The mule's long ears had gone flat. She knew what that meant; she could smell it.

He left the plow in the furrow and unhitched her as fast as his rapidly freezing fingers would move. The rain was heavier now, mixed with spits of snow. He scrambled onto the mule's back and let her have her head.

The last few furlongs were a nightmare of screaming wind and blinding snow. The mule stopped so abruptly that Gereint somersaulted over her head, fetching up against the barn door.

He picked himself up, cursing under his breath, and fumbled at the bolt. The wind ripped the door out of his hands and slammed it against the wall. The mule bolted past him.

He got a grip on the door and threw all his weight against it. The wind hammered at him. He roared at it—flinging all his anger and frustration into its icy teeth.

He could have sworn it was startled. It retreated just long enough for him to get the door shut and bolted before it struck like a battering ram.

The panels were oak, and had stood up to spring storms for a hundred years. They held. He stood in the dim stillness of the barn, in the warm smell of the cows, and scraped himself together as best he could.

The mule was as wet and frozen as he was. He rubbed her down and fed her a handful of barley and an armful of scavenged hay, then threw a blanket over her. When her shivering had stopped, his had barely begun. He nerved himself to face the storm again and cross the few yards between the barn and the house.

HIS MOTHER WAS not yet back from the village. If he was lucky, she would be stormbound until tomorrow. He was not sure he trusted himself with her just now.

He stirred up the fire, stripped off his wet clothes and put on dry ones, and warmed a mug of milk with honey. The wind shrieked in the eaves. There would be thatch to renew, he judged, when this was over; but for now he was dry and warm and out of the storm.

Alone, with no one to see, he let himself play with the fire, running his hands through the flames. They were warm, but not enough to burn; they felt like leaves of grass or quick cat-tongues, curling around his fingers. Idly he began to weave them, shaping them into a glimmering skein.

There was something else he could do, something he could draw out of air, some force or substance that he could shape into—what? He could not grasp it. The fire-weaving unraveled. He pulled back quickly before the flames scorched his hand.

Frustration was rising again. There was so much he did not know, that his mother would not let him know. Every time the magefinders came to test the young ones for their orders, she sent him somewhere out of the way and forbade him to have anything to do with those strange and glittering men and women. "Your life is here," she said. "There's no need for you to look elsewhere. You're born to farm this land, and you will farm it. I won't have you breaking your heart trying to be something you were never meant to be."

But that was just what he was doing. The closer to manhood he came, the more his body grew and changed, the stronger his magic became. He felt like a phoenix in a hen's nest, try-ing not to burn it to ash.

The fire roared up the chimney. He had a moment's power-ful temptation to let it take him—so powerful that he nearly let himself go; nearly fell in.

He pulled back in a kind of panic. The fire retreated to its proper bounds. The wind had abated somewhat.

The world seemed to be holding its breath. When the ham-mering began, at first Gereint thought it was some new mani-festation of his magic. Then he realized it was the door, and someone was knocking on it.

His mother would never knock; she would simply come in. It must be some stranger caught in the storm.

Maybe, he thought, it was a magefinder.

He would not dare to hope. He lifted the latch, keeping a good grip in case the wind came back, and opened the door.

A man stood on the step, wrapped in a cloak, with snow thick on his hood and shoulders. Shadows of others stood behind.

Gereint looked inside himself for the tingle of alarm. There was something, like a trickle of heat down his backbone, but he did not sense any danger.

"Messire," said the man on the doorstep, "of your courtesy, may we beg shelter for ourselves and our horses?"

That was not a local accent, or a lowborn one, either. Gereint swallowed past the lump of excitement and said, "Of course, sir. How many horses?"

"Twelve, messire," said the man, "and six men. If you have room in barn or byre—"

"Of course," said Gereint. He retrieved his winter cloak from its hook and wrapped it around him.

THE HORSES WERE soaked and shivering, and the men were in no better case. The storm was closing in again. Gereint herded them all into the horse barn. There was only the mule in it now, with a pair of goats to keep her company; the cart horse had gone to market with Enid.

Twelve horses were a fair crowd, and half of them were stallions—fine glossy beasts under the wet and cold. The rest were geldings, sturdy pack animals who had no objection to being squeezed in two to a stall. They were all well fed, well shod and caparisoned, and the device on every bridle and saddle made Gereint's heart leap nigh out of his breast.

A blood-red rose, embossed on leather or enameled on silver. It was a small thing, deceptively simple, but it meant the world.

These were Knights of the Rose—more than mages, and more by far than simple fighting men. Great arts and powers belonged to them. They were defenders of the realm and protectors of all that was holy. The Young God himself had founded their order. The Twelve Paladins had been its first Knights.

Ever since Gereint was old enough to remember, he had

loved to hear stories about the Knights. Before he outgrew his illusions, he had dreamed of becoming one—before he learned that only noblemen could enter the ranks, and he was as common as the dirt under his feet.

And they were here, in Gereint's mother's barn, rubbing down their horses and feeding them oats and barley from their own stores and hay from the loft. It was almost more than Gereint could bear. For a panicked moment he thought of sending them back out into the storm—not far, just to the next farm, but far enough that he would not have to face them.

That would be cowardice, not to mention murder. He could endure them for a night. Just to remind himself of what dreams were—and of what he could never hope to be.

They seemed human enough, and not averse to work, either. When they professed themselves content to bed down in the loft above the horses, Gereint heard himself say, "Oh, no. There's room in the house, and my mother would box my ears if she thought I'd made guests sleep in the barn."

"By all means, we must not have that," said the oldest of them. He was a lean grey wolf of a man, but the lines around his eyes and mouth spoke more of laughter than of sternness.

One or two of his men might have demurred even so, but his glance brought them to order. "We're safe here," he said, "and the horses are in comfort. I for one will be glad to sleep warm and dry tonight." He bowed to Gereint and smiled. "You have our thanks, messire."

Gereint blushed and tried not to fall over his own feet. He mumbled something, he hardly cared what, and led them all back through the snow to the house.

2

The storm raged unabated through all the rest of that day and into the night. Gereint's guests ate spring lamb roasted with herbs and drank the strong dark ale Enid brewed herself, and shared loaves of brown hearth bread that they declared was better than the bread in the houses of their order.

"Though maybe not as good as what they bake on the Isle," said the youngest. He was younger than Gereint and somewhat outspoken. His name was Ademar.

"You've been to the Ladies' Isle?" Gereint asked.

Ademar nodded. "Nobody goes over the mountain to the secret places, but we often visit the port and the harbor."

Gereint sighed. "I've never been even a day's walk outside of Rémy," he said.

"I've been everywhere," said Ademar. "After a while, every place looks alike. All the chapter houses are built to the same pattern, imitations in greater or lesser scale of the mother house in Fontevrai. The land changes, but less than you might think. The whole world is just like everywhere else."

"But the bread is better on the Isle," Gereint said.

Ademar drew himself up, offended, but a sardonic glance from one of his fellows made him duck his head and blush. "He's very young," the older one said—not that he was so very much older himself.

They were, Gereint discovered, two Knights in black and three Squires in deep blue, and Ademar, the youngest, in dark green, which marked him as a Novice. Gereint knew what those ranks meant. Knights were highest, and then Squires, and Novices were initiates who had not yet passed the testing to be members of the order.

They were good company, once he decided to let himself enjoy them. They knew more songs and stories than Gereint had ever heard. And they would talk about magic.

They were mages. They did not speak of that—Gereint did not expect them to; what they did was a great mystery. But they could tell stories about the magic that was in the world, the daimons and spirits and mystical beasts that inhabited it side by side with mortals, and the arts and powers that were common to all orders of mages.

Gereint drank in every word. They hardly made sense to him now, but he remembered each one, to bring out later and study, turning over in his mind like a handful of jewels. They might have to last him for the rest of his life.

He had expected to be glad when a glance from the eldest brought them all to their feet, but he was not. It was all he could do not to beg them to stay with him for yet a while. Of course they could not. It was late; they had a long way to go.

Gereint stayed by the fire as they went up to bed, staring into the embers. A shadow fell across him. The younger Knight, who had said very little all evening, was standing over him.

He scrambled to his feet. "Messire?" he said. "Is there something I can get for you?"

The Knight shook his head. His name, Gereint had heard from the others, was Mauritius. "I have a question," he said. "If it's a dire insult, you're free not to answer."

Gereint was taller than the Knight. Lately, he was taller than most people—a great gawk, his mother said. Even standing a head higher than this man, he felt small. "I'm hard to offend, messire," he said. "By all means ask."

Mauritius nodded. His eyes were keen, taking in all of Gereint. There was no telling what he thought. "You must be—what? Eighteen, nineteen summers?"

"Sixteen," Gereint said. "I'm big for my age."

One of the black brows twitched upward. "Indeed. You speak of a mother. Your father—dead?"

"I never had one," Gereint said steadily. "I'm godborn."

The brow rose again, somewhat higher. "Your mother needs you here, I can see. I presume that is why you were never tested for one of the orders."

Gereint's chest was tight. "She said there was no need. Magic, like the glass that makes it, is for the wealthy. We are honest farmers. We belong on the land."

Mauritius frowned. "There's no glass at all here. Not in the windows, not in cup or jar, not even a bit of enamel to ornament a plate. It's not poverty, I can see that—you're clearly prosperous. Is she afraid of magic, then?"

"She doesn't believe in it," Gereint said. "She says there's no point in it. It's useless glamour and expensive foolery."

"I see," said Mauritius. His tone was colorless. "You should, if you can possibly gain her consent, present yourself to be tested. Power unrestrained is deadly dangerous, and power such as yours . . ." He shook his head. "For your own safety, lad."

Gereint could hardly breathe. Getting the words out was almost more than he could do. "Are you telling me—are you saying I have—"

"I haven't tested you," Mauritius said, "and this is not the place or the time—but you brought us in from the storm. You're like a beacon in the dark. How often is it breaking loose? More lately?"

Gereint opened his mouth, then shut it again. "I don't—I'm not—"

"The older you get," said Mauritius, "the stronger it grows, the harder it is to control. Have you heard of wild mages?"

Gereint shook his head.

"Thank the good God," Mauritius said, "they're very few. They burn out, most of them, before they damage anyone but themselves. But those that do . . ." He shivered. "Get yourself tested, boy. At least find a priest who can teach you wards and bindings. Rein it in before it runs off with you."

"What if I'm not allowed?" Gereint asked, so low he almost hoped he was not heard.

The Knight's ears were sharp. "Then you should consider

her safety as well. Get it done, learn to control it, or you'll go up like a torch."

Gereint sucked in a breath. "How strong am I? Can you tell?"

"Strong," Mauritius said. He looked Gereint hard in the face. "You're not crowing about it. Good. That means there's hope. Let it scare you—and learn how to master it."

"I hope I can," Gereint said.

Mauritius clapped him on the shoulder—startling him into speechlessness. "I think you can, if you do it soon enough. I'd hardly urge a son to go against his mother's wishes, but when the magefinders come through this summer, seek them out and give them my name. Tell them what I told you. They'll find a way."

Hope was such an unfamiliar thing that Gereint hardly recognized it. He hunted for words to thank this man who had given him so great a gift, but Mauritius was already gone.

Gereint almost wondered if he had been there at all, but the Knight's presence lingered, dissipating slowly. It had a clarity to it, like light shining through glass: red and gold and green and a flash of breathtaking blue.

Gereint blinked. He had never seen that way before— straight through the world, as if it were made of glass itself— and yet it felt like the most natural thing imaginable. As if he had been as blind as a newborn kitten, but now his eyes were open and he could see.

He curled up by the fire, since his own room was full of Knights and magic. The embers died slowly. Memories were unfolding in his head. Fire and magic; wind and storm and a riding of Knights.

He was coming to a decision. It needed time. He was almost afraid to face it, for fear he would wake and find it all a dream.

That would be cruel. But Gereint knew the world was not kind. His mother had taught him that, though she would say she was only trying to protect him. Against what, she never said.

She would be back as soon as the roads were clear. The wind

had died down some while since, and the snow had thinned considerably. By morning it would have ended. The sun would come, strong with spring, and melt the snow. By evening it would all be gone.

The Knights would be gone then, too. And the bars of Gereint's cage would close in. He would burn inside them until there was nothing left, not even a drift of ash.

THE KNIGHTS LEFT in the morning. The road was knee-deep with snow, but the sun was bright and their errand was urgent. Gereint watched them ride out of the farmyard on their glossy stallions, with their pack train behind them.

Whatever was in those panniers, they set great store by it. There was a sheen on it like a coating of ice or clear glass.

Those were wards, he thought. He had never seen anything like them before, but somehow he recognized them.

The whole world looked different this morning, and not only because of the snow. Mauritius' words had awakened something in Gereint. Or maybe it was the Knights' presence here where magic—Gereint's aside—was never allowed to come. Even the village wisewoman stayed away; the animals delivered their young without her help, and when Gereint or Enid or one of the hired hands in season was hurt or sick, she dosed them with her own concoctions and left the rest to God.

Now he knew why. He was changing so rapidly inside that he hardly knew himself. Parts of him were opening that he had not even known he had.

The Knights were almost over the hill. A few more moments and they would be out of sight.

His mother was coming down the other road. He could not have said how he knew. It was like everything else this morning: so new he did not understand it. The Knights would be out of sight before she came close enough to see.

Gereint bolted into the house. He scrambled together whatever he could find—a change of clothes, his new boots, a few oddments and the little bag of coins that he had been saving for the end of the world.

This was the end of the world he had known. He wrapped everything in his good wool cloak, along with a loaf of yesterday's bread and a thick wedge of cheese. Last of all he thrust his hunting knife in with the rest, in the leather sheath he had made for it.

He slung the makeshift pack behind him. All the stock were fed and the morning chores were done. His mother would find nothing to fault when she came back, except his absence.

He almost gave it up and stayed. But the Knights were gone and the sun was climbing, taking the snow with it. He set off at the same steady lope that carried him on the track of the red deer in autumn.

It felt as if he were shedding his skin—sloughing off his name and family and the whole dragging weight of the farm, scale by scale. At the top of the hill he paused to draw breath. The Knights were halfway across the valley, headed for the river and the bridge. He took a deep breath and set off after them.

3

Duke Urien's messenger stood in the Lady's receiving room where no man had been in all the years since Averil came to the Isle. He had the grace to look uncomfortable as well as ungainly: rough and bearded and clashing in armor in that place of light and peace.

His presence was a shock but not a surprise. Averil was here on sufferance, to learn but not to stay. Her proper place, ordained for her by birth and duty, was in the Duchy of Quitaine in the kingdom of Lys.

He had come to call her back to it. It was rude, she knew too well, but she did not wait for him to speak. "Yes," she said before she lost her courage. "I'll come."

He blinked, opened his mouth, then shut it again. "Time is short, lady. Your father asks that you come soon."

"Is he ill?" she asked. "Is he dying?" As she spoke, she felt an altogether unexpected pang of the heart. She hardly knew her father: he had sent her away soon after she learned to walk.

Still, he was her father. Blood called to blood.

But the messenger shook his head. "He was well when I left him, lady. Nevertheless, the sooner you can come, the better for us all."

Averil glanced at the Lady who sat silent, watching. The Lady's expression did not change.

"Tomorrow," Averil said. "In the morning. I'll be ready."

The messenger bowed again, lower than before. His gratitude washed over her. He had no magic, and therefore no protections; his emotions hung in the air like wisps of smoke.

She would have to learn to live among such people, to shield herself because they could not. She had been trained for it all her life. But however long she had prepared, it still came too soon.

The messenger bowed a third time and left in an aura of relief. Averil should go if she was to be ready by morning, but she stayed a moment.

The Lady Margali rose from her chair. She was not tall, but she held herself perfectly erect, so that she seemed to tower over Averil. Her magic was so pure and her mastery so great that she looked like a glass full of light.

Averil bowed for the blessing, but it was not immediately forthcoming. The Lady laid hands on her shoulders and said, "You are sure of this?"

"I have to go," Averil said.

Lady Margali lifted a brow. "You've had a foreseeing?"

Averil shrugged, uncomfortable. "Nothing so lofty. I feel it, that's all."

"What do you feel?"

Averil looked down at her hands. She had been trained in the highest of high magic. She was not supposed to have odd premonitions or peculiar sensations of things that might happen, or could, or would if the stars aligned to make it so. Learned magic indulged in no such fancies. It was all perfectly controlled.

There was wildness in her. She fought it with all the learning she had—but it was not enough. It might never be enough.

She looked up into Lady Margali's face. It was wise and kind. She had always treated Averil fairly, with strictness when that was required, and gentleness when there was need.

She was still the Lady of the Isle, where control was always perfect and magic was contained in the artifice of enchanted glass. Wild magic, magic without law or order, had no place in her world.

Averil put on a smile. It was wobbly, but it steadied. "I've always known I can never take full vows. I'm a Lady of Lys, not of the Isle; my fate is to rule in the world and to marry a man of equal or greater lineage and breed heirs in my turn. I know my duty, Lady. I've never found it in me to refuse it."

"That is true," said the Lady. "It's a pity, in its way. You have great gifts."

"The greater the gift, the more need for control," Averil said. "I've been well taught. When I go, I'll keep the Isle in my heart. All that I learned here, I'll remember."

"I know you will," Lady Margali said. "Go with my blessing, child, and the goodwill of the Isle. If ever you have need, call on us. We will answer."

Averil looked up, startled. That was a great gift. It was never given lightly.

Lady Margali nodded. "I feel it, too. Something is coming. Before you enter Lys, learn all you can of what is happening there. Never go blind into battle."

"You think I'll have to fight?"

"I think the world beyond our walls is a perilous place. Not all is as it seems, and even what is true or honest may twist into falsehood. Look to the Knights for help, and to those they trust. In all else, be wary. Trust no one without surety. Your heart is your best guide, with the knowledge that you gained here. We have trained you for more than the arts of contemplation and peace. In your way, you are as much a warrior as any armored Knight."

"It's going to be bad, isn't it?" Averil said. "Whatever I'm sailing to."

"When you go over the mountain," said Lady Margali, "Knights will be waiting in the Havens. They will instruct you."

That was all she would say. Averil bowed her head one last time.

Lady Margali laid her hands on it in blessing. She spoke no words. All those had been said.

Averil left as the messenger had, because it was time. So simply and so completely, her life on the Isle ended.

BY CUSTOM THERE was no feast of farewell when an acolyte left the Isle for the outer world, but that night's dinner was not the usual fare. The bread was festival bread, baked with herbs and crumbled cheese, and the dull and daily lentils were cooked with garlic and onions and pungent spices. Instead of ale, there was liberally watered wine; and at the end, everyone had a sweet cake and a bit of honeycomb.

It was feast enough for the purpose. Averil's gaze went round the circle of the hall, remembering each face: Lady and acolyte and servant, white gown and grey and homespun brown. Some met her eyes and smiled. She had no will to smile back.

She was no longer required to attend the night office, but when the bell rang, she rose from her hard narrow bed in the dormitory, put on her grey gown for the last time, and joined the procession of acolytes to the chapel. The power of its luminous glass was all but stilled, the tall windows dark. Nothing roused in them that she could sense, except what always woke during these midnight rites: stillness and peace, and heart's ease.

She let it fill her until all her fears slipped away. She could not say she was eager to face what her heart feared was ahead of her, but she was as ready as she could be.

AVERIL WOKE IN the dark before dawn, somewhat surprised that she had slept at all. Two of the servants stood over her cot.

She rose softly and followed them through the rows of sleeping acolytes. For one or two she might have stopped, but if she did, she would not be able to go on.

Her guides led her to the bathhouse, where a basin was waiting and water was steaming over the hearth. They bathed her as if for a high ritual, washed and combed her hair and plaited it more elaborately than she would ever have done for herself, then dressed her in the clothes to which she must now become accustomed. White linen shift, so fine it felt like a sin, and embroidered over-shift, and gown of deep blue silk sewn with pearls and crystals on bodice and hem and flowing sleeves. It was so stiff it could stand on its own, and so tight she could hardly breathe.

"It's the latest fashion in Lys, lady," the servant Grane said. Her hands lingered on the silk; she sighed faintly.

Averil bit her tongue before she offered to let the woman have the gown. What possible use it would be for riding on muleback over the mountain and down to the harbor, she could not imagine.

The answer to that was waiting for her when she emerged from the bathhouse. Her father's messenger stood with a company of armed men, all mounted on horses. In the middle of the line was a gilded litter supported between two mules.

Averil shook her head firmly. "Oh, no. I'll do whatever is proper once we're off the Isle, but I am not going over the mountain in that. Give me a horse, or a mule at least, and find me something fit to ride in."

The men exchanged glances. They had been taxing her protections with gusts of emotion that told her she must have grown up well, or at least acceptably pretty. Now she caught a whiff of disapproval from one or two, but the rest looked as if they were fighting back grins.

"A horse," Averil repeated. "Riding gear. Now."

Grane and her sister Gerda were deeply disappointed, but they followed Averil back into the bathhouse and divested her of the ridiculous gown. In its place and with much clucking and fluttering, they dressed her in a gown hardly more practical but with fewer pearls and, particularly to the point, a skirt divided for riding.

They made it clear that was the best Averil could expect. She determined to order properly useful riding clothes at the earliest opportunity. In the meantime she mounted the placid gelding that was waiting, while the man who had been riding him settled—with surprisingly little disgruntlement—for one of the mules.

Then they could go. The sun was just coming up, casting long light across the valley and staining the mountain walls with gold and red.

The sunrise chant echoed sweetly from the chapel. Averil's heart sang the words as she so well remembered them. They carried her out of the Ladies' shrine and through the grove and past orchards in full and dizzying bloom, down along the edge of the lake.

Then in silence, with morning light growing bright around her, she rode up the first steep slope onto the mountain's knees. The lake gleamed below; the spires of the chapel were a jagged jewel beside it.

Already she was too far away to see the procession out of the chapel or the Ladies seeking out their day's duties. All of that was gone, withdrawn into memory.

Averil faced forward. It was a long way up the mountain and a long way in the heart from this world to the one she had been born to.

For a moment she quailed. She could not do this. She was not fit for it. She knew nothing but the Isle and its secrets.

Her father had abandoned her here when she was a tiny child, casting her off in grief after her mother's death. She knew him through letters—one each year, stiffly formal and full of learned instruction—and such stories as her teachers knew, and a portrait in enamelwork that he had sent her for her name-day when she was nine years old. For years she had hoped that he would find another duchess and breed a more welcome heir, but he had no eyes for any woman but his lost Alais.

Now this near-stranger had called her back, and forces were moving in the world that she barely had the wits to comprehend. She was a girl, a child, fifteen summers old. What did she know of anything that mattered?

She straightened her back and lifted her chin. She knew how to learn—and that, as her teachers had taught her, was the key to everything. She would listen and study and use what skills she had. She would master that world as she had mastered this.

Already they were halfway up the first ascent. There were three more, each steeper than the last, and then the summit, where the Ladies' power rose in a wall of light that none but those they accepted could pass. Averil could see it above her with eyes of the spirit, as transparent as the clearest glass—but light shifted subtly along it and made it visible.

That was the edge of the world she knew. Everything beyond it was strange.

She was ready. She had to be. This was not a choice. It was what she had been born for and what she was trained to do.

4

The Havens lay within a circle of stone. The Isle dropped sheer into the sea on all of its sides save only here, somewhat west of south, where a long curve of black sand slanted upward onto a rolling level.

The harbor was deep and sheltered, calm even in the worst of the winter storms. In the days when Romagna's empire ruled the world, its workmen had built the sea-wall and stretched a chain across the harbor's mouth.

The wall was still there. So was the chain, sunk in the seabed but protected by works of magic. If it was ever needed, it would rise and bar entry to the enemy's fleet.

There had been no such invasion for time out of mind. The old port city had shrunk until half of it was in ruins; the rest was built over with makeshifts and odd bits of flotsam. In the past few reigns of kings in Lys, the city had begun to grow again and take on new beauty.

When Averil came to the Havens from the inner Isle, she found an odd match of crumbling age and raw newness. Spires rose on the eastern edge: a newly built cathedral of the Young God. Like the city itself, it was half raw stone and half scaffolding.

The streets were full of people: makers and builders, traders, seafarers and the odd pirate. Averil, riding among them in her ring of armed guards, heard a babble of tongues. Some she recognized, but most she did not.

There were almost no women. Those few she did see were dressed like servants, or else leaned out of upper windows or idled in doorways, displaying a telling quantity of breast and leg.

Outrage gusted through her. This was the Ladies' Isle. How dare these creatures taint it with their presence?

She met a pair of painted eyes, all afire with indignation, then flushed in sudden shame. These were women, too. How dare she fault them for making their way as best they could?

The whore's ripe lips curled in scorn, but her eyes were tired. Averil gave her what solace she had to offer. It was not much, at speed and at increasing distance, without a burning glass to strengthen it, but it was better than nothing.

She received no thanks for it. She had not expected any. The fact she had done it was enough.

Her escort left the broad thoroughfare that ran down from the mountain and turned into a narrower street. The end of it was the half-grown bulk of the cathedral. Midway along it, they stopped in front of an unprepossessing gate. There was nothing to mark it for a house of any consequence, except the rose carved in the wall above the arch.

The gate opened. Only one man followed Averil within; he held the bridle of her horse while she dismounted, and handed the rein of the mule that carried her bit of baggage to the groom who waited in the courtyard. Then, with a low bow and a murmured word, he left her.

The groom barely glanced at her before he led the horse and the mule away. She stood alone in the sunlit space, listening to the distant clamor of the city.

There were wards here. After a moment she saw where they were set: in the panes of the circular window that looked down on the gate, then sustained in bits of unshaped glass set along the wall in seemingly random order. Each was placed to catch the light in its own particular way.

It was cleverly and beautifully done, in simplicity so pure that it must be the work of a master. She said as much to the man whose step she heard behind her. His startlement brushed her with a faint scent of scorched linen.

She turned. He was a tall man, still black-haired but with his beard gone iron grey, dressed in cotte and hose of black wool.

Like the house, his attire was scrupulously plain. Only the

scarlet rose embroidered on the breast of his tunic indicated what he was: a Knight of the Rose.

She counted six golden thorns on the stem of the rose. He ranked high, then. She met his calm dark eyes and saw there the same power that she had seen in elder Ladies.

He bowed, not too low but low enough for honest respect. "Lady," he said. "My name is Bernardin. I bring greetings from your father and gratitude from us all for deigning to come so quickly."

Averil's brows rose. "Bernardin? Knight Commander of the Rose and Lord Protector of Quitaine? That is an honor."

He bowed again, lower this time. "The honor is mine, lady. Will you come within?"

She inclined her head as a lady should. He led her across the courtyard and through a low door into sudden darkness.

The flash of panic dissipated quickly. There was no danger here—not to Averil. The Knight's presence was clear and strong in front of her.

Slowly her eyes focused. Darkness became lamplight in a passage. At the end of it, a flight of steps ascended to another door.

The door opened on clear daylight in a small but airy room. Bernardin said, "Here you may rest and, if you wish, bathe— the bath is yonder, behind that door. I'll send someone in an hour; then we'll dine."

Averil was not hungry, but in an hour she was sure she would be. She thanked the Knight, then added a smile that made him blink.

She knew better than to laugh at his maiden blushes. Knights were neither cloistered nor necessarily chaste, but like the Ladies, they seldom had time to spare for distraction.

He retreated in good order. She barred the door behind him and dropped her stifling clothes where she stood, then dived into the bliss of a bath.

DINNER WAS PLAIN fare but plenty of it, such as Averil was used to. She shared it with Bernardin and a pair of silent

Squires, served by a Novice who turned scarlet every time her eyes fell on him.

That was growing old very quickly, but Averil could not see what to do about it. Smiling at the boy only made it worse: he nearly poured wine into her lap instead of her cup. He retreated in confusion that she dared not try to soothe lest she reduce him to drooling idiocy.

When Averil had eaten all she could, Bernardin rose and held out his hand. He had an air of anticipation, rigidly and carefully controlled, but enough escaped that she could taste it.

It was sweet and fiery on her tongue. She let him lead her out of the stark plainness of the dining hall, down a long corridor into luminous splendor.

Like the Ladies' chapel, this hall was made of glass. It was not large, no more than nine yards across, but the power that shimmered in it drew its strength from the sun itself. Its heart was a burning glass, warded and shielded in lead: glass and matrix, fire and earth.

If Averil had been alone, she would have taken a long hour to explore the images wrought in enchanted glass on every wall and curving upward into a gleaming vault. There was no stone in this place except the black paving of the floor—and that too was glass, forged deep in earth and cast up from the mountain's heart. The fabric that held the walls together was metal, a work of the Maker's art so intricate and so potent that Averil stood in awe.

Bernardin led her to the center, where a silver rose was inlaid in the floor. "I beg your pardon," he said, "for burdening you with so much so soon—but time is short. We sail with the morning tide. By tomorrow evening we make landfall in Lys, and then time will be shorter still."

With an effort she turned her mind from the glory of that hall to the solid humanity of his face. There was warmth in it but steel beneath. Duty drove him—just as it drove her.

"I'm ready," she said steadily.

His nod became a bow. His hands rose. He gathered the light of that place and spun it before her, until she looked down on the orb of the world.

Slowly it swelled and grew and shifted until she seemed to stand on a high hill over the land of Lys. It was a green country, cut through with the silver lines of rivers. To the west a rampart of mountains divided it from the kingdom of Moresca; in the east a broad river marked the boundary of Gotha, where fertile farmland gave way to deep and haunted forest. North was the cold spume of the sea; blue ocean lapped the shores in the warm and singing south, until the land curved away and another mountain wall dropped sheer to the remnants of Romagna.

Averil traced the lines of magic across the living earth, straight lines of leys and curving lines of the power of life and spirit that every living thing fed on—and, woven throughout, the wildness that was never far from the surface of any living place. Westward between the cold sea and the mountains, it was strongest; it sang to her, luring her away from the strait-ened path of order and discipline.

She wrenched her mind away before the wildness consumed it. There was nothing here that she had not seen before; such living maps as these were commonplace in the acolytes' schoolroom. This was larger, that was all, and more intricate. It was a work of art in its own right.

Then it changed. Maybe Bernardin had altered the spell, or maybe this was part of its magic. The land turned to glass. Great shapes moved beneath, a slow shifting of coils and a gleam of scales.

She shuddered, but she had no power to escape from the vision. It changed again to what at first she thought must be an invasion of ants. Then she realized they were men—armies.

They spread like a stain of blood, welling up from the heart of Lys, where a city lay athwart its river: golden Lutèce with its sixty towers and its royal chapel that rivaled the Ladies' chapel on the Isle in power and glory. Now there was a canker in its heart.

The canker wore a crown. She could not see his face—the magic did not choose to be so precise—but all too easily she could see what he intended. He was taking domains one by one, duchies and counties that had owed allegiance but not submission to the king since the kingdom began.

He was not conquering solely by force of arms. Sometimes it was poison; sometimes a dagger in the dark. But always, once the lord was gone, a slither of scales took his place, a creature who spoke the king's words and carried out the king's wishes.

As Averil began to understand what was becoming of the kingdom, she saw why her father had called her home. The fallen domains were scattered from end to end of Lys, but a nearly perfect ring of them surrounded one particular duchy between the Wildlands and the warmth of the south.

Slowly but surely, the king's noose was tightening around Quitaine. Averil was still deep in the vision, but when she looked for Bernardin he was there, standing like a bulwark between Averil and the powers that threatened the kingdom. "How much time do we have?" she asked him.

"Not long," he answered. "I hope long enough to see you settled in Fontevrai."

"So soon," she said. She shook herself before her courage failed yet again. "Tell me honestly. Is my father ill? Is he dying?"

"What do you see?"

So, thought Averil: Knights taught by answering question with question, just as Ladies did. For some reason it made her smile, though there was no mirth in her.

She narrowed her eyes. The vision resisted—it wanted to keep its grand scale. Only slowly would it focus on the jewel of white and green and silver that was Fontevrai.

She dropped like a hawk stooping, down into the sprawling stone hulk of the duke's palace. Through the glass of its windows and the crystal of its wards, she brought her father into focus.

He had aged greatly since his portrait was taken, half a dozen years ago. His dark hair had gone white; his fine-drawn face was haggard and his eyes were weary. He was sitting under an arbor in a garden with a pair of wolfhounds at his feet and a book in his lap. The hand that turned the page was thin; it trembled.

And yet, as Averil looked closer, she saw the strength in him. He was a mage in his own right, a scholar and a loremaster. In youth he had trained to be a Knight; he had left before his vows were taken, just as his daughter had left the Ladies, but his studies had continued.

The protections that lay like a glimmering matrix over the duchy were his. Other powers sustained them, a web of mages in every town and village, but they served at his command.

Averil bowed to his mastery. If Quitaine was under siege, its duke defended it well.

But he was old. He needed his heir, so that when he died, she would be ready to continue what he had begun.

Part of that, inevitably, was that his heir should find and secure a husband. She could rule and wield magic, but a woman did not lead armies. And she would need armies if she was to stand against the king.

It was a cold thought, but duty and policy were not warm things. Averil knew her duty. She had been raised to perform it.

She withdrew carefully from the vision, sealing off each glimmering shard. She was aware of Bernardin watching, taking care not to interfere. This was a test of sorts, and she meant to pass it.

She opened her eyes on the outer world. It seemed dull and flat after the pure light of the vision.

Bernardin knelt at her feet, head bowed. It had cost him no little strength to sustain this vision for her.

That was a debt she could repay. She laid her hand on his head. Light coalesced around them both; she poured it into him.

He looked up, startled. She did not see why he should be. Any acolyte of the Isle could do this—though maybe not as easily as she did. She had a talent for it.

She drew back her hand before she spent too much of herself. He was restored in any case, rising slowly, only to bow in front of her. "Lady," he said.

He meant it in many different ways. She opened her mouth to point out that she was not and would never be a Lady of the Isle, but in the end she did not say it. He had given her the title of his own choice. It was an honor and a tribute.

5

The king of Lys walked slowly through his dome of paradise. Its walls were sheets of glass joined by a matrix of high magic. The sun shone through them in all seasons, even in the dead of winter, feeding the rich and humid heat of his personal Eden.

The scent of earth and moisture and fecund decay filled his nostrils. Strange greenery and stranger flowers burgeoned around him. Bright and exotic birds flitted through the branches; vivid insects darted and swarmed and crawled. In cages of glass beneath the blossoming canopy, supple shapes coiled, scales gleaming, tongues flicking.

Only a few of the cages were enclosed. From most, their occupants could come and go, gliding out to bask or hunt or feed. In this paradise, serpents were welcome—and human creatures must move with care, because many of those that slipped underfoot or wound around branches were deadly poisonous.

Clodovec the king had no fear of them. He paused beneath a fan of deep green leaves. A shape of incandescent green uncoiled from the heart of one broad leaf, investigating his face with the flick of its tongue. He stood perfectly still, with barely the flicker of an eyelid, while that most deadly of serpents assured itself that he was indeed its master.

The air stirred behind him, but he did not move. The snake left its resting place and poured itself down over his shoulder, coiling around his arm. Its head came to rest in the cup of his hand.

If he moved suddenly, its fangs would sink into flesh. Even his magic would be hard put to save him before the venom stopped his heart.

The sheer exhilarating terror of it made him smile.

The air stirred subtly. He sensed the presence behind him, the power banked and subtly warded and the breath softened as much as mortal might. "Father Gamelin," he said.

"Sire," said his counselor, coming round slowly to face him.

The serpent slept in the king's hand, its lidless eyes gleaming. Gamelin rather reminded the king of the snake: slender, elegant, and deceptively quiet. He looked like a humble priest, gowned always in black among the glittering plumage of the court, but there was no mind more subtle and no magic more dangerous than his.

He was the Serpent's most dearly loved servant. Clodovec by contrast was merely an acolyte—albeit a royal and exceedingly powerful one.

Someday he would be more. He lidded his eyes lest the thought escape and extended his smile to the priest. "You see I'm at my prayers. Is your message urgent?"

"Not so much, sire," Gamelin said. He bowed to the serpent that was so dear a child of the great one, moving with exquisite care.

The serpent raised its head. Clodovec did his best to calm the beating of his heart and quell the uprush of fear. The black tongue flicked; the narrow head swayed. Clodovec barely breathed.

Abruptly the snake reared up, darting back onto its leaf. Clodovec retreated as quickly as he dared. A drop of cold sweat trickled down his back. Suddenly, fiercely, he wanted a woman.

This was not the time for that. "So, then, Father," he said. "What needs my immediate attention?"

"Perhaps not immediate, sire," Gamelin said, "but soon. Duke Urien's heir has left the Isle."

Clodovec's brow twitched upward. "So soon? He's found a husband for her, then?"

"It seems not," said Gamelin. "We're pressing him hard. He's panicked, perhaps."

"My dear and formerly beloved brother-in-law does not panic," the king said. "What does he know that we do not?"

Gamelin spread his hands. "Sire, that I cannot tell you. I've cast the crystals and invoked the aether; but there is nothing."

Clodovec frowned, running his fingers through the perfumed curls of his beard. The scent of musk and ambergris sweetened his nostrils. "Is it possible that the treasure has been found?"

Gamelin stiffened, though he kept his face expressionless. "We know the Knights keep it. But if he had found it, we would know. There has been nothing."

"Except a summons that we did not expect until the girl had come of age and been betrothed."

"It is possible," said Gamelin, "that he has foreseen his death. He's an old man. Old men die."

"That would be grievous to his people," Clodovec granted him, "and convenient for us. I'm sure, Father, that you can discover what brought about this turn of events."

Gamelin bowed low as a good servant should, but Clodovec caught the glitter of his eyes. He was as deadly as the green snake—a fact Clodovec could never allow himself to forget.

He was also highly useful. He left Clodovec with new possibilities to consider and new plans to ponder. So: Urien thought he might die soon? That prophecy might well fulfill itself.

Clodovec had tasks of his own to perform, but he delayed a while longer. The center of the paradise was a globe of crystal as tall as a tall man—a little taller than the king. A dark shape coiled in it. Magic had made it and prayer sustained it; but it was only an image.

He knelt in front of it. Somewhere among the intricate web of the Knights' powers both earthly and divine was the living reality of which this globe was a reflection. Somewhere the Serpent in its true and most sacred self was imprisoned.

Clodovec prayed that the great power, the holy and exalted one, supernal Chaos, would break free. That was his deep desire and his most intense purpose.

The world could not know, yet, what Clodovec intended. The Young God's Church ruled it with a hand of iron and bitter magic—and it was the Young God who had bound the Serpent.

The Knights were his loyal servants and the Ladies were their ancient allies.

Clodovec hated them all. He had honed that hate to a fine edge, nurtured and cherished it until it was a weapon of unequaled potency.

Someday soon, all that would change. He would find the Knights' most precious and most secret treasure. Then he would free the prisoner. And then . . .

Then the world would be such a paradise as this shrine to the Serpent. Grim laws and straitened order would be broken. Mankind would be free as it had been before what the Serpent's beloved called the Fall—when the Serpent was bound and the joy of sublime disorder went out of the world.

Clodovec was a passionate man, but he was also a practical one. He breathed a last prayer and rose. The globe darkened until it seemed no more than an orb of stone set for ornament in the king's exotic garden.

As he made his way into the less secluded portions of the palace, a thought wandered aimlessly past. What if—just suppose—Duke Urien knew where the Serpent was imprisoned? And what if his daughter had some part in that secret?

It was a peculiar thought, but not as preposterous as Clodovec might have liked. Quitaine was the wealthiest of the duchies in Lys, and its ruling family was famous for the depth and purity of its magic. Only Clodovec's own family stood higher in the ranks of the blessed—and the duke's late duchess had been Clodovec's sister. Duke Urien's heir was doubly and powerfully royal.

Time was when they would all have been called the children of gods. Lys was no longer pagan, whatever Clodovec hoped it would become once the Serpent was freed. A malleable young girl raised in the cloistered solitude of the Isle, an elderly and infirm father . . .

Clodovec began to smile. Urien thought himself clever, bringing his heir home in time to bind her to his magic before old age took him. But clever men seldom considered that others might see as clearly as they.

While the duke's heir was on the Isle, Clodovec could not

touch her. In Quitaine, however well guarded she might be, she was still within his reach. And once her father was dead, she came under the wardship of her next closest kinsman: her mother's brother, the king of Lys.

Even if she knew nothing of the great secret that the Knights kept, she was a rich prize. One way or the other, Clodovec could not fail.

Clodovec liked to win battles. Even better was a plan well executed, with no more bloodshed than absolutely necessary.

He snapped his fingers. A servant appeared as if from air. He gave orders that he had every expectation would be obeyed.

Then he did not rest—a king's duties were never so light as that—but he allowed himself to be, for the moment, content.

6

Gereint stalked the Knights for two days, partly because he did not want them to pack him off to his mother again and partly because he was afraid to hope that they would let him stay. As long as they did not know he was there, he could keep pretending that he could ask them to take him in. He would never get so far above himself as to dream of becoming a Knight, but if they would only teach him to control the thing inside him, he told himself that would be enough.

By the evening of the second day, his rationed provisions were running low. He thought of begging at one of the farmhouses he passed on that winding road, but he was not starving yet.

He crept close enough that night to hear the Knights talking around their campfire of how they would reach their chapter house the next day. People were waiting there to take their treasure onward.

Even among themselves they did not say what that treasure was. Gereint might have guessed that it was gold or coin, but the tingle in his spine said otherwise. Whatever was in those boxes and bags that seemed so ordinary, it was a work of magic, strongly and all but invisibly protected.

Tonight they were looking forward to their return home but regretting a little that the journey was over. Their conversation was easy, quiet, of lives and people that were unfamiliar to Gereint.

He would not have called it gossip, but it had a flavor of market talk. There was nothing high or noble about it.

He found it reassuring. Knights and mages and descendants

of Paladins though they might be, these men were as mortal as he was. They might not be too far above it all to help a farmer's son.

Even being close to them seemed to be keeping his magic within bounds. It stayed coiled inside, as close to sleep as it could ever be.

The Knights ended their conversation and wandered off to their tents. Gereint slithered backwards toward the nest he had made in the bracken.

Something blocked his way. He scrambled up, caught his feet on one another and fell sprawling.

The Knight Mauritius looked down at him, standing tall against the stars. Gereint lay where he had fallen. His heart was beating hard. "Sir!" he said, breathless.

Mauritius held out a hand. Gereint hesitated, then took it and let the Knight pull him to his feet. This time he stayed on them.

"You are tenacious," Mauritius said. "Didn't you notice the aversion spell we set on anyone who might be stalking us?"

"Is that what it was?" Gereint asked. "I felt something, but it was meant to guard against danger. I don't mean any harm."

"What did you feel?"

It was a bit odd, hearing that calm voice in the dark, asking a teacher's questions. Gereint answered as best he could. "It was a little like too much sun on a summer day and a little like frozen fingers thawing in front of a fire. It wasn't really aimed at me. I let it go past me and it stopped."

Mauritius' face was a shadow on shadow, but Gereint had the distinct sensation that his brows had risen. "Come with me," he said.

"Promise you won't send me home," Gereint said, "at least until you've heard what I have to say."

"I can guess," Mauritius said. His hand fell on Gereint's shoulder. "Come."

MAURITIUS LED GEREINT to a place near the horses where he could spread his blanket and catch what sleep he could for the rest of the night. In the morning he was greeted without curiosity, fed a loaf of bread sopped in watered wine and given one of the remounts.

No one asked if he could ride. They all acted as if they had been expecting him. He was not one of them—they did not go that far—but he was not an outcast, either.

Gereint supposed it was because they were mages. They knew things.

He kept his mouth shut and his ears open. They were not going to give away secrets while he was there, but he could learn much from voices and expressions and bits of conversation. Most of it did not fit together yet, but in time he was sure it would.

As they rode in sunlight that had more than recovered itself since that last, unwontedly late storm of snow, a most peculiar sensation filled him. At first he was horrified, fearing it was his magic breaking loose after all.

Then he realized what it was. He was happy. He rode from confusion into uncertainty, and he could still be sent back to his mother—but he wanted to laugh and sing.

He did neither, of course. If he was ever going to learn self-control, this was the time and place to begin.

THE CHAPTER HOUSE of Saint-Émile guarded the road to the sea. The light was different there, with a strange clarity along the western horizon; the air had a faint, sharp smell. Gereint might have followed that smell to its source, which his companions said was the sea, but the grey stone walls of the Knights' house drew him in.

They called it a house. He called it a castle—not a large one and built around a villa from the old days, but there could be no doubt that it was a house of war.

It was a house of magic, too. Strands of it wove through the walls and arched above the low square towers. Gereint's skin prickled as he rode through the gate.

He glanced at the others. They seemed unconcerned, carrying on their conversations through the gate and into what was obviously a stableyard. People were waiting there to take the horses; some wore Novice green, but others seemed as common as Gereint, stablehands in plain clothes like his and with only the faintest glimmer of magic about them.

He thought he might be handed over to the grooms like one of the horses, but Mauritius came to him while he stood at a loss and said as he had last night in the bracken, "Come."

For once in his life, Gereint was mutely obedient. He had been in a castle a time or two before, running errands for his mother to the lord of Rémy. Messire Henri's castle was more impressive than this, but it had not reduced him to silence.

Magic was woven into the fabric of this place. Every stone, every court and passage, was full of it. And yet the people living in it took it for granted.

They were as incurious about Gereint as his companions on the road had been: sparing him a glance at most and reserving their smiles and greetings for his guide. Mauritius returned both with the ease of a man in his element.

Gereint tried to study how he did it. Not that a farmboy would ever need such easy grace, but it was a wonderful thing to see.

He was so caught up in the people that he barely noticed where Mauritius was leading him. When they stopped, he found himself in a small bare courtyard, face to face with an image from a church window: a knight in full and gleaming armor, great sword uplifted to smite the neck of a cowering worm.

He blinked hard. The sun was full in his eyes, hovering just above the wall. The shining figure resolved itself into a man in cuirass and greaves, hacking at a block of padded wood.

He was hacking most handsomely, turning it into a kind of dance: stroke and turn, back and forward, stroke, counterstroke, flashing whirl of blade through lucent air, spinning into sudden stillness.

Gereint looked into a face somewhat younger than Mauritius' but much sterner, standing rather higher than his own. The fair skin was flushed with exertion, the blue eyes glittering, but there was a deep quiet inside them. They saw through all of Gereint's masks and pretenses, down so deep he almost could not feel them any longer.

He turned to face them there, all the way inside his mind. At that, they widened. They were the color of glass in the window of a church, bluer than blue, with the light of heaven shining through them. He basked in it.

"Enough." The voice was soft and deep. It lifted Gereint out of himself into the waning sunlight.

Gereint saw what the Knight was trying to do. He lent it the slightest hint of a hand, the whisper of a stroke to bring them both smoothly and cleanly back to the outer world.

HE CAME TO himself sprawled against a wall, aching in every bone, with such a pounding in his head that he could barely see. The air smelled like the aftermath of thunder.

With ringing ears and sinking heart, Gereint pushed himself to his feet. People gathered near the center of the court, where a figure in armor was lying.

He had done that—or his damned bloody magic had. This time it had done worse than destroy a barn or a hayrick: it had struck down a man.

He slid along the wall, aiming for the gate, which at the moment was unguarded. God knew where he would go or what he would do there, but he could not stay here. He could not stay anywhere. If even this strongly protected place could not stop him, what in the world could?

He walked straight into a wall he could not see. He sensed it too late, just as it stopped him cold.

Two grim-faced men appeared, one on either side, and gripped his arms. He made no move to resist them. They half led, half dragged him out of the courtyard and into the heart of the castle.

GEREINT SPENT THE night in a small bare room. There was a cot and a stool and a chamberpot and little else.

The cot had a sheet of rough-woven linen and a harsh woolen blanket. The only ornament in the room, if it could be called that, was an enameled rose hung on the wall over the cot. There was strong magic in it, a warding spell that enclosed all four walls and the door.

When Gereint had been there for a while, sitting listless on the cot, a boy brought a frugal dinner: bread, ale, a pickled onion. The boy neither spoke nor met Gereint's eyes. He was as heavily warded as the room.

Maybe Gereint was going to die for what he had done. That would not be a terrible thing. He had been dangerous before; now he was deadly.

He left his dinner uneaten and lay back with his arm over his eyes. Memory kept sliding away from those brief but devastating moments in the courtyard.

He rolled onto his face. Part of him wanted to dissolve in tears, but there were none to shed. They were burned out of him.

Maybe he slept. His dreams were dark and formless. Sometimes he thought he heard hissing and the sliding of scales.

Morning was grey, with the damp heaviness of rain. The men who came to fetch him were twins of the silent pair who had brought him to the room the night before. He followed them in mute obedience, hoping only that, whatever was in store for him, it would be over quickly.

THE ROOM TO which his two guards took him was hardly larger or more ornate than the one where he had spent the night—except for the window. It was narrow and tall and made of colored glass like a window in a church. Even on this grey day, it glimmered with light.

Gereint was hardly aware of the guards' retreat beyond the door. The window drew him to it. There were figures wrought of glass and paint and lead, but they seemed to shift and change, so that the closer he peered, the less certain he was of what they were.

A whole world lived in the glass: fields and forests, rivers and streams, a sea of tossing waves and shining spume. Beasts and birds ran and crawled and flew. Human shapes passed as shadows, faint sketches in ink on the lucent glass.

He raised his hand to touch it. It melted around him. He

stumbled through a blur of many-colored light into a space of singing stillness.

The blue-eyed Knight was standing there, alive and breathing and to all appearances unharmed. Others stood with him, cowled in grey. The rose glowed blood-red on each mailed breast.

"Kneel," said the Knight he thought he had killed.

He had no will to refuse. The floor was hard and cold. The blow that fell on his shoulder rocked him sorely but did not fell him.

The Knight's eyes shone as brightly as the glass through which Gereint had come. "The road is hard and the labor is long. Far more fail than reach the rank we hold. You may burn yourself to ash or you may turn to living light. Will you venture it? Do you dare?"

Gereint gaped like an idiot. "But I'm not—I wouldn't—I almost—"

"Do you dare?"

"I'm not a nobleman. I can't control my magic. I have no—"

"Answer me," said the Knight.

Gereint could not breathe. Whatever he could possibly have expected, it was not this. They should be putting him to death, not offering him their world.

He could refuse it. They were giving him that choice. But if he did, he would not live long. If they did not kill him, his magic would.

He wanted to live. It was cowardly, but there it was. To be a Knight, or to have the chance of being a Knight, was too high and terrifying a thing to think about just then.

He focused on the thing he had come for: to learn the mastery of his magic. He would get that—or if he failed, the Knights would dispose of him.

A wave of calm washed over him. He had flung himself into air, and the air had caught him. He was shaking, but that was his body offering its own opinion. It seemed faint and far away.

"Yes," he said breathlessly. "Yes, I dare."

7

Gereint was a Postulant. That was the first thing his two watchdogs told him. They led him out of the room of the testing by a perfectly ordinary door, down a passage to another room in which a bath was waiting.

"You'll be cleansed," said the taller of the two, "and your old life taken away. Then you'll be a Postulant—one who begs admission to the ranks."

"So I'm not there yet," Gereint said as they stripped him of his clothes.

He could not help but notice how their noses wrinkled. The one who carried off his clothes looked as if he had drawn the short straw.

He resented that. He was clean—he bathed all over every week. He even knew what hot water was.

Gereint moved toward the steaming basin, but the smaller guard stood in the way. "You'll beg at the gate for a year," he said. "Then you'll be tested. If you pass, you'll become a Novice. Most Postulants don't pass. Some of them die."

"I'm dead if I don't try," Gereint said. "Are you a Postulant?"

"I am a Novice," the boy said with dignity—he was no older than Gereint, if that. "Postulants aren't strong enough to stop you if you let go again."

Gereint wanted to declare that he would never do such a thing, but that would have been false. He had been raised to tell the truth. He set his lips together and let the conversation die.

The Novice pointed him toward the basin and scrubbed him in silence. He suffered the indignity of what was clearly a rite of passage, though he wondered if the ritual required that he be scrubbed raw and his hair combed through ruthlessly for lice that were not there.

He swallowed his objections. It was a test, and he was determined not to fail it.

When he was cleaner than he had ever imagined he could be, both Novices dressed him in linen underclothes, very plain but well made, and tunic and hose of brown wool belted with leather, with leather shoes that seemed cut to fit his feet. A folded armful of wool and linen proved a change of clothes and a cloak and hood and a bag of useful objects: comb, razor for the beard he had yet to grow, scrap of mirror, and odd objects that he did not immediately recognize.

"If you have to ride abroad," said the smaller one, whose name was Simon, "you'll be issued boots and riding gear. Everything else you need in your life is here."

It was a small life and not very heavy, but Gereint thought that was fitting. He was still too stunned to make sense of it all.

His stomach growled loudly. Gilles, the taller Novice, slid a glance at him. "I should think you would be no stranger to hunger."

Gereint's temper flared. "Why? Because I wasn't born in a castle? My mother farms a rich steading, which her father farmed before her. What we don't eat or use, we sell in the market. Maybe we don't dress in silks and jewels, but that's because they're wasteful. There's always food in our bellies and clothes on our backs. We live the way we choose to live."

The Novices looked as startled as he felt. Simon seemed to be fighting back a grin. Gilles flushed and scowled. "Knights are noblemen," he said. "There are other orders for commoners. Most likely you'll be sent to one of them, if you don't destroy yourself first. You won't pass the tests here. You're not bred for it."

"Your superiors seem to think otherwise," Gereint said stiffly.

"Our superiors are in a panic. You should have been reined in years ago. Because you weren't, you're a threat to yourself and everyone around you. They did the only thing they could think of to get you under control."

"Maybe it will work," Gereint said.

"Maybe you'll die," said Gilles. "I hope the rest of us don't die with you."

Gereint pressed his lips together. He could see how long a road he had to travel, mapped in that well-bred face.

He was not going to turn back. He was as stubborn as a mule, his mother liked to say—and that was honestly come by. He got it from her.

HE NEEDED EVERY bit of that stubbornness. A Postulant's life was not nearly as hard or the days as long as a farmer's, but he had little in common with the three Postulants who shared the dormitory with him. For one thing, they were half his age. For another, they already knew more about magic than he did.

He could hardly blame them for that. Except for Gilles, none of them—of any rank, clear up to Knights—seemed to care what station he had been born to. But he was an oddity.

In the schoolroom, at least, he managed to hold his own. He could read and write—that much his mother had insisted on— and he had a way with numbers. His fellows were far better read, but he was quick-witted. With a little effort, he could keep up with them.

He could ride—not elegantly but well enough to stay on— and God knew, he could look after the horses. The stable-hands and the master of horse were duly appreciative.

That rather made up for his complete lack of skill with weapons—except for the bow. He could shoot; he had hunted for the pot since he was small. Sword and shield, spear, lance, mace and battleaxe were altogether alien to him.

Noblemen grew up with weapons in their hands. They were descendants of Paladins, bred for war. Gereint was bred to dig in the dirt.

He persevered, though the one part of this life that he had expected was yet to appear. He was taught no magic.

When spring was nearly past and the orchards had swelled

into full bloom, he summoned up the courage to ask the question that burned strong in him. He approached Mauritius, because of all of them, that was the one who seemed least disconcerted by his existence.

Evenings were long in this season, and the light lingered well after the sun had set. That evening between vespers and midnight, the air was full of sweetness: apple blossoms and peach and pear, and in a corner of the cloister, one cherished lemon tree that elected to bloom with the rest. Even stone walls and strong protections could not keep it out.

Gereint had been tending a horse with the colic. The horse was up and eating a little; he was reasonably sure the crisis was past.

It was one of the Knights' horses, a fine bay stallion. Mauritius had come to look in on the beast, since he had a particular fondness for it. "My family breeds them," he said as they leaned on the stall door, watching the horse alternate between dozing and nibbling at the handful of hay in the manger. "He's exceptionally well bred and exceptionally talented, but he's a bit fragile."

"He's a prince," Gereint said. "Mortal life is too much for him."

He held his breath as soon as he had said it, because it was not the wisest thing to say to a nobleman, but Mauritius smiled and nodded. "He is that. You have a good hand with him."

Gereint shrugged. "I'm hopeless when it comes to the sword, but horse-doctoring I do know."

Mauritius leveled a keen gaze on him. "Is it very bad with the other boys?"

Gereint shrugged again. "It's no worse than I expected. I don't really belong here, do I? I'm just here until you decide what to do with me."

"Who told you that?"

"I can tell," Gereint said. "It's obvious. I'm the only commoner here who isn't a stablehand or a servant. Can't you just give me bindings that work, or else take the magic out of me and let me go?"

"Do you want to go?"

"No!" said Gereint before he stopped to think. Then, when his mind had caught up with his mouth: "No, I don't. I'd rather be a Knight than anything in the world. Just the little I've seen of this place and this life, and what you are and what you do . . . it makes me want it more than ever. But I was brought up to be practical. If there is an order of mages that will take me, it's not this one."

"What makes you think that?"

Gereint started to snap at him, but caught himself in time. Mauritius was not trying to mock him. He honestly seemed interested in Gereint's answer.

Gereint spread his hands, taking in the whole of the chapter house—including the high-bred stallion who had come to investigate his fingers. "You are all princes. I don't even know who my father is. My mother has never told me. But one thing I do know. He's not one of you."

"You're sure of that?"

Gereint's heart wanted to leap with hope, but as he had said, he was practical. "I'm sure. I can't tell you how I know, but whatever my blood is, it's not a part of yours or any Knight's. Sometimes I think my mother lay with an incubus. That would explain a great deal, wouldn't it?"

"You're young to be so jaded," Mauritius said. "Have you ever thought about who—or what—the Paladins were? They rode with the Young God against the Serpent, to be sure, but where did they come from?"

"I heard they were lords of the Young God's country, who came to serve him when the Serpent rose and tried to eat the sun. He gave them their powers and made them great, but they were wellborn before he found them."

"So the priests say," Mauritius said. "It's convenient and keeps the common people from getting above their station. But it's not exactly the truth. Some of them were princes, yes, but some were not. Peredur the Beloved, the youngest and one of the most powerful, was godborn like you—son of a harlot. It's said his father was a daimon, one of the immortals who dwell in the aether, who walked in human form one day in the port of Kasara and saw the woman plying her trade in front of their goddess' temple. She was beautiful, but more than that, she was strong, and she took pride in what she did. He loved her for that and left her with child—and when that child was as old as you, the Young God chose him.

"Do you think," said Mauritius, "that we should be any more exacting in our requirements than the Young God?"

"I am not a Paladin," Gereint said.

"Not yet," said Mauritius. "I spoke for you, you know—but I'm not the only one. Others see what's in you. You belong with us, I think. I don't know why or what will come of it, but I am as sure of that as you are that your father wasn't of our order."

"It's not going to be easy," Gereint said.

"Would you want it to be?"

Gereint laughed, startled. "No. I suppose not. Everything's better if you've worked for it."

Mauritius applauded him. "You see? You do understand. And as for your question—what makes you think you haven't been learning to control your magic?"

Gereint opened his mouth, then shut it. "Why should I think I have been?"

"Look inside," Mauritius said. He clapped Gereint lightly on the shoulder, rubbed the nose of the stallion who was now notably more alert and left Gereint to chew over what he had said.

There was nothing inside but confusion. Tiredness, too— he had been up at dawn and it was well on the way toward midnight. He was required to attend the midnight office, then if he could, he would sleep until dawn, when a new rite called him out of bed.

That was if the stallion continued to get better—which seemed certain, but with horses one never knew. Gereint expected he would sleep in a stall tonight. It would not be the first time.

He could see no magic anywhere. It was all order and discipline, lessons in books and lessons in weaponry—with the bruises to show for it—and the daily round of duty and ritual. The clarity of vision that he had gained on the journey was still there, but it saw only the world of mortal light and mortal faces.

He stopped short and ran through that thought again. He could see no magic. The fullness of his days, with each hour mapped, left no room for excess.

It was like a framework of wards, a web of protections laid on him by the shape and structure of each day's work. Even sleep was kept under control, constrained within the round of holy offices.

"It can't be that simple," he said to the air.

The air did not answer. The stallion snorted wetly. Gereint heard the soft and unmistakable sound of manure falling.

That was the sound he had been waiting for. He laughed. It was that or howl at the moon.

The stallion would be well. Whether Gereint would be the same . . . he could not tell. His whole world had changed. Everything was new, and he was not sure he understood it.

He had to remember what it was like to dream—then make it real. That was what magic was for.

8

Gereint woke with a weight on his chest. When he shifted, it fell with a thud to the floor. He sat up bleary-eyed.

His nostrils twitched at the smell of leather. He stared at a pair of boots and a parcel of folded leather and linen.

Gilles the Novice looked as little disgruntled as Gereint had ever seen him. "Get up and dress," he said, "then find your breakfast. You ride in an hour."

Gereint tried to knuckle the sleep out of his eyes. He did not succeed very well. The Postulants' dormitory was deserted except for the two of them, but he was sure he had not slept past the dawn bell. It was still dark outside.

He peered at the Novice. "Ride? Where?"

"Fontevrai."

"Where—"

"Fontevrai," said Gilles in the singsong of the schoolroom, "is the greatest city of Quitaine, the duke's seat and a famous center of learning in its own right. We are in the county of Montmerci, which offers fealty to the duke in Quitaine. Our house, accordingly, looks to the mother house of the order, which is in Fontevrai. Where, messire Postulant, you are being sent, because no one here has the patience to deal with you."

Gereint was awake. He was not happy about it, either. "I'm going to Fontevrai?"

"Yes, messire lackwit, you are going to Fontevrai." Gilles flung the boots at him again. "Move, or you'll miss breakfast."

Gereint pulled on such clothes as he had never worn before: tight leather breeches and close-cut linen shirt and leather jerkin with the blood-red rose embroidered on the breast. It all fit well, as did the boots. There was a belt, too, and a long knife, but no sword. A Postulant carried weapons only in practice.

He belted the knife at his waist and tried not to feel like a fool as he walked out stiffly in his new boots. He could tell by the smell of the air that it was early—long before dawn—but the cooks were up. The bread in the refectory was fresh and still warm, and there was barley porridge to go with it, and a cup of new milk sweetened with honey and strengthened with wine.

For this place, it was a feast. He was the only one there to eat it; he ate quickly, torn between excitement and anxiety. He had done nothing, surely, to warrant being sent away.

Gilles left him without a word of farewell. He could not say he was sorry. Gilles had his uses, but he was anything but a friend.

Just as Gereint finished the last of the milk, a new Novice came to fetch him. His spirits lightened immeasurably when he saw who it was. "Ademar! You're coming, too?"

Ademar sighed vastly, but Gereint could feel the lightness in him. "I'm always on the road. They seem to think my gift is for incessant travel. I'm a mage of peripateia."

Gereint laughed. "I'm glad to see you," he said.

"Ah," said Ademar. "Well. You'll make the journey a little bearable, I suppose. Mauritius is coming, too."

Gereint's heart leaped. But he said, "Tell me the truth. Why am I being sent away?"

"You're not being sent *away*," Ademar said. "You're being sent *on*. It happens to many of us. Saint-Émile is small and not well equipped to educate a mage of your particular talents."

"Or lack thereof," Gereint muttered.

Ademar arched a brow at him. "Believe me, the other Postulants are consumed with envy. They have to stay in this backwater. *You* get sent to the heart of it all. Even some of the Novices are ready to slip a blade between your ribs—then cast an illusion and put on your face and go instead."

"They could do that?"

"Messire," said Ademar, "don't play the yokel with me. *I* can see what's behind it."

"But can they really—"

Ademar rolled eyes at his stubbornness, but gave him the answer he was looking for. "They're not supposed to. It doesn't mean they won't."

"So now I have to watch my back," Gereint said.

"You should always watch your back," said Ademar. "You're not in your mother's hay barn anymore. This is a dangerous world."

"You mean," said Gereint, "that I used to be the most dangerous thing in my world. Now there are things more dangerous than I am."

"You can say that," Ademar said. "Quick, up. They'll be riding off without us."

GEREINT WAS NOT the only reason for the riding to Fontevrai. There were messages for the mother house and the quarter's tithes from the chapter house's lands. Altogether, two Knights and four Squires rode with the caravan, and four Novices and one Postulant.

Gereint was put in charge of the horses and mules. He was glad to do it; it kept him from stopping to think of what he was riding to and what might become of him.

It was a quiet enough journey, all five days of it. Nights they spent in chapter houses of the order, slipping into the daily rites and offices as if they had always been there. What Ademar had said in Gereint's mother's house was true: every house of the Knights was like every other.

And yet they were all different. The differences were subtle, but to Gereint they seemed obvious. It might be the light or the air or the lie of the land; although the shape and structure of each house was the same, the wards that protected it and the magic that filled it were, in each place, subtly or more visibly distinct.

He was beginning to think—in error, he hoped—that people did not see things as he did. Even these strong mages seemed oblivious to currents of magic that threatened at times to overwhelm him. It must be his lack of training and his still laughably feeble discipline.

He was holding on. He clung to that. He had not lost control in sixteen whole days. The last time had been hardly more than a slip of the will, a broken pot in the kitchen and its contents dissipated into the aether.

When they were somewhat more than a day's ride from Fontevrai, a rider met them on the road. It was a Squire, well armed and mounted on a fast horse. He rode straight toward Mauritius and the second Knight, Odilo; they drew away from the others, talking in low voices.

Gereint tried to listen, but their voices were like a buzzing of bees. When he tried harder, a splitting headache drove him back. He retreated to the horses, trying not to wince when his steps jarred his aching skull.

The Knights' colloquy ended quickly. The messenger rode on. So did they, no faster or slower than they had before.

And yet there was a new sense about the Knights of tightly reined-in urgency. Whatever was waiting for them tonight, they were eager to face it.

He drew deep breaths, fighting for calm. All this time he had been waiting for something to happen, some burst of magic or attack by bandits. He had been disappointed to discover that the life of a Knight, for the most part, was overwhelmingly mundane.

This could be more of the same: a new shipment of wine or a finer dinner than usual. But surely that would not warrant a messenger and secrecy.

The road seemed to stretch longer, the closer they came to sunset. The town they were aiming for was named Morency; the chapter house there was very large. Next to the mother house in Fontevrai, it was the largest of them all.

Gereint could feel it long before he came to it. It felt like an edifice of light hovering just below the horizon. Slowly it rose into view of the eyes as well as the mind: a row of squat grey towers rising out of a grove of trees.

The town that lay between was nearer a city. Gereint realized, looking at it, that until now the caravan had been traveling by back roads and byways, stopping in out-of-the-way villages.

He did not delude himself that their circumspection had

been for his sake. He had never seen a town larger than Rémy. This city was a profound shock.

If he had not been protected within the wards of the caravan, he would have collapsed from the assault on his senses. So many walls, so many people, so many sounds and smells.

He felt the magic rising in him, rumbling like summer thunder. Desperately he clung to the discipline he had learned: the ordered beauty of the evening office, each word shaped and fitted to the next, set in a matrix of sacred music. He rode the long melismas of the *Lord, have mercy on us*, note by note and word by word, until the storm diminished and the magic sank back down beneath the surface of his awareness.

He sagged against his horse's neck. The gelding plodded calmly onward, following the horse in front of it.

Gereint straightened as best he could. The chapter house was close, promising a refuge. He drew in a long breath, then another. It steadied him a little.

Fontevrai was going to be worse than this. He had to be prepared. There would be teachers there, masters who would give him what he needed—but first he had to survive his arrival.

It was better now. The evening office finished itself in his head; he let the midnight office follow.

The caravan had slowed to a crawl. It was the end of the long late-spring day. People were leaving the market all at once, clotting in the streets and alleys and barring the way with their carts and wagons. Even a company of Knights could not force its way through.

The crowds were maddening, but the helplessness of it, in a strange way, brought Gereint back to himself. It was so ordinary a thing, so unexceptional a frustration. If even Knights could be caught in a market-day crush, that made it all less overwhelming.

9

$\approx$

Between the Isle and the town of Morency outside of Fontevrai was ten days' steady travel, making no haste but not dallying, either. For Averil it was a passage between worlds.

She had sailed from the Havens to the port of Careol on the mainland with her escort of Knights and a cargo of wool and tin from Prydain. In Careol a larger escort was waiting, double the number of Knights and a dozen guards in the deep blue and silver of Quitaine.

There were also a pair of maids, soft-spoken young women with quiet eyes and a strong gift of magic. Averil recognized them as acolytes who, like her, had left the Isle before taking Ladies' vows.

One was small and round and dark. The other was like Averil, tall and fair-skinned, with hair more red than gold. The dark one's name was Jennet; the fair one was Emma.

Averil found their presence comforting. The Knights were loyal and respectful, but they found her presence disconcerting. Only Bernardin seemed comfortable with her, and he was preoccupied with matters of his order and his position in the duchy. He gave her as much time as he had to spare, but that was not much.

Jennet and Emma had been sent to educate Averil in the manners and customs of a highborn lady. "Not," said Jennet, "that you're lacking the finer arts—but there's a difference between a lady and a Lady."

"Yes," said Emma. "A lady has to pretend that men rule the world."

"It's a delusion," Jennet said, "but it's persistent; and men grow terribly petulant if you let slip the truth."

"That's foolish," Averil said. "Why would we want to foster a delusion?"

"Because the order of society depends on it," said Emma. "Order is not always based on truth or reason. So we play the game and learn to be subtle. And that keeps chaos at bay."

Averil shook her head. None of it made sense to her, but if this was the game she was required to play, she would find a way to play it. She listened and learned and kept her thoughts to herself.

MORENCY'S CHAPTER HOUSE received the duke's heir with honor but without fanfare. She was led to the guesthouse as she had been in the other houses where they stopped for the night, and fed the richer fare that was reserved for guests.

Averil was learning to eat white bread and fine spices and to stomach bits of meat and the overwrought and oversweetened delicacies that were all the rage in noble courts. She would much rather have had brown bread and refectory ale, but as with the rest, this was the game and she must play it.

Tonight it seemed she would be dining alone. The Master of the house was occupied elsewhere.

She was a little surprised. Tomorrow she would go on to Fontevrai. She might have expected some message from her father, some sign that he was waiting for her.

She choked down a bite or two of her dinner and laid the rest aside. Sleep might be a useful diversion, but the sun was still well above the horizon. She contemplated sending someone to the chapter house's library to see if there was anything there for her to read. Something edifying and deadly dull would do admirably.

Just as she was about to send Jennet on the errand, a Novice knocked and, diffidently, entered. He would not look at her except in glances; she had to strain to hear his mumbled words. "Lady, our Master bids—he requests—he asks if you will receive him."

"Of course," said Averil.

The boy bowed, mumbled unintelligibly and fled.

Averil scowled after him. "What is it with these men? Haven't they ever seen a woman before?"

"Now and then," said Jennet, looking up from the needle-work that absorbed her whenever she was not obliged to play the servant. "It's beauty that robs them of sense."

"I'm not—"

Jennet's ironic glance stopped her. "You were a gawky child, weren't you? Like a yearling filly. But yearlings grow, and awkwardness transforms into grace. Your mother was the most beautiful woman in Lys. You're the image of her. A bit raw yet and still with growing to do, but in your day you may excel her."

Averil looked down at her hands. They were long and thin and the little fingers were slightly crooked. The skin was fash-ionably fair, but it was dusted with pale golden freckles; she had calluses that her maids deplored, marks of hard work in the fields and orchards of the Isle.

She was not going to let that go. They might ply her with potions and cantrips and baths in asses' milk, but she would keep her honest self. The world's order could learn to suffer it.

THE MASTER OF the house did not keep her waiting long. He was a gaunt man and old, but very strong in his magic: she could feel him long before he passed the door. Bernardin was with him, accompanied by another, much younger man, dark and wiry, with a narrow intelligent face and a keen glance.

They bowed to her. She acknowledged them with an incli-nation of the head.

These men at least would look at her without blushing and fleeing. They studied her, Bernardin as much as any, as if what they had to say depended on what they saw. She felt as she of-ten had on the Isle when her teachers tested her, judging her either worthy or unworthy to continue with their instruction.

She could not tell if she passed muster. That too was familiar. She waited them out as she had learned to do, in polite silence.

At length Master Huguelin said, "We have word from your father, lady, and a request to which you may object—but he begs you to comply."

Averil had been braced for an hour's worth of courtly meandering. His directness took her by surprise.

She could sense the Knights' amusement. The dark one in particular, whose name she did not yet know, seemed to find the proceedings more than usually diverting.

She turned her hands palm up and put on her most open and innocent expression. "Yes?" she said.

Master Huguelin's eyes glinted under the bristling grey brows. "He asks, lady, if you will surrender your rank and your finery to the maid whom he has chosen for her resemblance to you. Will you take her place and her apparent rank?"

The air seemed to chill. The easy amusement of the moment before was gone. Even the dark Knight had gone somber. "May I ask why?" Averil asked quietly.

It was the dark Knight who answered, bowing and offering her his name: Mauritius. "Your father believes, lady, that the duchy is in danger. There may be no need for such a pretense; in that case, you may exchange places once more and no one be the wiser."

Averil turned to Emma. "Did you know?"

Emma lifted a shoulder. "It was a possibility," she said. "I'll wear a glamour, of course. I've studied you faithfully. I won't shame you."

"It's not shame that troubles me," said Averil. "You could die."

Emma met her gaze steadily. "I know," she said. "I'm not afraid."

Averil considered a world in which such a deception might be necessary, and knew a moment's fierce longing for the serenity of the Isle. She straightened her shoulders and drew a long breath. Her hands were shaking. She laced her fingers tightly together and willed them to be still.

"It may be nothing," Bernardin said. "It's a precaution, no more. If you are a target, that will become obvious fairly quickly; then we can take measures to defend you."

"You haven't taken them already?" Averil asked—still quietly, but there was steel in her tone.

"We have, lady," Bernardin said, "but circumstances have grown worse since we left for the Isle. Proensa has fallen to the king's forces. Its duke and duchess are dead; their lone heir is simpleminded and cares for nothing but his toy soldiers. The king has declared himself the new duke's guardian. Your father fears, lady, that he may be planning a similar stroke here."

"We have time, surely," said Averil. "If Clodovec is occupied with Proensa—"

"The king has already left it in the hands of his loyal general Mauritius," said the Knight of the same name. He arched a brow at Averil's look of inquiry. "My brother, yes. We have little in common."

Averil nodded as she considered that. "So my uncle is coming here."

"We believe so," said Bernardin. "If he follows the pattern he's set, he'll dispose of the old duke and try to make you his puppet."

"You don't think he'll kill me?"

"Your father thinks he may," Bernardin said. "I believe he'll try to suborn you first. As far as he knows, you're an innocent, not much more dangerous than the bearded infant in Proensa."

"My mother was a Lady of the Isle," Averil said, "and she was the king's sister. He'll know what I'm capable of." She was surprised to find herself so calm. It was shock, she thought. She was prepared for this—she had been raised for it—but it was coming fast and hard.

"Lady," Emma said, "I am willing to do this, and I am aware of the risks. If your father asks it of us, then he has excellent reason."

Averil had no doubt of that. "I'll pray his visions are fears, not foresight." She rose and bowed. "My lady."

Emma looked rather thoroughly disconcerted.

Averil met her eyes. "We'll begin now. A glamour can change the face and voice, but the manner doesn't lie. You must *be* the heir of Quitaine."

"That is true," Mauritius said. "And you, lady—can you be her loyal servant?"

"More easily than I can be her lady," said Averil.

"Now that," said Jennet wryly, "is all too true."

"That's well, then," Master Huguelin said. "In the morning, you go—with your places reversed." He held out a pretty thing: a pendant of enamel on a silver chain. The device upon it was the silver swan of Quitaine swimming in a deep blue field.

Emma shivered slightly as she took it. Averil blinked. Then—although she was prepared for it—she stared.

So that was what she looked like. She never had troubled with mirrors even when her maids pressed her to try. She had seen that face limned in glass in the Ladies' chapel. It was the face of the Lady Magdalen, the Young God's beloved.

It was beautiful, yes, she thought dispassionately—rather exceptionally so. Beauty to enthrall her people and lure a strong husband. She was as well bred as a fine mare, and quite as valuable.

This image of her had no calluses on its hands and no freckles to mar its milk-white skin. It was a little too perfect— but people would expect that. They would not be expecting Averil's true self, dressed as a servant and making no effort to hide her flaws.

She smiled. This was a terribly dangerous thing that Emma did, but Averil could see the humor in it. It kept her from collapsing in terror—or from ripping the talisman from Emma's hand and blasting it into shards.

They were all bound to this game, some by choice and some by birth. Averil was cursed with both.

She opened her mouth to dismiss the Knights, but that was no longer her place. Emma lifted her hand instead and held it out for them to kiss, which they duly and properly did.

The older Knights took their leave without further acknowledging Averil, which was also proper, but Mauritius paused. He was smiling. "You'll do," he said.

"I'm glad you approve," said Averil.

He grinned like a boy. "You will most definitely do. Don't

change a bit of yourself, lady. Fools will see you as what you seem to be, and the wise will know the truth."

"Is the king wise?"

"Now that is a question," said Mauritius. He saluted her as Knight to Knight. "Good night, lady and servant."

It was only after he was gone that Averil realized he had not answered her question. That made her heart go cold, but her smile refused to fade. Whatever came of this, in one Knight's mind at least, she had done well.

10

After all their haste to reach Morency, the travelers from Saint-Émile dallied for three days in the chapter house. Gereint gathered that they were waiting for something, but no one was forthcoming as to what it was.

He had more than enough to do with looking after the horses and mules and being required to join in arms practice with the half-dozen Postulants who were in this house. They had other lessons and duties as well, but he was excused from those. Teachers in the mother house would examine him and determine what he was fit for.

Here, he was fit to clean stalls, haul hay and acquire new bruises in his attempts at armed combat. He would not have said he was content, but the delay had an unlooked-for effect: it calmed him. He stopped waking in the night, gasping in formless panic. He could contemplate the road ahead with more anticipation than dread.

Late on the third day, a new company of Knights came riding in. These, he had heard, came from the Isle, and they brought a great treasure.

They seemed no more or less laden with riches than any other caravan of Knights that Gereint had seen—except for what they escorted: three women, mantled and veiled, on palfreys as genteel as their riders. Gereint wondered if they were Ladies from the Isle. He had never seen one, let alone three.

He saw precious little of these, between the veils and their being swept away into the guesthouse. He happened to be closest and therefore most convenient for taking charge of their horses, which he did willingly. Maybe if he was lucky he could catch a glimpse of the fabled Ladies.

The horses had little to say except that they were hungry and tired and had been ridden with appropriate respect. He took off their saddles and bridles and rubbed them down, settled them in stalls with water and full mangers, then cleaned the saddles because he had been taught to be thorough.

By then night had fallen. He had a bed in the Postulants' dormitory, but the hayloft was closer and quieter. He made himself comfortable there, bathed in starlight and wan moonlight from the high window.

There was no glass in the window, which at first seemed unremarkable—but as he lay there, he reflected that in Knights' houses, every opening was warded with glass. Even if it was no more than a crystal hung on a thread, it was there, laden with protections and shimmering with magic.

There was nothing here. It was a plain square opening high under the peak of the roof, with a shutter fastened back.

Someone had been lax. Unless it was intentional that there was a gap in the wards. If someone wanted to get in, maybe. Or let someone—or something—in.

Gereint shivered. He had grown up in a place completely devoid of either wards or magic, without even a shard of glass—and here he was fretting over one unguarded window.

He knew little and understood even less. Strange how clear that was as he lay here, alone but for the horses and mules asleep below. The city was a distant presence; even the chapter house with its rooms full of mages and apprentices seemed remote, its power muted.

He was neither awake nor asleep: half in a dream, half aware of the world around him. He lay buried in straw, warm and at ease, as a dark figure ascended the ladder into the loft.

It moved softly but without stealth, as if it belonged here. No spark of alarm kindled in him. He watched in dreamlike calm.

The shape was human, wrapped in a hooded mantle. It seemed unaware of him, treading softly among the heaps of hay and bundled straw toward the unguarded window.

The window still made his stomach clench, but the night visitor did not trouble him at all. He would find that strange when he was more awake. Now, it seemed to fit into his dream.

The figure stopped below the window. From its stance, he thought it might be looking up.

It raised hands that glimmered white in starlight. Something bright shone in one palm. It was a crystal, clear and many-sided. Starlight filled it. Gereint could hear singing, high and inhuman, welling softly from the stone.

The stone left the figure's palm as if drawn up by strands of starlight until it hung in the center of the window. There it stayed, glinting.

The subtle sense of wrongness—of defenselessness—vanished. Gereint's body went limp with relief. The figure sighed, a profoundly human sound.

Something moved beyond the warding: a flutter and a slither and a scrabbling of claws. The cloaked mage stood very still. Even in the dark, Gereint could see the tension in the shoulders.

Whatever it was gave up the effort. Long after the fluttering had died away, the mage stood motionless. Starlight faded from the crystal, but the wards held. The house was safe.

The figure turned and walked slowly back the way it had come. Gereint hardly dared to breathe. It passed by him without seeming to see, gliding down the ladder and out of sight.

IN THE MORNING Gereint would have thought he had dreamed it all, but when he looked up in the grey light, he saw the crystal glittering in the window. The wards were secure, their pattern unbroken.

The youngest Postulant of this house came between Gereint and the window. "When the sun comes up," he said, "you're to ride to Fontevrai. Have the horses ready."

"You're helping me," Gereint said. The boy sulked, but he surprised Gereint by not only staying but making himself useful.

Maybe that was how to talk to noblemen, Gereint thought. Never ask. Simply assume obedience.

Between them they had the horses saddled and the mules laden by the time the sun broke the horizon. The city was awake beyond the house's walls. The Knights were long since up and about their day's duties.

A doubled caravan would ride to Fontevrai: the riders from Saint-Émile and those from the Isle, playing escort to the veiled ladies. Gereint saddled their horses himself, carefully—even before his able assistant told him who they were. "It's the duke's daughter and her maids," the boy said. "She's been on the Isle all her life. Now she's coming home to find a husband before the old duke dies."

Gereint had never seen a duke's heiress before. He doubted he would now, either. Between veils and guards, there was little chance a mere groom could catch a glimpse of so lofty a face.

That hardly stopped him from hoping he might. "I suppose she's beautiful," he said—not meaning to say it aloud. "They all are, aren't they, those noble ladies?"

The boy shrugged. "I never noticed."

He was very young. Gereint bit his tongue on whatever else he might have said. The boy would never understand.

People were coming out of the house, dressed and armed to ride. The ladies came late and last.

They were heavily veiled as before, faceless and silent. Gereint could not help but think of his mother with her bare, weathered face and forthright manner. These highbred flowers were as unlike her as spirits of the aether.

He kept his place, well back in the line, as the caravan clattered through the gate. The ladies rode guarded in the center. Not only weapons protected them; the wards were so strong that Gereint's ears buzzed.

He fixed his eyes on the road in front of him. Knights were not priests; they were not forbidden the love of women. But they did not marry, and highborn ladies must. These ladies were forbidden not only because he was a commoner but because he wanted to be a Knight.

His body knew none of that. If it had known, it would not have cared. Between his mother's stern eye and his burgeoning magic, he had had little enough opportunity in Rémy to do what other young men his age insisted came naturally. It had never prevented him from thinking about it, or suffering from dreams that left him spent and sticky in the mornings.

He shifted uncomfortably in the saddle and did his best to focus on yesterday's humiliation in the fighting court. He could count his mistakes in bruises. As he ran through each one, trying to remember exactly how the arms master had corrected him, the last and most devastating commentary persisted in filling his head. "You're overgrown and badly balanced," the old man had said, "but you're not any more clumsy than you should be. There's talent in there somewhere, waiting for you to find it. You can be a fine fighting man. What you lack above all is faith. You don't believe that you can do this—or, truth be told, that you should. When you give yourself permission to learn, then you will."

Gereint was not sure what that meant. Maybe he did not want to know. He glared at the road, his strange mood gone notably stranger.

By nightfall they would be in Fontevrai. Maybe there were answers there, and help for his troubles. Neither of which he would gain from mooning after women whose faces he could not even see.

11

Averil was glad to be leaving Morency. It was a hand-some enough town and the Knights' house was large and well run, but there were strange undertones. It was not only her father's command and the spell that bound Emma to wear an alien face. It was the place itself.

She had sensed the break in the wards. It felt like a gap in well-forged armor—all the more disturbing because the rest was so carefully wrought. She could not tell why it was there or what it was for, but she knew she could not let it stay. She had to mend it.

It was a simple working, less complicated than many she had done on the Isle. As soon as it was done, as if the working had brought it, a creature of the aether came to test it.

The creature was not one of the airy beings that she had seen dancing above the sea as she sailed from the Isle. It came from a darker and stranger place.

It was a spy, she thought. Surely it had not come to find her—because if it had, that implied a conspiracy from within, as well as art enough to leave a single gap in the wards with-out breaking the structure of the whole. And why, if she had been able to sense it, had none of the Knights or their acolytes been able to do so?

So many questions, and no answers that she could find. She was well out of that house, though she did not delude herself that what she went to could be any better. This was a foretaste of the life she would be living. She would have to learn to bear it.

AVERIL HAD NO memory of Fontevrai. She had been sent away in her nurse's arms when her mother died soon after bearing her. And yet she knew the city as she knew the duchy: from long lessons and deep study.

She knew that it was the greatest city in the south of Lys, greater even than Tolosa in Proensa; that its castle had been built a thousand years ago in the fall of Romagna and rebuilt seven times since, most recently in her father's youth. She knew that it was set on a long high hill over the river Mireille, and that the fields that spread wide about it were planted with barley and rye, a golden treasure of grain that fed half the duchy. Its apples were famous and its pears were so sweet that songs were sung of them; the wine of its vineyards had graced emperors' tables in Romagna and was still a favorite of the Sacred Curia in that ancient city.

And most certainly she knew that its University was renowned for its scholars of law and medicine, philosophy and theology and above all the art of magic: both the learned magic of the Book and the high magic of the Making. Nine orders of mages called this city their own, and highest of them all was the order of the Knights of the Rose.

Books and tales and teaching did not prepare her for the subtle things. The shimmer in the air and the trails of magical workings hovering on the edge of vision; the intricate pattern of wards and magic. The scent of roses and the river, and the hot smell of the glass foundries in their quarter by the western wall.

She could not say that she was coming home. Home was the Isle, no matter what blood and duty told her. But this was a place where, if she chose, she could belong.

The western gate was elaborately carved in the pale golden stone of this country, in patterns too intricate to take in all at once. Bits of glass were inlaid in it. Where the carving pierced the stone, brilliant colors filled the openings, bright as jewels in the sunlight.

The Isle was wrought of magic. So, in its way, was Fontevrai. Its foundations were older than Romagna; the first of the Paladins had laid the first stone and the Lady Magdalen had wrought the first wards.

They rode in with pomp and trumpets, in crowds and cheering and a rain of flowers. Emma, wrapped in a golden glamour, sat a milk-white mare beneath a canopy of midnight and silver. The train of her deep blue gown trailed to the flower-strewn cobbles, and her hair streamed down her back like molten gold and copper, bound about her brows with a garland of white roses.

She was everything a duke's heir should be, a regal beauty bestowing her glance and the lift of her hand on her adoring subjects. And they did adore her. Averil, anonymous in servant's garb, saw how their eyes warmed and their faces softened. They had fallen in love.

That was the glamour's intent. Everyone was fixed on that shining figure; the rest of the riders faded into insignificance.

Emma's back was straight and her courage steadfast. She would hardly be human if she did not take pleasure in so much adulation, even knowing it was not meant for her. Averil could only pray that pleasure was all Emma took from it; that it did not cost her her life.

The procession ascended from the gate to the citadel, the duke's palace with all its banners flying. Armored guards came out to meet them, an escort of honor dressed in the livery of the silver swan. They bowed low before the supposed heir and flowed smoothly around her, sweeping her into the palace.

Jennet had managed to stay with Emma, but Averil found herself jostled in the rear among the squires and servants. The high ones went off to a different courtyard than the one to which the tide of people and animals carried her.

This was older, darker, less lofty and elegant than the newer portions of the palace that she glimpsed through distant archways. The animals here were mules and serviceable cobs, stabled cleanly and comfortably but without excessive sentiment.

She could look after a mule—she had done it often enough on the Isle. Since no one around her seemed inclined to give

or receive orders, she lent a hand where one seemed necessary, forking hay and hauling water buckets and rubbing down
sweaty backs and tired legs.

It was hard work but peaceful. The half-dozen stablehands
dwindled as the day lengthened, until only one other stayed
to finish the watering and feeding: a large young man with
rumpled fair hair and big, callused hands. She vaguely remembered him on the road, riding a mule with more practi-
cality than grace.

He seemed not to remember her at all. Unlike the Knights,
he could look at her without falling down in a fit; if her beauty
dazzled him, he gave no sign of it. They worked side by side
in silence, needing no words for work that they both knew
well.

Averil had had such companionship on the Isle. It was familiar, and welcome—though after they were done and she
had gone to find her maids and a bed, she realized she had
never asked his name.

Well, she thought: he had not asked hers, either. He smiled
and nodded and went on his way. She surprised herself with a
stab of loneliness.

Jennet and Emma were waiting for her, surely. And so was
her father. She had been avoiding that meeting.

She could keep on avoiding it. She should wash off the stink
of the stables—there were baths for the servants in the ancient
part of the palace, left over from Romagna—and she could
sleep among the servants, too. In the morning she could come
to it fresh in mind and body.

She got as far as the baths before Jennet found her. She was
dripping wet but she was clean, and she was wringing out her
hair when she looked up into that round and disapproving
face. "Lady," said Jennet, "we thought we'd lost you."

"Don't call me that," Averil said, though they were alone in
the room. "I'm your equal here. You have to remember."

"You will never be my equal," Jennet said, but she forbore
from adding Averil's title. "Your f— the duke is asking for
you. I'm to take you to him."

Averil took a deep breath and nodded. "Help me," she said.

Jennet was already moving to comb out Averil's hair and braid it. Even as Averil contemplated getting back into her stained and redolent clothes, the maid shook out a clean linen shift and a brown woolen gown: plainer even than the others, but much more finely made. They were servant's garb only in color and cut. In fabric they were subtly exquisite.

Averil would have to speak to her about that, but for the moment they would do. She let Jennet help her into them, because Jennet insisted. Then there was no avoiding it further. She had to face the man who had refused to look at her when she was born and who had never seen her since.

DUKE URIEN HAD aged greatly since the portrait he had sent his daughter. His hair had gone white and there was no black left in his beard; he was stooped and shrunken and his hands trembled. But his eyes were dark and clear, taking in his daughter with no expression that she could discern.

She was not sharing her thoughts, either. While he studied her, she studied the room in which he had received her: a small room, much less ornate than she might have expected, with a table and a scattering of chairs, and books everywhere. They lined the walls and marched in rows down the center, heaped on the floor and the table. Leaves of parchment, pens and brushes, blocks and bottles of ink lay scattered among the books.

It was a scholar's haven. She would have loved to bury herself in it—and maybe one day she would. Tonight she was under examination, as was he.

She was not about to break the silence once she had bowed to him and offered appropriate respect. She stood with her hands folded and her eyes lowered, saving her glances for the books nearby. The titles on their spines were almost too distracting.

At last he said, "We'll not be speaking often. It won't be appropriate. You understand, I hope."

She nodded.

"Also understand," he said, "why I did what I did. Do you regret your years on the Isle?"

She was careful to breathe slowly. "No," she said. "I do not."

"And yet you'll not forgive me."

"What is there to forgive? Fosterage is an honorable institution. You chose the Isle, for which I was well suited."

"And now I've torn you away from it."

She looked up then, because she had a need to see his face. It was no more transparent than ever.

Still, when she saw it in front of her, she knew what she had to say. "You have your reasons."

"You trust me?"

She thought about it. He was wise enough to wait. In time she said, "I believe I do. You may care nothing for me, but this duchy is your heart. You'll protect me in order to protect it."

"Your mother was my heart," he said, so starkly simple that her own heart clenched. "You are her blood and bone and her living image. You too are my heart—as little as I may have shown it."

"You did as you thought best." The words sounded cold, but they were all she could think of to say.

His faint sigh held a life's worth of regret. He straightened painfully. When he spoke again, he spoke nearly as coldly, as duke to servant. "Jennet will assign you your duties. Those will be light—but in order to preserve the illusion, they must be both visible and credible."

"I understand," Averil said. "I'm moderately competent as a ladies' maid. I know somewhat of herbs and simples and the lesser arts of healing, if that would be useful. And I make a fair stablehand."

He winced at that—slightly, but she could tell it was heartfelt. "Tonight you rest in comfort. In the morning the deception continues. Sleep well. Try to think well of me."

"I've never done otherwise," Averil said.

If she had been someone else, she would have dared the chill between them and embraced him, even kissed him. But she could not make herself move. He bowed somewhat stiffly. She bowed in return.

Jennet was waiting to take her to a room nearby: quiet,

secluded and as subtly luxurious as the clothes Averil wore. She was tired suddenly, to the point of exhaustion. There was no struggle left in her.

She went where she was led and lay where she was told. Sleep took her with such force that even as she gave way to it, she knew that there was magic in it.

12

Gereint more than half wished he could hide in the duke's stables, looking after the horses and mules and occasionally, if he was lucky, sharing the evening's duties with the redheaded stablehand. She had been a pleasant surprise. When he had time, he would occupy it with memories of her expression and how she had moved, and how her plain and practical servant's gown had not quite managed to hide the shape of her body.

It was an excellent shape, strong as well as graceful, and tall enough that she could look him easily in the face. That was not common. He quite liked it.

At the moment he had orders, and he was not fool enough to disobey them. He presented himself, late but obedient, at the mother house of the Rose.

It stood in the upper city below the duke's palace. Part of it was built into the rock that rose sheer from the river. From the street it looked like a long stone wall broken occasionally by gates. Only once Gereint was inside did he realize how strongly fortified it was and how much ground it covered. It was larger than the whole city of Morency.

It was too late and he was too befuddled to understand what he had been sent to. Saint-Émile had seemed imposing enough to his village-bred eyes. This was beyond his reckoning.

First he had to choose a gate. The largest seemed too obvious somehow. It was brightly lit and glinting with jeweled glass; guards in shining armor stood on either side of it. Even so late, it was open and waiting—inviting, one would have thought.

Gereint slid on past, evading the pool of light from the gate. He passed by half a dozen more before one seemed right.

It was a small gate, half in shadow; if it had been full dark he might not have seen it at all. At first in fact he thought it a trick of the light. A briar rose grew up out of the stone paving, twining around the posts and the low stone lintel. Its blossoms were as red as blood; their scent made the night dizzy.

Gereint raised his fist to pound on the gate, but it opened before he touched it. A very old man stood in it, gnarled and stooped, raising a lantern to peer into Gereint's face.

Whatever he saw seemed not to horrify him. He nodded, hooded eyes glinting. "Come in, messire," he said.

Gereint bowed as low as he could. A Knight this old, he reasoned, must have been a master in his day—even if he was ending his days as the guardian of a very small gate in a very large house. It seemed a pleasant duty, standing watch amid the scent of roses. Gereint should be so lucky, if he came so far.

The old man smiled a remarkably sweet smile. He stood back, beckoning Gereint inside.

Gereint entered with only the barest hint of hesitation. "Straight ahead," the porter said, "and left at the arbor. From there you'll know the way."

"How can I—" Gereint began, but the porter was gone—vanished. A wind moved among the roses, scattering a shower of petals on Gereint's head. They felt like a flicker of laughter.

This was magic. Gereint had never imagined such a thing: the lightness of it; the simple joy in what it could do.

He took the joy with him down the long shadowy path. The arbor at the end overflowed with roses. He paused to fill his head with their fragrance, then turned left as he had been instructed, toward a row of arches and a torchlit colonnade.

The torches led him. They brightened as he approached, then dimmed as he passed. More magic. And so, after joy, he discovered ease: the casualness with which the light swelled and faded.

He had never thought magic could be easy or joyful. All he knew was fear. In Saint-Émile he had learned anything but magic, and never seen anyone working it. He had thought the Knights made a great secret of it, but this place was brimming with it.

He could fall down in confusion or he could go on and hope for answers. He came to the colonnade and turned where the light told him to go. If it was a test of trust, he hoped he was passing it. Otherwise he could hope he died without too much pain.

He stopped in front of a door. It was a perfectly ordinary door of wooden panels bound with iron. The bar slid easily; the door opened on darkness that lightened slowly into a gold-tinged twilight.

A man stood there: the first human figure Gereint had seen since he left the porter. He was wearing Novice green, and he greeted Gereint with a smile. "Good," he said. "You came quickly. You still have time for dinner."

Gereint frowned. "I'm early?"

"You're exactly on time," the Novice said. "Usually when the new ones come, they choose another gate. It can take them days to find their way here."

"During which time they die of thirst or starvation?"

The Novice grinned. "There are pools in the gardens, and there's always fruit on the trees."

"All I saw was roses," Gereint said.

The Novice's brows rose. "Really? You *are* blessed." He cocked his head as if listening. Gereint heard nothing, but the Novice nodded as if in response to another's voice and said, "We're coming." He turned, beckoning to Gereint, and set hand to what had seemed a solid wall.

The wall slid back. The same golden light shone beyond, but the surroundings were much more familiar: a training court, empty in the dusk, and beyond it a mess hall notably larger than that in Saint-Émile but of much the same shape and ambience. It was nearly empty now, but there was ample provender to be had still, and a handful of Postulants and Novices to share it with.

Gereint's guide did not ask him if he minded sitting at the

most populous table. When he hung back, the Novice pulled him down to the bench in the midst of the crowd. A cup and a bowl appeared in front of him.

He ate and drank blindly, buffeted by the others' good cheer. This was nothing like Saint-Émile.

They did not know who he was or where he was from. None seemed to have noticed that he was twice the age of the usual Postulant. They were much more intrigued by the fact that he had come in through the rose gate, by the straight way.

He had already guessed that it was a test, but he had not known how much it mattered. It was as if one choice, and one gate, could tell them everything they needed to know.

He knew nothing at all. When he had eaten as much as he could hold, his Novice extricated him neatly from the crowd and bore him off to a dormitory. There were bodies in the beds, snoring softly.

Gereint realized that he was exhausted almost beyond sense. There was a bed in front of him, as narrow and starkly plain as his bed in Saint-Émile. He had no memory of falling into it. Between night and morning was not even the shadow of a dream.

THE MASTER OF Novices studied Gereint from every angle. Gereint endured his scrutiny without, he hoped, twitching too badly.

It had been a long morning, full of sometimes inexplicable tasks and tests. The examinations in weaponry and horsemanship he could understand; he had proved that he could read the vulgar tongue fluently, Romagnan haltingly, and a handful of other languages little or not at all. But he could not imagine why he had been asked to distinguish among seven different kinds of sand, or what it meant that he had chosen one particular crystal out of a bowlful of them. It had something to do with magic, he supposed.

Now this seemingly gentle Knight with a blind eye and a

withered hand was looking him over as if he had been a cob at a horse fair. Any moment he expected the man to pry open his mouth and peer at his teeth.

After what seemed a very long time, the Master of Novices said, "You present an interesting challenge, messire. An impossible one, we might think—but you came through the rose gate. The porter spoke well of you."

"I'm too old, aren't I?" Gereint said. "It's too late for me."

"Some might say that," said the Master of Novices. "But the porter likes you. And you came by the straight way. If we all survive you, you'll be a credit to the order."

"You believe that?"

The Master's brow lowered over his one good eye. "*If* we survive you. You're a patchwork of half-knowledge and ignorance. Your magic has nothing resembling either order or control. Still, I think you can be taught. The Squire Riquier has asked to take you in hand. He's aware of the risk and declares himself unafraid of the consequences."

"And if he dies of it?"

"You should think better of yourself," the Master of Novices said. "Riquier has two highly useful gifts: endless patience and an exceptional talent for setting and maintaining magical protections. And, he says, he likes you. Between him and the porter, you come unusually well recommended."

God knows why, Gereint thought—catching himself before he said it.

It seemed the Master heard it regardless. He gripped Gereint's shoulder with his one good hand and shook it hard enough to rattle Gereint's teeth. "Never cast the dark glass on yourself. See the truth, but see it clearly. The darker the light by which you see, the more likely you are to lose control of your magic."

Gereint stared at him, mute inside and out. The Master of Novices nodded as if in satisfaction. "Go. Eat something. Then find Riquier."

Gereint did not know if he should bow, kneel, fall flat on his face—or simply duck his head and run for it. He hoped Riquier was patient about answering questions. Gereint had a thousand of them, and those were only the ones that came immediately to mind.

THE SQUIRE RIQUIER turned out to be Gereint's guide of the night before. This morning he was dressed in a Squire's dusk-blue cotte instead of the worn green he had been wearing when Gereint met him.

Gereint frowned. "I thought you were a Novice," he said.

"I was," said Riquier, "until last night."

"They made you nursemaid me right before you were elevated?"

"Why not?" said Riquier.

Gereint had no answer for that as for so much else. Riquier grinned and clapped him on the shoulder and said, "Don't look so scared. You wouldn't be here if we didn't think you could do it."

"That's not what some people said in Saint-Émile."

Riquier's grin vanished briefly. In that instant, Gereint saw what a formidable man he could be. Then he was smiling again. "Some people don't know what they're talking about. Come—the sooner we start, the closer you'll be to proving them all wrong."

Gereint had to smile at that, if weakly. Riquier pulled him along until he mustered wits to do his own walking, showing him all the ways of the mother house, its halls, dormitories, refectories, practice courts, chapels, retiring rooms and above all its library. Somewhere in the middle there was a meal, and after the library Gereint had an hour to rest.

Tomorrow, his guide told him, he would begin lessons in earnest. Today was for learning what the mother house was.

There was a great deal to learn. But Gereint had known that. One skill he still had to acquire: how to ask questions and—even more to the point—understand the answers.

"MAGIC," SAID RIQUIER, "is very simple at its heart. Humans have divided it into orders and rules and levels of mastery, but all of it is only this: light that shines through everything that is. Glass gathers and shapes it, but magic needs only itself."

"Is that what wild magic is?" Gereint asked.

Riquier's eyes widened slightly. "You've heard of that, have you? None of us understands wild magic. We do know that without order and control, magic is deadly dangerous. Everything we do is aimed at protecting us from that."

Gereint nodded. They were in a rather incongruous place: in one of the stables, excavating a particularly filthy stall. Riquier's words were punctuated by the scrape and thrust of his shovel.

Somehow that seemed fitting. Gereint spread lime where Riquier had cleared away the worst of the muck.

Riquier paused, leaning on his shovel. "Here in the order, we control magic on two sides: through the lore of the Book and the arts of the Making. We all have to be scholars in order to be mages, and we also are required to be artificers. We make the glass through which we wield our powers."

"And the arts of war? Where do those come in?"

"Those are our rite and sacrifice. We defend the order and the realm. We guard the Mysteries for which we were founded."

"Mysteries?"

Riquier's patience was as inexhaustible as the Master had said, but Gereint could tell he had walked close to the edge of what the Squire could or would tell him. Riquier went back to his digging, thrusting rather deeper than strictly necessary.

Just when Gereint had decided that that was one question to which he would not receive an answer, Riquier said, "I'll tell you this once, and not again until you've passed the tests and proved yourself worthy. I'm telling you because if I don't, you'll try to find the answers for yourself—and that is more dangerous than you can understand. You are old enough and strong enough and I think wise enough to keep this secret between us."

"If you don't think I can," Gereint said, "don't tell me. I promise not to go looking."

"You won't be able to help it," Riquier said. "Now listen.

Every child knows the mystery of faith: how the Young God struck down the Serpent and brought order into the world. Before, there was no order, no reason and little sanity. Magic ran wild and mortals were enslaved to it. Then the Young God came, born in mortal flesh but created of living light. He led his band of followers against the Serpent and destroyed it, but in the doing was himself destroyed. His Ladies and his Paladins bore his body away from the field of battle and buried it in a secret place. Then came the great miracle: on the third day, when the Ladies came to seal the tomb with rite and power, they found it empty, with marks of supernal fire upon it.

"That much, every priest and true believer knows. It's the foundation of our faith, the truest proof that the Young God was indeed a god.

"What the priests never tell and very few of them know is that one thing was left of the Young God after he was lifted up to heaven. His shroud was lying on the stone. Burned into its fabric was the image of his body as it had been composed in death.

"That is the first Mystery," Riquier said, "and the first of the treasures that we keep: the shroud with its image and its memory of divine power. The second Mystery is the spear with which the Young God pierced the Serpent, that then was turned against him. Half a dozen holy houses venerate a spear that they claim is the very one. In truth it is with us. His blood is mingled with the Serpent's still, clotted on the cold iron."

Riquier stopped. His head was bowed. Gereint thought he was done, but he spoke again without lifting his head. "Then there is the third Mystery. I shouldn't tell you this at all, or speak of it to anyone not initiate. But my orders are to answer any question you ask. There is a third charge that we keep." He paused to draw a long breath. "The Church teaches that the Serpent was cast down and destroyed. So it was—in a manner of speaking. The Serpent is living chaos and the embodiment of eternal night. It existed before creation and will exist when creation is destroyed. Although its power was broken and driven out of the world, it was not killed. The Young God's spear weakened it, but it was the Young God's death that over-came it. Then the Paladins bound it with the power that came to them from the Young God, and the Ladies wrought for it a prison where it would be bound perpetually.

"That prison, we guard. What it is, where it is, what it's made of, no one below the rank of Knight Commander is per-mitted to know. We only know that it exists, and that this above all is the reason our order was founded. Every art we practice, every fragment of lore we know, comes simply to this: assuring that the Serpent never escapes from its prison. For if it does, all order will be scoured from the world and all kingdoms will fall. Mortals will once more be enslaved, bound to serve the Serpent and its disciples. We will never be free again."

When Riquier stopped then, he did not go on. Gereint would not have wanted him to. There was so much to understand—too much.

The world he had known as a child was irrevocably changed by the fact and knowledge of magic. Now he had a glimpse of what magic was for.

It was more than he could take in all at once. A lifetime might not be enough. And then he had to understand that he had been called to this duty—this great guardianship, which no one in the wider world had ever heard of.

He realized that he had dug a hole past ankle-deep, and that Riquier had done nothing to stop him. He filled it again with teeth-gritted concentration.

Then he went on to the next stall, blindly, not caring if Riquier followed. He could not think, not now. He had to sim-ply be. If he could do that, he convinced himself, the rest would be easy.

13

Within two days of the heir's arrival in Fontevrai, the suitors began to gather. They must have been circling like vultures along the border, waiting for a new and nubile victim.

Averil should try for fairness of mind. She was born to marry; it was her destiny and her duty. One of these men, or one like him, must stand beside her when she ruled the duchy.

Still, on the outside as she was, unknown and unacknowledged, she found their flocking and chattering faintly ridiculous. It was also faintly repellent.

Emma played her part admirably. She danced, chattered, laughed. She let herself be seen in court and in the gardens and from the balcony of the ladies' solar. She was a vision of red-golden beauty, created to drive a man mad.

Averil had a maid's duties: fetching and carrying whatever the supposed heir might be presumed to need, looking after her gowns and jewels and waiting on her pleasure. For Averil this was a light burden. She had hours free when she could explore the palace or the city or bury herself in her father's library.

She saw the duke often enough from a distance, but he did not acknowledge her and she was careful not to invite his or anyone else's notice. With her head down and a veil over her hair, she was simply another servant girl going about her business.

When she had been six days in Fontevrai, she was enlisted with all the other servants to prepare a grand banquet: the formal feast of welcome for the duke's heir. She fetched linens and spread them on long tables in the hall; then she laid out trenchers and spoons and arranged cups and bowls to the steward's order. The cups for the lowest tables were silver, for the nobles' tables gold, and for the high table, crystal so fine it sang when the air touched it.

She had been feeling strange since she woke before dawn. Her dreams had been vague and formless; she remembered nothing of them, but they darkened her mood.

It was a glorious day: clear, bright, warm but not unbearably so. The scent of roses in the gardens was intoxicating. The hall was banked with them, heaped in vases and bowls and woven into garlands along the edges of the high table.

All that fragrance made Averil feel slightly ill. The sky, as brightly blue as it was, seemed to weigh on her. Beneath the chatter of voices and the strains of song and sacred chant, she kept hearing the hiss and slither of darker things.

EMMA SAT IN Averil's place at the feast, at the high table beside the duke. She was crowned with white roses and dressed in white samite, a shimmering vision beneath the jeweled glass of the high windows.

Averil watched from behind a pillar. She had eluded whatever duties the steward might have found for her; she was a shadow, a silent presence on the edge of that glittering assemblage.

Six of the twelve courses had come and gone. In some distant otherworld, her stomach was clenched with hunger. She had not eaten since at least the night before.

It did not matter. She had to be here. There was no sense or reason in it, and it certainly was not jealousy of the woman who wore her face and accepted the homage that was meant for her. There was great danger in that place. If Averil had not believed it before, in this long evening, for no clear reason, she was sure of it.

The duke was happy tonight. He was frail and age lay heavy on him, but he was smiling, basking in the light of the lady beside him. Even though he knew that she was a glamour and a deception, he let himself be glad that his heir was here, alive and safe.

The suitors had risen and begun to dance in front of the lady. It was an energetic dance, with much stamping and shouting. The glitter of their jeweled ornaments and the sheen of their silken cottes made Averil's sight blur.

Her head ached; she was dizzy and her stomach heaved. The hissing that she had heard earlier was loud now, drowning out the suitors' war-chant. They were doing battle for the image on the dais, vying for the gift of her favor.

Something flashed in the corner of Averil's eye. In the first instant she thought it the reflection of light from a cup or the flash of a jewel, but it was too jagged and swift—and it was in flight, winging from the shadows on the hall's edge. There was something—she could almost see—

It was aiming toward the dais. Averil's body would not obey her. She could only stand and stare and watch that half-visible, half-perceived dart leap toward its target.

The high ones on the dais seemed both blind and oblivious. They laughed and bantered and drank from their crystal cups.

The duke stiffened. Averil's eyes had been on Emma, but the false heir showed no sign of trouble. The dart that had seemed to be aimed at her had flicked aside.

The duke was its target. Averil heard, or fancied she heard, cold laughter.

Even his guards did not know. They stood like armored images behind the dais.

Averil fought with every scrap of will she had to break the spell that bound her. She could not move forward at all, but she found she could move sideways, sliding along the wall as if pressed between a wall of stone and one of air.

The duke was sitting motionless. The dance of suitors had risen to a crescendo and ended with a stamp and shout. Emma laughed and clapped her hands.

Averil collided with what she took for a pillar, until it yielded. She looked up startled into Bernardin's face. He seemed as spellbound as the rest, but his eyes were on the duke.

She gripped his arms and shook him hard. He blinked and shuddered.

She slapped him.

His hand flew up. She braced for the blow, but it fell short of striking her down. His frown was more puzzled than angry. "What—"

She pulled him with her along the wall, wading as if through water. They were caught between worlds, between the careless revelry of the feast and the cold stillness of hostile magic.

The duke's eyes were blank. The dart gleamed in the hollow of his throat. It was sinking deeper, absorbing into the flesh.

Bernardin broke free of the spell and sprang ahead of Averil toward the dais and the duke.

The duke crumpled into his arms. A ripple of silence spread outward from the dais. In its wake ran a murmur of shock, then outrage, then horror.

Averil, anonymous and unregarded, slipped in behind Emma's chair and said in her ear, "Stand up. Take charge. Or they'll stampede like cattle."

Emma's glance was as wild as any of the rest, but Averil's brisk tone and sharp words shocked her into, if not sanity, then at least obedience. She rose unsteadily, but her voice was clear. "Please. In God's name. Give us room."

They were little enough as words went, but they spoke to the spirit of order that was ingrained in every child of Lys. Panic turned to simple fear. People retreated, drawing away from the duke lying limp in the Lord Protector's arms.

DUKE URIEN LAY in his hard and narrow bed. It was a scholar's bed or a monk's, just as the room was a scholar's room. Books walled it, rising above the windowframes and heaping on benches and tables and chests.

The duke's eyes were open, but whatever they saw, it was not the age-darkened beams of the ceiling. His hands lay strengthless on the coverlet. He barely breathed.

His court physician had found nothing to cause this sudden sickness. The dart was gone, melted like ice. Only its poison was left, seeping slowly through the duke's body.

The masters of the nine orders of mages had come and gone. Like Mestre Orazio, they had thrown up their hands and professed themselves at a loss. There was magic in this sickness— on that they all agreed—but it was nothing that any of them could recognize.

Emma had been carried off to her rooms. She had fainted most convincingly and been fluttered over by half the suitors and her whole flock of maids. Now there was only Averil, invisible as ever, and Bernardin sitting silent beside the bed.

The Lord Protector's head was bent, his chin propped on his fist. There was a deep line between his brows. He was on guard in more ways than the eye could see, but he was no more certain of what had struck down his duke than any of the rest.

Averil sat across from him and let the shadows withdraw. When she was sufficiently in the light, his eyes widened. She suppressed a smile.

"Lady," he said, bowing where he sat.

She waved that aside. "You didn't see it, did you? No one did."

"What should I have seen?" Almost he added her title again, but he wisely left it to silence.

"The dart," she said, "that came from the shadows. It must be glass, I thought, but it melted like ice. You didn't see it at all?"

He shook his head. "You are sure? It was a dart?"

"I saw it," she said.

His frown deepened to a scowl.

"Do you recognize it?" she asked. "Is it a kind of magic you know?"

"It need not be magic at all," he said. "Magic in the dart, poison in the tip: that, I have heard of. But what the poison is, if Mestre Orazio and his order have no knowledge, I can hardly say. My art is to protect and defend, not creep and destroy."

"Would the king know?"

"The king," said Bernardin slowly, "is no friend to our order.

We rejected him, did you know? He came to us with hopes of becoming a Knight, but he failed even to pass the gate of the mother house."

"Why did he fail?"

"Is that significant?"

"Can you say it's not?"

Bernardin sighed. He sounded ineffably tired. "He failed because his magic was sufficient but his heart was not. He lacked a certain quality of spirit."

"He was weak?"

"Not at all," said Bernardin. "He was very strong. But his strength was and is unsuited to our discipline. A Knight lives to serve the kingdom and the order. Clodovec lives only to serve himself."

"So he hates you," Averil said. "What is my father to him, then? Simply an obstacle?"

"Your father is the greatest lord in this part of Lys, and wields more influence, and more wealth, than the king himself. Yes, I think the king is behind this—but what he has done or how to undo it, none of us knows."

"Then we will learn," Averil said.

Bernardin nodded. After a pause he said, "Lady, in his incapacity, under normal circumstances I would rule as regent. Now that you—or your image—are here, that office should go to you. Will you take it? Will you remove the glamour from your servant and stand in the light?"

"If I do," said Averil, "will I be in any more or less danger than I was before?"

"You were a target then. You'll be more of one now."

Averil looked down at her tightly laced fingers. "I have to think," she said. "Double the guard on my image and secure the protections."

"It's done, lady," Bernardin said.

She realized that he had given her her title twice, and she had not corrected him. She shrugged slightly. Everyone here knew who she was.

She rose and shook out her skirts. He rose also and stood as a guard stands, waiting.

"Stay," she said. "I'm only going to the library."

"You should be guarded," he said.

"If I am," she pointed out, "and I but a servant, won't that raise questions we don't want answered?"

He gave way to that—not easily, but he could see it as well as she. She smiled at him, wearily, and bent her head. "Look after my father," she said.

14

Gereint found life in the mother house both exhausting and exhilarating. With Riquier for his teacher, he was up before dawn and laboring—studying, learning, practicing with weapons—far into the night. Riquier shared a philosophy with Gereint's mother: the harder the difficult child was made to work, the less time he had to get into trouble.

The morning after the feast in which the duke fell, word of his indisposition hummed through the refectory. Gereint heard it without great interest. It was nothing to do with him; he was more concerned with the dozen books he had been given to read, most of them in languages he had never heard of.

"You'll learn them," Riquier had told him the evening before when he dropped the lot of them at the foot of Gereint's bed. "Starting tomorrow, after mess duty and stable duty, and after your hour with the sword."

Mess duty and stable duty were more pleasant than not. The hour with the sword was as humiliating as Gereint had expected. After he had washed off the sweat and blood, he trudged toward the library, where some crabbed and ancient scholar no doubt was waiting to enlighten his ignorance.

The mother house was a maze, but he was learning its ways. From the hall of the sword to the library, the shortest way ran across a courtyard and skirted the stables, then traversed a kitchen garden, the lower kitchens and the passage to the Knights' dining hall. There were a number of doors off this passage, most of which were perpetually locked.

The one that led to the library was at the end of the passage and up a flight of worn stone steps. This morning, the door at the bottom of the stair, which had always been barred with magic as well as an iron bolt, was unlocked.

Gereint knew better than to give way to curiosity. He would have gone past like a virtuous Postulant, if he had not staggered and almost fallen.

Something was inside. Something enormous; something wonderful. It was singing.

The song tangled his feet and brought him down. It filled his head; it unraveled the knots deep inside and sent skeins of magic curling and glimmering outward.

He swayed on his knees, blinking and gaping. The door was open. Many-colored light fell in shafts across the floor.

There were wonders inside. All of that wide, high room was lined with tables and pedestals and cases. In those cases were the most marvelous things Gereint had ever seen.

They were made of glass. There was silver and gold; there were jewels. There were baser metals and finely carved wood and sculpted stone. But those were mere ornament. The true art and power resided in the glass.

Here was magic. Gereint had seen the glass in churches and chapels and felt the protections on the Knights' houses. He had been reading of the art of the Maker and the Loremaster and learning of great works and mystical enchantments, but until now, he had not known what those could be.

These were works of the Making, power captured in earth and fire and then given shape through the crystalline substance of glass. Some were shaped by mortal breath, others molded within a matrix of metal or stone.

He knew he should not go in. But the glitter of so many workings drew him irresistibly, and their song silenced any misgivings he might have had.

He walked down aisles of wonderful and incomprehensible things. Each was meant for a purpose. Maybe someday he would learn what it was.

He kept his hands tightly clasped behind his back. Sometimes he paused, bending to peer through a tunnel of glass into shining infinity or pausing to marvel at a pane of clear glass that looked out on no world he had ever seen.

He had forgotten his teacher waiting in the library above. All he could think of was this miracle of manifold magic.

Near the end of the hall was a space set apart. A long table stood there. On it was a beautiful, a glorious thing. It looked like a reliquary made of gold and jewels, rich with enamel-work, but inside it, instead of the bones of a saint, was magic.

It looked like a white-hot coal suspended in a sphere of glass and gold. He could almost grasp what it was meant to do. It concentrated magic; but for what, he was not exactly sure.

He leaned closer. He would never touch it, he was not that great a fool, but he needed to see it clearly. He bent until his nose was hardly a palm's width away from the luminous center.

Had it been glowing that brightly before? It gathered light—that was one of its properties. It tugged at his magic, tempting it out of its bonds.

Oh, no, he thought. He was not going to give way. He had learned a little since he left his mother's house. He could turn away from temptation.

The working was blazing brightly now, as if the sun had come down out of the sky. It was trying to capture Gereint's magic and bind it.

He stopped it with a single stroke like the quick cut of a blade snipping a thread.

The heart of the working shattered. Gold and jewels fell, their bindings loosed. Shards of glass tumbled to the table and scattered across the floor.

Gereint felt nothing at all. That would come later. Whatever he had done before to prove that he was not worth saving, this was worse. Much, much worse.

He could run away, but where would he run to? Wherever he went, he was still Gereint. He would still be a danger to every person and place he came to.

The shards of the working were deadly sharp. He lifted the largest. It was almost as long as a dagger, and its edge drew blood even from so light a touch.

He could hope he would bleed to death before anyone found

him. It was a feeble hope. The eruption of so much magic could not have escaped the Knights' notice. They would be here soon.

Maybe not soon enough. He set the point of the shard to the vein of his wrist, gritted his teeth and braced to cut.

Fingers closed over his. He looked, not into Riquier's face as he might have expected, but that of the Knight Mauritius.

Very gently but without any possibility of resistance, Mauritius freed the shard of glass from Gereint's hand. "Come," the Knight said equally gently.

Gereint eyed the knife at Mauritius' belt. He was fast, but he had no doubt the Knight was faster. Still, if he could just . . .

Mauritius' hand came to rest on that inlaid hilt. He bowed, ushering Gereint ahead of him.

Gereint had reached the point of perfect despair. It was almost a pleasure, like pain that had pierced too deep to be felt any longer for what it was. He went where he was told, secure in the knowledge that this time there was no hope left.

THE FATHER GENERAL of the order was a personage so august that Gereint had seen him only from far away, officiating at services in chapel. From across the worktable in a cluttered study, he looked like any other man of middle years—younger than Gereint might have expected—but there was no denying his strength.

This magic did not beg Gereint to touch it. If he had dared, it would have seared him to the bone. That was a temptation of its own, but the impulse to take his life had passed. For better or worse, he was bound to this body until someone or something else released the binding.

The ruins of the working lay on the table in front of the Father General. He brushed it with a finger and sighed. "This," he said, "was the masterwork of a Knight Major who aspires to become a Knight Commander. He wrought it with his own hands and his own magic, unassisted by any other, as proof of his fitness for the higher rank. Nine years he spent perfecting it. His heart and soul were in it, and all the mastery that he had. There will not be another like it in this world."

With each word, Gereint's shoulders bent lower, until he was almost on the floor. "I'm sorry," he said. "I didn't—I can't—"

"Of course you are sorry," Father Vincent said. "You have a good enough heart. But your magic is nearer to wild than any man's should be."

Gereint lifted his head. "There isn't any hope, is there? There never was. Even if I had been taught, I don't have a kind of magic that can be controlled. I was born wild. I'll never be safe, nor will anyone who comes near me."

"That may be," said Father Vincent. "Or it may not."

"So you'll send me away. Or kill me. I'd rather be dead, sir, if you don't mind. Every time I go anywhere, sooner or later this happens. What if next time someone is killed? Better I die first."

"That too may be," Father Vincent said, "but it's not for you to decide. The Lord Protector needs someone quick and unobtrusive to run his errands. Riquier will go with you—he's been assigned to the palace. Your lessons will continue."

"So," said Gereint, trying not to be bitter, "you're sending me away after all."

"Riquier asked for you," Father Vincent said.

"Why?"

The Father General's lips twitched. It dawned on Gereint that he had been unconscionably forward with the Grand Master of all the Knights. But before he could scramble together an apology, Father Vincent said, "Riquier believes that there is hope. He also believes that he can teach you."

"Riquier is a fool," said Gereint.

"Then so am I," said Father Vincent. "I agree with him."

Gereint shook his head vehemently. "There isn't anything anyone can do. Unless . . ." He swallowed, nearly choking. "Unless you can take it away. Kill the magic. Take it out of me."

"That would kill you," said Father Vincent.

"Then let it," Gereint said.

The Father General shook his head. "Despair is a sin, messire. Go with Riquier. Try to find a little of his faith in you."

Gereint dug in his heels. "Not before I learn something—anything—to stop these eruptions."

Father Vincent nodded slowly. "That's reasonable enough." He touched Gereint's forehead, then heart, then hand. "From the mind to the heart and the heart to the hand: so is magic ruled and contained. There's a cantrip for you, messire. Remember it whenever the bonds threaten to break."

"But I don't understand—"

"You will," said Father Vincent.

"But—"

The Father's General's patience was vast, but it was not inexhaustible. The flash of his glance cut off what else Gereint would have said, and sent him in search of Riquier.

15

Riquier had already gone to the duke's palace. He had left a message for Gereint, with instructions to pack his belongings and bring them to the white tower within the citadel. There were also new clothes, which fit much better than Gereint's already outgrown ones, and a servant with a bath and a pair of shears.

A good hour later, scrubbed clean and with his hair cut and combed into something resembling order, Gereint shouldered his bag of belongings. He hardly expected a grand farewell, but he was touched when he left the Postulants' dormitory to find all the Postulants and a good number of Novices waiting to see him off. Not one of them castigated him for what he had done.

It seemed Riquier's faith was catching. He was standing straighter as he made his way to the gate and feeling almost as if he believed in himself. This was not a trivial task he had been given. If he had been passed on like a badly chosen name-day gift, at least he was going somewhere useful.

The gate he had been sent to opened on the great square of Fontevrai, across from the cathedral with its soaring towers. The citadel rose on its high rock above the square, with the ducal palace in its heart.

There were guards at the gate of the mother house, but there was also a porter, the same ancient man who had let Gereint in through the rose gate. Gereint greeted him with a smile that wobbled only a little.

The old man smiled back. "Ah, messire. Precisely on time as always. Here; I have a gift for you."

Gereint blinked. "Sir, you don't need to—"

The porter ignored him, drawing from his purse a pendant on a silver chain. It was a pretty thing, finely wrought in enamelwork in shades of red and blue and green and gold, with a twining pattern that beguiled the eye. There seemed to be no magic in it, and nothing remarkable apart from its pleasing shape and color.

"Keep it with you always," the old man said. "When the bonds threaten to break, remember your cantrip and let this be your focus. It will help you."

Gereint bowed. This was a gift of pure kindness. He let the porter hang it around his neck, slipping it under his cotte and shirt. It was cool against his skin, but it warmed soon enough, until he could almost forget that it was there.

The porter's smile saw him out of the gate and into the square. People were coming and going, most on foot, some on horseback or in carriages. He threaded his way through them, keeping his eye on the duke's palace.

It was farther away than it looked, and the way to the gate was steep. That was for defense, he had learned: a charge on horseback was not so easy, going straight uphill, and arrows flew better down than up.

It made for a fair trudge in the hot summer noon. He was sweating when he came to the gate and presented his orders.

The guards there examined the parchment minutely, and one of them tested the seal with a flare of magic. Only when he was well satisfied would he allow Gereint to go on. "Third court," he said, "in the white tower."

Gereint wondered if he should bow. The guards were already engrossed in the next arrival, a mounted nobleman with a large and glittering escort. It was gratifying to see that a prince received the same scrutiny as a lowly Postulant of the Rose.

Gereint was letting himself be distracted. He squared his shoulders and forayed into the maze of courts and halls and passages.

He lost his way twice and had to ask for guidance from supercilious servants, but he found the third court soon enough, and the white tower rising above it. That was impossible to mistake: there were roses growing up the front of it and carved in stone over its gate. Its guards were Squires in bright armor, who seemed to be expecting him. One said, "Ah. Good. Up the stair; fourth door on the left."

That proved to be a dormitory, deserted at this hour, with a bed over by the far wall that appeared to be unclaimed. Gereint laid down his traveling bag and stood for a while, simply breathing. He felt as if the world had been spinning out of control, then completely without warning, it had stopped. He could not imagine what he was supposed to do next.

"Gereint!"

The familiar voice brought him about. Riquier was grinning at him. "There you are. Took you long enough. Did Father Vincent take too many strips off your hide?"

"Not more than a dozen," Gereint said wryly. "I was surprised. I thought he'd have my whole hide, and my head with it."

"I talked him out of that," said Riquier.

"Why?" Gereint demanded as he had of the Father General. Riquier shrugged. "I have a feeling."

"What—"

"Sometimes," said Riquier, "it's best not to examine such things too closely. Now come with me. The Lord Protector has a few moments to spare, but they aren't many and his patience isn't what it should be. You'd best pay your respects while you can."

Gereint's courage almost failed, but Riquier had him by the arm and was half-dragging him out of the dormitory. Unless Gereint wanted a fight, he had to give in to the Squire's urgency.

WITH SOMEWHAT OF a shock, Gereint recognized the Lord Protector. He was the Knight who had led the caravan from the Isle, escorting the duke's heir. He looked harried now;

even as the Squire and the Postulant ventured into his work-room, a man in the duke's livery left at a fast trot.

Lord Bernardin greeted Gereint with a scowl and Riquier with a sharp word. "You're sure he can do it?"

"I am, messire," Riquier said.

Bernardin grunted. "I need someone quick, cool-headed and discreet. I also need someone who knows the city as well as anyone born in it."

"Messire—" Gereint began.

Riquier's voice rose over his. "Give us the rest of the day. By morning he'll know everything you need him to know."

"You trust him?" Bernardin demanded.

Riquier nodded.

"Do it," said the Lord Protector.

"WHAT EXACTLY AM I supposed to be doing?"

Gereint had waited the better part of an hour to ask the question that had been burning in him. Riquier was in the midst of building a fortress of books, heaping them on a table in a library nearly as wondrous as the one in the mother house.

The Squire paused in opening a massive tome. "Bernardin needs a runner he can trust: someone to carry messages, run errands, and be his eyes and ears in places where the Lord Protector would be too conspicuous."

"And you persuaded him to choose *me*?" Gereint's voice had risen to a squeak. "He needs a master spy, not a farmboy with pretensions."

"A farmboy with pretensions is exactly what he needs," Riquier said. "You're not a nobleman and you don't look like one. You've been a hunter. You know how to make yourself disappear." He beckoned. "Come here."

Gereint came warily. Riquier was standing in the middle of a tower of books. Each one, Gereint happened to notice, had a bit of glass set in the cover: a gleam of enamelwork, a crystal, or a scrap of mirror.

They were books of magic. Gereint turned to run, but the spell was already on him. Instead of bolting away, his feet carried him into the center next to Riquier.

The Squire had a roundel of glass in his hand: a lens, it was called. It gathered magic and focused it. He turned it on Gereint.

Gereint opened his mouth to protest. He of all people could not be this close to magic or be a part of it.

The words never came. He looked into that point of light, and a sigh escaped him.

It was knowledge: as pure and simple as that. The wild magic stirred within Gereint, but the words of the Father General's cantrip sent it back to sleep. Other words, words as crystalline as the glass that conveyed them, flooded into his mind. Images flowed with them, bright and clear, giving the words substance.

The citadel of Fontevrai, the city that surrounded it, the duchy whose heart it was, poured into Gereint and became a part of him. What would have taken years to learn by reading and doing was the matter of a long afternoon.

He came out ravenous from the trance of the spell, to find the table laden with food and drink and Riquier already diving into it. Gereint fell on it as if he had not eaten in a month. He hardly noticed what he ate, except that it filled the echoing cavern of his stomach.

When he came up for air, every plate and bowl was empty, and Riquier was grinning at him. Gereint belched nobly and sat back in his chair. "If I'd known learning was this easy, I'd have done it this way long ago."

Riquier's grin faded somewhat. "You wouldn't want to make a habit of it. You'd burn out. But," he said, "now and then, isn't it a pleasure to be a mage?"

"Who'd have thought it?"

"You should," Riquier said. "Now go to bed. The Lord Protector will be needing you in the morning."

Exhaustion struck Gereint like a blow. He might have argued that he was not to be sent to bed like a child, but he was out on his feet. He made his own way to the dormitory, and he must have put himself to bed, because when he opened his eyes again, the sun was coming up and the morning bell was ringing.

GEREINT'S FIRST CHARGE as the Lord Protector's errand boy was to stand behind Bernardin in his workroom and remember the face of each person who came and went. If a name went with it, he was to remember that as well. He was not told why; he was simply told to do it.

It might have been monstrously tedious, but he found the various faces fascinating. They were of all ranks and stations, and they came for different purposes, which he took care to remember. Most had to do with the defense of the duchy. Nearly all said something of the duke's indisposition—the cause of which none of them knew, though they were working hard to discover it.

In the late morning the stream of faces dwindled to a trickle, then stopped. Bernardin rose and stretched, then sighed heavily. "Come with me," he said.

Gereint would have been glad to escape and rest, but the day was far from over. The Lord Protector led him through a door he had undertaken to notice, small and hidden behind a curtain in the workroom. It opened on a passage of no distinction whatever, dim-lit by lights that burned without flame— magic again, bound in spheres of glass.

It was not a long passage. It went up a stair and then down one and turned three times. It ended in a door and another passage, which in turn led to a starkly plain room full of books and summer sunlight.

The duke was lying on a bed no wider or softer than the one Gereint had slept in the night before. Gereint recognized him not so much from his portraits as from the way Bernardin looked at him in love and worship and tightly restrained despair.

Gereint wondered if he should bow or kneel, but the Lord Protector was doing no such thing and the duke was past noticing. Gereint trailed behind Bernardin until they both stood by the bed.

As plain as the bed was, the coverlet was rich and strange. It was woven or embroidered in a pattern of shimmering scales. It seemed to stir although the duke hardly breathed, flexing as if alive.

He opened his mouth to ask about it, but Bernardin spoke first. "This is your lord and liege," he said. "You owe obedience to the order always, but while the order stands in Quitaine, this is the lord to whom we offer fealty."

"Not the king?" Gereint asked.

"The king is no friend of ours," said Bernardin.

"Still—" Gereint began, but then he stopped. These were high matters, well above him, as his mother would have said. He decided not to argue but to keep his mouth shut and listen.

And all the while he dedicated himself to obedience, the duke's coverlet stirred and shimmered, seeming more alive the longer he looked at it.

16

At the end of a long day of waiting on the Lord Protector, Gereint was ready to fall over. But there were books waiting in the library in the white tower. Riquier had given him a grammar of Helladic and written down a row of letters that were not quite like the ones Gereint already knew. Tomorrow, the Squire said, those lessons would begin.

Gereint thought longingly of his bed, but he was finding it hard to resist a new book. He copied the new letters onto a scrap of parchment until hand and eye and mind all remembered them. Then he opened the grammar, peering at it in the light of the oil lamp he had brought with him.

A step sounded near the door. In the silence of the evening, it seemed unnaturally loud.

It was a woman in a servant's gown and smock, laden down with books. She laid them on a table near the door—reverently, which told Gereint she must know how to read them—and touched the sphere of glass that stood on a pedestal near the end of the table. It swelled into clear white light.

Gereint's brows rose. It took a fine hand with magic to do that. His brows rose farther as she slipped the kerchief from her hair and let it fall. He recognized that coppery-gold mane—and the fine-drawn face, too, with its gold-dusting of freckles across the nose. And, now his mind had caught up with his eyes, the body under the smock, tall and graceful and most sweetly curved. It seemed his acquaintance of the stables was a scholar as well as a stablehand.

Either she had not seen him or she did not recognize him. He supposed he should say something, but shyness shackled his tongue. He ducked his head and tried to focus on the book in front of him.

He had almost succeeded when a shadow fell across the page. He looked up into her face. She was not quite smiling. "You're studying Helladic?" she asked.

He gulped, blinked, then scraped together the wits to nod. "Starting tomorrow. I'm staring at it tonight—giving myself a leg up, as it were."

"Does it work?"

"I'll let you know."

She sat across from him. Her smile was more in evidence now. "I remember you. You were in charge of the horses on the road from Morency. You're a Postulant? Not a Novice?"

Gereint shrugged. He was somewhat surprised that he did not feel either embarrassed or irritable. Her question was honest and offered no judgment. "You know what they say. Better late than never."

She laughed. It was infectious; he caught himself grinning. "So they do!" she said. "Messire Bernardin thinks well of you—I heard him tell one of his Squires that he thinks you'll do."

"Servants hear everything," Gereint observed.

"Invisibility comes with the office," she said. "I know your name. I heard Bernardin say it—Gereint, yes?" He nodded. "Mine is Averil," she said.

"Averil," said Gereint. His tongue savored the name.

He offered his hand. She took it in strong callused fingers. Her grip was as forthright as a man's.

It was not easy to think with her so close, being so very distinctly a woman, but that firm handclasp helped him to focus. After a moment he found he could carry on a conversation as if she had been—almost—one of the Knights. "Are you sworn to an order?" he asked her.

"I was trained on the Isle," she said with no sign that she shared his confusion, "though I left before taking vows. I've been trying to keep up my studies."

"You're well ahead of me, then," Gereint said. "I've mastered mucking stalls and plowing fields, but the finer arts are mostly new to me."

"I can muck a stall and plow a field," she said. "If you'd like company in exploring the finer arts, I'm here most evenings."

Gereint flushed. All his hard-earned composure had fled. "Oh! Oh, no. I wouldn't want to slow you down. I really do know nothing."

"Teaching is how we learn," she said, not the least bit put off.

She sounded almost prim. That focused him somehow; he frowned at her. "Did someone put you up to this? Is this Riquier's way of lightening the burden? Not that I mind," he added hastily, "but you don't need to play games. I know what an ignoramus I am."

"I don't play games," she said, "and I don't know a Knight named Riquier, though I have a cousin or six by that name. As for your ignorance or lack thereof, we all start somewhere. Here, for example." She drew his book toward her and tapped the page. "Wouldn't you rather learn together than alone?"

"I wouldn't know," he said.

"Then that's the first thing you'll learn." She gave him back his book. "Tomorrow, then?"

He meant to make excuses but no promises and so escape, but her eyes were so clear and direct that he heard himself say, "Tomorrow. Unless—"

"Tomorrow," she said, smiling but firm.

AVERIL DID NOT know why she had said what she had. She was lonely, to be sure; and so was he, big awkward boy that he was, with so much magic in him that he could hardly contain it all. Part of her wanted to bristle like a cat. The rest wanted to teach him how to control himself—if only for her own peace of mind.

It was a distraction, which she needed. For all that the orders of mages could do, her father was sinking deeper into his dark dream. This morning the healers of Saint Raphael had thought they had the poison at bay—but as they finished working their spell, the poison came back in full force.

Averil was not ready to fall into despair. Not yet. But all the common remedies had failed. She needed something uncommon—something she had not thought of yet.

She could sleep on it, for what good that might do. The night might bring answers—or the morrow. Somewhere there was hope for her father.

AFTER THE FIRST day, Gereint spent much less time in the Lord Protector's workroom and much more of it running through the palace and the city. The spell of knowledge that Riquier had worked in him was well rooted now, spreading branches that blossomed and bore fruit: a deep awareness not only of the city and its people but of the land beneath and the powers that ruled the earth and air. He had become a part of Fontevrai, deeper and stronger than he might have dreamed possible.

In the evenings he went to the library. Averil was always there with her books. They had fallen into a habit of reading together, and when he had questions, she had answers for them. It was a rather painful pleasure, being so close to her, smelling the sweetness of her hair and trying not to let his eyes dwell on the curve of her breast under the smock, but he taught himself to live with it. It was good discipline.

Sometimes he saw her during the day, performing menial tasks, fetching and carrying for the duke's heir or one of her ladies. She would never acknowledge him then. He was a Postulant of the Rose, ranked well above a simple servant.

He thought that was absurd, but if he had learned nothing else, he had been indoctrinated with the importance of order in the world. Where the world could see, it was best if they kept their respective stations. But in the library, by lamplight, he was the pupil and she was the teacher.

If he dreamed of other things, alone in his bed afterwards, that was no affair of hers—and no fault of his, either. Dreams came and went as they would. They were like wild magic: powers in their own right, little susceptible to human control.

She was more than she wanted to seem. How much more, he was beginning to suspect. Her servitude was a pretense. She knew how to keep her head down and her bearing humble, and she was no stranger to hard work—but the way she spoke and carried herself in the library in the evenings, she was no simple serving girl. She was a mage and a powerful one, with arts that he could only guess at.

He kept quiet. If she wanted to tell him what she really was, she would. Meanwhile, no one else appeared to see the truth. Her illusion was almost perfect. Gereint would never have seen through it if he had not spoken to her night after night in the library.

He had been a week in Fontevrai before he saw the ailing duke again. He had run an errand to the mother house of Saint Orderic, bearing a message bound in a talisman of gold and jeweled glass. When he came back, Bernardin was taking a turn at watch over the duke.

Gereint might have waited or found something else to do, but the door-guard said, "He asked to see you," and held the door open. There was no easy way to slip out of that. Gereint stepped slowly across the threshold, tensing at the crackle of protections, but they let him through without challenge.

They were stronger than they had been a week ago. If any new attack came, it would fail.

Gereint did not think there would be one. There was no need for it. The duke was fading slowly but all too surely. Even from the door, Gereint could see how grey and shrunken he looked.

Bernardin sat by the bed with his head in his hand, breathing like a man in a light sleep. Gereint had been about to announce himself, but he let the words die before he spoke them. He moved softly across the room.

Midway between the door and the bed, he checked his stride. Someone else was there, wrapped in shadow. His heart knew her—and leaped—before his eyes took in the familiar shape.

Averil was watching over the duke. Gereint decided it was courteous to let her stay invisible. He finished his advance toward the bed and stood by it, and waited for the Lord Protector to wake and notice him.

While he stood waiting, he kept his eyes carefully averted from Averil. They came to rest on the duke instead, and fixed there.

The coverlet was even more intricate than he remembered, and even more beautifully embroidered. It must have some significance, since everything else was so very plain.

He would ask Averil tonight. She always knew the answers to his questions, or else knew where to find them. Meanwhile he had lessons to recall; he rested his mind in them while Bernardin drowsed and the duke sank slowly but surely into death.

"IS THERE A reason why the duke sleeps under a dragon's hide?" Gereint asked.

Averil frowned. She had been reading a book of theology while he struggled and cursed over his Helladic grammar. His question had come out of a long day's reflection, but to her it must have seemed drawn out of empty air.

"Dragon's hide?" she said. "What do you mean?"

"His coverlet," Gereint said. "It's an amazing thing—I've never seen or heard of anything like it."

Her frown deepened. "Why? What do you see?"

"It must be embroidered, then," he said. "All those scales—they gleam as if they were alive. There must be magic in the working, or else such art that it might as well be magic."

She rose, then reached across the table and pulled him to his feet. "Show me," she said.

He blinked, baffled. She pulled him with her out of the library.

IN LAMPLIGHT THE duke's coverlet was even more wonderful than in daylight. The scales of it were iridescent, with a shimmer on them that Gereint could not resist. He reached to touch the edge of one.

His finger sank through it to something so familiar that for a long moment he could not recognize it. Then his sluggish brain knew the roughness of woven wool.

He stared at his hand half-submerged in glistening scales. "What—"

"Tell me exactly what you see," Averil said.

Her voice was soft and might have seemed calm, but it had an undertone like shivered bronze. He answered as best he could. "Scales," he said, "larger than my hand. They look like silver or steel, with the shimmer of the rainbow on them. They seem alive. It's almost as if they breathe."

Her breath hissed. She spoke without looking at the Knight who stood guard. "Find the Lord Protector. Bring him here."

The Knight bowed—which Gereint found most interesting— and left at the run.

While they waited, Averil sat beside the bed. She seemed to be trying to see what Gereint saw. If he squinted hard, the scales grew translucent; he could just see the dark wool blanket beneath.

His head was full of questions, but he was feeling shy again—and guilty, too. If he had spoken of this a week ago, when he first saw it . . .

BERNARDIN CAME SO quickly that he must have been nearby. There was no sleep in his face; his eyes were hollow with the lack of it.

Gereint hardly needed Averil's prompting to tell the Lord Protector what he had seen. As Bernardin listened, his face grew even more haggard. When Gereint was done—it was, after all, a short tale, albeit a weighty one—Bernardin glanced at Averil. "Do you see this?"

She shook her head. "If I try hard, I can almost catch a glimpse of something, but that may only be desire overcoming sense. I do believe him, even so. I think he's seeing the spell that's on my f—that's on my lord."

"No doubt," said Bernardin. "Tell me, messire. Can you see inside it? Is there anything there but scales?"

"I can't—" Gereint began, but he paused. His eyes narrowed. If he tried too hard, he would be as blind as the others. He had to stop trying and simply be.

When he did that, he saw the framework beneath the scales. It might be the stitches of embroidery or the matrix of a magical working. He traced them with his fingertip, not quite touching the coverlet.

He saw Bernardin's eyes widen. "Can you see?" he asked.

The Lord Protector nodded. He leaned forward. Averil leaned with him.

"I've never seen anything like it," said Bernardin. "This is no magic we know or practice. Yet it is most certainly magic. What it might be . . ." He leaned even closer, until his beard nearly brushed the shimmer of scales.

"I have seen it," Averil said, almost too low to hear. "Or something like it. Underneath the surface of the Isle, in the chapel that is sometimes called Perilous. It's old magic, unimaginably old. Magic of the great disorder. Serpent magic."

Bernardin straightened slowly. Beneath weathering and old scars, his face had gone pale. "That magic was suppressed long ago and all its followers either put to death or stripped of their powers. This cannot be—"

"Nothing ever truly dies," Averil said. "That's one of the first lessons we learn on the Isle. Magic is neither created nor destroyed. It simply and perpetually is."

"So we say of our magic," Bernardin said. "But this—" He shook his head more in disgust than in denial. "Dear God in heaven, if this has risen again, my lord's fears are more than well founded."

"This must be what's been felling the lords of the demesnes without perceptible resistance," Averil said, "which means that the king has been exploring forbidden magics. He's not even trying to hide it."

"He'll have seen no need," said Bernardin. "We would never have guessed if it had not been for this young man."

"That speaks poorly of our powers in these latter days," Averil said.

Gereint did not know where to look. It was no new thing for him to see what no one else could see. They of all people should have been different.

The knowledge left him half elated and half dejected. Elation overcame the dejection and made him say, "This helps, doesn't it? Can you find a way to cure him?"

"I hope so," Averil said. Bernardin said nothing at all.

17

The Lord Protector was closeted for the rest of that day and much of the night with masters of the magical orders. Gereint had thought he would be put to work running errands for this sudden council, but he seemed to have been forgotten. Even Riquier had no time for him: he sent Gereint to the library to make his own way through the day's lessons.

Gereint did his best. But the longer he glowered at history and philosophy, Romagnan and Helladic, the deeper his resentment grew. He had discovered the cause of the duke's sickness. Should he not at least have received some acknowledgment?

He had never cared for such a thing before. It was a sickness. He flung his books aside and went in search of something useful to do.

There was a surprising amount of solace in cleaning out the stables—attacking cobwebs after the stalls were swept and bedded and the horses groomed until they shone. There was even more comfort in company: Averil had had the same thought. She fell in beside him with her skirts kilted up and a broom in her hand.

He got his breathing under control—it always did speed up when she was that close—and slanted a glance at her. "They didn't need you, either?"

"They think I'm too young to understand," she said. He would have thought she was calm about it, but her eyes were narrowed and her lips were tight. "We know what you saw. Tell me what you think it means."

Gereint paused in knocking down a whole kingdom of spiders. "You know how little I know about anything."

"Guess," she said.

He opened his mouth, then shut it. After a moment he said, "I would guess that if it's the king who's cast the spell or who ordered the spell to be cast, then we should look to him for a way to undo it. He must have found books that escaped the purges. If we could find those . . ."

"Or," said Averil, "there is a secret order of mages from the old time. The king obviously found them. What if there are still mages or powers beyond mages who know how to fight these forgotten orders? We should at least look for them, to discover whether they exist."

Gereint nodded. "I'm sure the council, which we are too young and ignorant to attend, is debating exactly this. It's obvious, isn't it? After all."

"The truth was obvious to you," Averil pointed out, "but to no one else who stood in that room, including the Grand Masters of the orders. I don't think we can trust that anyone sees what we see."

"We *are* young," Gereint said. "We *do* know little. Or I do. You're far beyond me. We need someone older and wiser to advise us."

"Bernardin," she said.

"But he's the one—"

"He's the one who listened to you," Averil said. "We'll go to him in the morning after he's had a chance to rest. If we're lucky, he's already thought of all of this, and we can put our fears aside. If he hasn't, he'll hear us. I'll make sure of it."

Gereint pressed his lips together. Bernardin was the one who had dismissed them both from the council. But he was disinclined to argue.

He went back to clearing cobwebs. So, after a moment, did she.

While he worked, he watched her out of the corner of his eye. For once he was thinking of more than that she made his blood sing.

A thought was growing in him. It was the way she had said

she would make Bernardin listen. It was also the way she moved through the duke's palace, as if she could go where she pleased and do as she would.

Suppose . . .

He left the thought hanging while he finished the task he had set himself. When the last cobweb was banished, he put the broom away. Averil had found something else to do: sorting out the room where the saddles and bridles were kept.

That was a gift of the Young God. Gereint thanked Him for it and decided to reckon it an omen.

ONCE OR TWICE in the course of running errands for the Lord Protector, Gereint had ventured into the women's wing of the palace. He had never gone as far as the heir's rooms, but he knew where they were: high in the innermost tower, opening on the rose garden that was planted on the roof of the great hall.

The lady had been secluded since her father was struck down, heavily guarded and going out only to reassure the people—and her mob of suitors—that she was alive and well. It was convenient, Gereint reflected, that few people ever saw her close up. She was always off at a distance, as remote as a statue in red gold and ivory.

What he had seen of her made him think of the serving maid whose magic was so strong and whose manner, when she let down her guard, was so unconsciously imperious. Averil was not nearly as perfect a beauty, but Gereint did not think anyone was.

He was going to see what he could see. His Postulant's livery got him past the first two ranks of guards, but the suitors who filled the receiving room were a difficulty. They had got up an uproarious game of dice, with parties and factions and wagers so high they made Gereint wheeze. For him they were riches unimaginable. For these spoiled princes, they were an afternoon's diversion.

Some were younger than he was. Some were more than old enough to know better. They were all playing for the richest prize in the kingdom. One of them said that repeatedly, slurring as the wine went to his head.

Gereint attracted no more notice than the servants who moved softly through the crowd, replenishing cups of wine and rolling the suitors into corners when the drink got the better of them. He made his way gradually toward the inner door. She would make an appearance; she did every day, offering a glimpse of her face.

"Whetting our appetite," said a man in flame-colored silk. The color suited his dark eyes and curling black hair, but the cut did not flatter his very tall, very narrow frame. He looked like a peeled carrot.

He had a pleasant voice and an engaging manner, and he seemed well liked within his faction. That could not be said of all of them. Some of the glances exchanged in that room had war and mayhem in them.

This was war in its own way. A highborn lady must marry and continue her line. It was a nobleman's duty to woo and win her, so that his own line might continue and so that his family might, if possible, grow richer.

This was the richest heiress in the kingdom. The man who won her would gain wealth and power beyond anything Gereint could imagine. She could have been hideous and they would still have pursued her; but she was a rare beauty. That, said the orange lord, was a distinct advantage.

Time was running on. Gereint began to wonder if the lady would deny them the light of her presence. One more round of the hall, he thought, then he would go.

It began as a ripple of silence. Whatever signal the suitors had caught, Gereint was too unschooled to catch it. They all turned toward the inner door like flowers to the sun.

There was a long and breathless pause. Just as Gereint began to grow dizzy, the door opened.

He was not as close as he had wanted to be, but he was tall enough and near enough that he had a clear view. She came like the sun, luminous in cloth of gold. Her face was ivory, her eyes were stars. Her hair was a fall of living flame.

He gasped, blinked and shook his head to clear it. The suitors were lost in the spell—and it was a spell, a working of magic to deceive the sight and cloud the mind.

If he narrowed his eyes and watched her sidelong, it shrank to a dizzying shimmer. There was living flesh under it, a woman tall and fair, but her face was subtly different from the one she wanted others to see.

Gereint let himself see the glamour again: this time to study it. The features were blurred with light and magic, but after not too long a moment, he nodded.

Under cover of her spell he slipped away. It tugged at him, but distantly. It was not meant for him. He was nothing that a lady of rank would ever want to marry.

He was singularly undismayed by that. Her world was as alien to him as the moon.

And so was she. For all her beauty and the power that lay on her, she left him cold. Not at all like Averil, who in all her imperfections, with her freckled face and her slight irregularity of feature and her very solid and practical and in no way ethereal self, enthralled him more completely than this lovely illusion ever could.

Averil lived in his dreams. This vision barely troubled his waking self.

He glanced back once before he passed the outer door. Suitors fluttered around her like moths around a candle. She nodded and smiled and murmured words that no one would remember after she had uttered them. It was all part of the spell.

It no longer touched him at all. He let the door fall shut behind him and passed between guards who cared no more for his leaving than they had for his going in.

THAT NIGHT AVERIL was in the library first. Gereint had hoped as much.

He paused just inside the doorway, looking toward the island of light near the far wall. Her hair shone red and gold; her head was bent, her finger tracing the lines of a crabbed and closely written book. There was ink on the finger and a smudge of it on her cheek.

She looked up. Her face lit at the sight of him. It was no glamour—it was honest light.

His breath came quick and shallow. The fragment of a dream brushed past him: his hands on her skin. It was like cream, rich and smooth.

He gritted his teeth and pushed the dream away. It *was* the same face. But this one was real, living and breathing, flesh and blood as well as potent magic.

He thought about saying something, but if she had wanted him to know, she would have told him. Whatever the duke's heir was doing playing the servant while someone else wore a glamour of her face, it was no business of his.

At last and mercifully, the awkwardness passed. She was still Averil. He sat in his place across from her and reached for his book.

18

The duke was getting better. The servants only dared to whisper it for fear of breaking the luck, but they were sure of it. The Lord Protector had called in the masters of the orders, and they had found a way through the spell.

Four days after Gereint told Bernardin what he saw in the duke's coverlet, he woke in a strange mood. His dreams had been odd; he remembered nothing of them, but he felt as if he had struggled his way to wakefulness through a forest of mist and shadows.

The air of apprehension lingered while he went about the morning's duties. He was learning not to disregard such things, but there was no one to confide in. Averil was nowhere to be found. Bernardin had troubles of his own. Riquier spared him an hour with the sword, but escaped before Gereint could find words to ask why he felt so strange.

Part of it was the conviction, which might be false but might not, that these absences and obstacles were the work of conscious will. Something wanted to blind and confuse him. Maybe it was not aimed at him precisely—a mere and lowly Postulant of the Rose—but at anyone who came close to the truth.

He tried to push the thought away, but it persisted. He did as he was told—stiffly, but no one seemed to notice. They were small duties, running messages to members of the duke's council, fetching a mage or two to add to the spells that were reviving the duke and venturing into the herb market of the city for one who wanted a potion of a very particular sort.

The duke, the servants said, was sitting up and talking. Better yet, he was talking sense.

For the first time since Gereint came to the palace, people were smiling. Hope had come back. But Gereint could not seem to share in it. The shadow on him had grown to a weight that crushed him slowly.

The potion proved unexpectedly difficult to find. The herbalist who had had it was not in residence—she had gone, a passersby said, to tend her aging mother in a village nearly as far away as Rémy. The one to whom she had referred her clients knew of the potion but had none to sell. "It requires nine distillations," she said, "four of them in the dark of the moon. That's four months at least."

"I don't think we have four days," Gereint said.

She shook her head, but as her eyes rested on Gereint, they softened. "There is one who may have it, or know of another and similar medicine. He's an odd one and may not oblige you, but you can do no worse than ask."

"I don't mind asking," Gereint said.

"He can be very difficult," she said. "Not violent, but . . . odd."

"Are you trying to tell me he's mad?"

"Not exactly," she said. "Just not like anyone else you may have met. He's on the street of the flower sellers. Ask any of them for Messire Perrin."

"Messire Perrin," Gereint repeated, to set it in his mind. He bowed and thanked her, which made her sputter, but her eyes were as warm as ever.

The flower sellers plied their trade near the western walls. Their quarter was full of gardens in which they grew their wares. It was a fashion in the ducal court to walk there and breathe the myriad fragrances; courtiers made a game of naming each. Gereint passed a gaggle of them doing just that.

None of them was likely to know the man he was looking for. He ventured into a shop spilling over with roses and hyacinths, lilies and something dazzlingly sweet that, the seller told him, was jasmine. She pressed a spray of it on him, "For your pretty eyes," she said—making him blush furiously.

She did not know where Messire Perrin was staying, but she sent him to another seller who might. He tucked the jasmine into his belt, where it wafted sweetness upward.

He had lost count of the flower sellers he had spoken to before he found one who directed him down an alleyway and up a flight of dark and narrow stairs into startling light.

One whole wall was glass. Even in the duke's palace Gereint had not seen any so clear or so perfect, in panes taller and wider than Gereint himself. He was so rapt in the wonder of it and in the beauty of the gardens spread below that it was a long while before he noticed the room at all.

It was bare and scrupulously clean. There was a bed in the corner, narrow and plain, and a chair and a bench and a table. One wall was a cupboard with tall wooden doors, secured with a lock that was only visible if one could see magic.

That was interesting, but not nearly as much as that wonder of a window. Gereint could not help but move closer to it, until he could touch a tentative finger to the glass.

No burst of magic flung him back. It was cool and smooth, without bubble or flaw.

"I never knew anything under heaven could be perfect," he said.

The presence he felt behind him had a voice deep and quiet, with an accent he had not heard before. "Perfection is attainable," it said, "if one is willing to pay the price."

Gereint turned. He had been expecting an old man, bent and withered, with a wild eye and an outlandish look. This man was older than Gereint and his hair was so fair it seemed white, but he was long years from old age. He was tall, broad in the shoulders and strong, with a face as cleanly carved as an image in a chapel. His eyes were like grey steel, fixed on Gereint with a peculiar intensity, but there was nothing wild about them.

He was dressed plainly, but his clothes were of good quality—Gereint had learned to recognize the same quality in the clothes the Knights wore. The man was no Knight; he wore the badge of no guild or order. And yet the magic in him was so strong that it made Gereint catch his breath.

"M—Messire Perrin?" Gereint never stammered, but his tongue felt thick and unwieldy.

"So they call me here," the man said.

"My name is Gereint," Gereint said. "I was sent to find a potion—it's called heart's ease, do you know it?—but Madame Laclos is gone away and Madame Guerin has none left and—"

"I know the preparation called heart's ease," said Messire Perrin. "It's for the duke, I suppose?"

Gereint stopped babbling, gulped air and nodded.

"I have none here," Messire Perrin said, "but there is something that may do as well."

He opened the cabinet as if there had been no locks on it at all. Inside were countless rows of drawers and shelves, a whole herbalist's shop in the space of a cupboard. His hand moved over the drawers, pausing once or twice, then darting with sudden decision. He drew out a vial of green glass with a wooden stopper.

"Three drops in a cup of wine should suffice," he said.

Gereint took the vial in a hand that wanted inexplicably to shake. "I was to pay Madame Laclos," he said. "I have—"

"I need no payment," Messire Perrin said.

"But—"

"No payment," the herbalist repeated. "But if you wish to offer a gift, I will accept that."

He tilted his chin toward Gereint's belt. For a moment Gereint gaped at him, thinking thoughts that were not at all becoming. Then he remembered the spray of jasmine, now considerably wilted but still sweet.

"This?" he asked. "But it's only—" He stopped. The man was an herbalist. The scent of jasmine was a beautiful thing. Maybe it had other properties, too, that Gereint knew nothing of.

He was oddly reluctant to let go of it, but it was little enough to give in return for the vial. He freed it from his belt and held it out.

In Messire Perrin's hands it bloomed again. The wilted flowers came to life; the shriveling leaves shone glossy green. He breathed deep of its fragrance and smiled at Gereint.

It was a remarkably sweet smile. Gereint caught himself

returning it. He did not know what he had done, but it seemed he had done well.

GEREINT'S SENSE OF well-being lasted most of the way back through the flower market before his morning's malaise came back in full force. The sense of impending disaster rocked him on his feet.

For the twentieth time he made sure the vial was safe in his purse. Then he began to run as fast as he could through streets so crowded.

THE PALACE WAS quiet. Nothing untoward had happened or seemed likely to happen. The physician in attendance on the duke took the vial that Gereint brought, with little enough thanks for his effort; then Gereint went to be humiliated in the practice court.

The day was in all ways completely ordinary, except for Gereint's meeting with Messire Perrin. That had been so strange that he could not think about it yet. He needed time to let it sink into his memory.

Averil was not in the library that night. That was not unheard of: sometimes she was called on for duties that kept her occupied until long after the sun went down. The long room felt oddly empty without her, and her place across the table seemed almost to have an echo in it. Gereint finished his evening's exercises as quickly as he could, put the books away and sat for a while, listening to the silence.

He should go to bed. It had been a long day, as they all were, and he was tired. But he could not muster the energy to stand up and walk.

He pushed himself to his feet. The lamp was guttering. He should have pinched out the flame before he left, but the dark was so heavy that he let the light die of its own accord.

He was walking in the dream that he had tried so hard to forget. When he left the library, instead of turning toward his dormitory, he went back into the duke's wing of the palace.

19

All that day, Averil had been uneasy. Her father was sleeping a great deal, but when he was awake, his mind was clear. He had no strength yet for affairs of state; but in the afternoon he was able to sit up for a while.

In the evening when she left him, he was sipping a cup of broth and wondering when he would be allowed more substantial nourishment. She should have been happy, not weighed down with dread.

She only stayed away for long enough to choke down a bit of supper and make a show of attending the false heir. As soon as she could, she went back to her father.

He was sleeping—real sleep, not the deep oblivion of the spell. Candles were lit, casting a soft glow on his face.

She opened the book she had been keeping by his bed and stared at the pages, but her mind was far away from the nature and properties of the spirits of aether. The order of the world was slipping again, uncovering the turmoil beneath.

The wild magic in her struggled to respond. Something was moving, creeping toward her. She strained her eyes—inner and outer—but nothing came clear.

Briefly and fiercely, she wished Gereint were there with his sight that was clearer than anyone else's. She could go and get him; he would be in the library at this hour. But she was inexplicably reluctant to leave the duke.

She closed her book and laid it aside. The soft thud of it touching the table was the only sound in the world except for the doubled hiss of her breathing and her father's. Whatever revelry still went on in the hall, no echo of it came into these rooms.

She could feel the Knights on guard at the door, a banked heat of magic under careful control. Their presence secured the protections on the duke. Nothing could get in; nothing could harm him.

And yet the air of apprehension grew more rather than less. The lamplight glimmered in the pendants of glass and enamelwork that hung from the beams and spun gently in the windows. Near the bed, the duke's scrying mirror shone darkly.

Had it been uncovered when she came into the room? The mirror had a silken shroud: it was crumpled around the base of the pedestal.

It was neither wise nor safe to leave such a mirror open to the aether. Averil tried to rise, but the silence was too heavy. It was like shifting a mountain.

The mirror's surface gleamed like oil. In the lamplit dark and the oppressive silence, it seemed that things were moving inside.

Averil strained every muscle and bone of body and magic to stand up, reach for the silk, cover the mirror. Fear was rising to choke her. The thing in the mirror almost had a shape. She almost recognized it.

The mirror's surface bulged. It coiled like molten glass stretched and twisted from the maker's rod, reaching toward the duke.

Averil had no spell to cast and no power to raise the protections that kept every enemy out except one that came through the portal of the mirror. She gasped for breath. She was drowning—dying.

The room exploded in light and fire. The spell on Averil shattered. She surged up. The mirror swayed on its pedestal.

It must not break—that would set the enemy's magic free. Averil lunged toward it.

Strong hands gripped hers, but not to stop her. Strong magic surrounded her. It shaped and firmed her own magic and strengthened her resistance.

She had never known such a thing, and yet it seemed perfectly right, as if it were meant to be. Her heart knew how to shape and wield it, to shield the duke and strike down the spell that hovered between them.

"Not yet," the other said. She looked into Gereint's eyes. Had she known before how clear they were? They were grey, which could make one think of rain and steel and honed flint, but she had never found anything in them but warmth.

Flint had met steel in them tonight. Out of the fire he said, "Capture it. Hold it. We have to know where it comes from."

It was a simple spell to work, and with his strength it was effortless. The working writhed, cut off from the mirror but denied its target. Averil and Gereint between them held it englobed as if in crystal.

Their hands were clasped, their fingers woven tight. So was their magic bound together, his the matrix, hers the fireborn glass, gleaming and splendid.

The enemy's working stretched and grew and turned transparent. In it they saw as through a window into the place where it was made. Two men were standing there: one drawn thin and fine with age, the other still more young than old, with beard and hair grown long and richly curled.

Averil caught her breath. Gereint's strength held her in the working or she would have fallen out of it. No one could mistake the King of Lys: only he in these days affected the ancient style of the long-haired kings.

"Now," said Gereint.

They brought their hands together. The spell puffed into dust. Gereint flung the cloth over the mirror, even as Averil sprang toward her father.

The duke slept undisturbed. His dream touched the edges of Averil's awareness, a dream of healing and peace.

Her knees buckled. Once again Gereint was there to hold her up. She allowed it for a moment, resting in his warm solidity, before she drew away.

He did not try to hold her. His head was up, cocked as if listening.

At first Averil did not recognize the sound. It was like wind shrieking in the eaves, but there was no wind in this warm summer night.

Women were wailing. The halls echoed with it. Someone nearby was dead—terribly and grievously.

Averil's heart went cold. Her father stirred; even as deep in dream as he was, he must have heard that eruption of grief.

The attack had never been meant for him at all. It was a diversion. While she defended a man who hardly needed it, her image—her false self—was dead.

EMMA HAD NOT died easily. Her body was so contorted and her face so blackened and swollen that it was unrecognizable. Only the red gold of her hair remained the same.

Jennet, calm and practical Jennet, was sobbing uncontrollably, weeping so hard her breath came in whooping gasps. Averil shook her until she stopped howling, then slapped her until she fell silent.

"Tell me," Averil said, sharp and cold.

That was not merciful, but mercy would have reduced the woman to even worse hysterics. Jennet's eyes that lifted to her were resentful, but they were also clear. She bit off the words with anger that cleansed and healed even while it lashed Averil. "It came through her mirror," she said. "A snake, greener than grass. It lay on her while she slept and bit her throat. Then it went back into the mirror."

"And you? What were you doing while your lady was dying?"

"I was lying open-eyed, with the weight of the world on me and no power to move."

Averil's breath shuddered as she drew it in. "Yes. Yes, that was how it was."

Jennet stared. She was coming back to herself more quickly than Averil could have managed. "The duke? Did he—is he—"

"He's safe," Averil said. "There was a diversion—and I don't doubt he would have died if we hadn't turned it aside. But he wasn't the target. Not this time."

"No," said Jennet flatly. "You were."

Averil shuddered. A great sickness rose in her.

She could not let it master her. The rest of the maids had run out screaming, filling the palace with clamor. That served her, in its way. It let her face Jennet in solitude except for Gereint.

He was watching quietly. There was no hint of surprise in him, though he must have heard and understood it all. He was on guard, she realized: he had covered the mirror and placed himself between Averil and the windows. Anywhere that magic could come in, he stood in the way.

She hated to lose his presence, but no one else could run this errand. "Fetch Bernardin," she said. "Bring him here quickly."

"He'll be on his way," Gereint said, "if I know—"

"Bring him," she said.

He stiffened as if she had laid a whip across his back, but he did as she bade.

"You could be kinder," Jennet observed when he was gone.

"Not tonight," Averil said.

Jennet shrugged. She was not sulking any longer. She was not smiling, either, but it would be a while before anyone did that.

As forgiveness went, it was feeble, but it was the best Averil could expect.

IT SEEMED A long while before the Lord Protector appeared. The shrieking and clamoring had died down, but that was only a lull. The whole palace would be awake by now and the rumors flying.

Jennet moved to compose the body as best she might, but Averil said, "Not yet. He has to see."

The maid nodded unhappily and backed away. Her hands were knotted so tightly the knuckles were white.

"If you need to go," said Averil, "go. I'll manage here."

"No!" Jennet's voice was fierce. "I won't leave you alone with that."

Averil did not have it in her to argue. Death should have no terror for her, nor should she fear the shades of the dead, but this ugliness was as much as she could bear.

Emma's spirit was not hovering as the souls of the violently slain so often did. Averil hoped—prayed—that it was free and not bound by some further ghastly spell.

Prayer seemed, on reflection, to be a useful occupation. She knelt and bowed her head and began to sing the psalms for the dead.

GEREINT HEARD THAT sweet lonely voice even through the shrilling of the women. It made a shiver run down his spine. What they had done in the duke's chamber—what they had wrought and what they had prevented—was more than he could comprehend. He needed time for it, and quiet.

He would not get that tonight. Bernardin had been on his way to the ladies' tower, as Gereint had known he would be.

Gereint found the Lord Protector in the solar. He hardly needed to say the words he had rehearsed. As the first of them tumbled out, Bernardin nodded brusquely and strode past him through the clamoring crowd of courtiers.

The door to the tower was hanging open, unguarded. Bernardin's glance promised ill for those who had abandoned their post. He ascended the stair with a young man's loping stride, two steps at a time and even three. Gereint was hard put to keep pace.

Nothing had changed in the lady's chamber. The dead lay as Gereint remembered. The maid Jennet stood over the body. Averil knelt by it with her bright hair streaming down her back, chanting in a pure high voice. She sounded like the stars singing.

Bernardin waited for the psalm to wind to its end. Then he said, "Lady, you have a choice to make."

Averil rose and turned. She had sung herself into a luminous calm.

Gereint felt his heart reaching out to her, yearning to be part of her. The thing they had done to save the duke was still there, bright and strong inside him. He dared to hope it might be the same in her.

She was focused on Bernardin, as if Gereint had never been in her world at all. "What choice would that be?" she asked.

"You know, lady," said Bernardin: "Whether to be dead and hope the enemy will betray himself, or live and show him for a fool."

"We know who he is," she said. "It's as we thought: it's the king. He has an accomplice, an old man who pretends to be a priest."

"You are certain?"

"I saw it in the mirror," Averil said. Gereint noticed that she had not said which one. "He was careless; he didn't try to hide himself."

Bernardin nodded, then let his head fall forward as if it were too heavy to lift. "All the more reason, lady, to make your choice now. He won't wait to take the duchy—he'll be here as soon as his army can march."

"Three days," she said. "That was in the mirror, too. He'll come to the heir's funeral, if there is to be one."

"Will there?"

She hesitated. Her back was straight, her face composed, but Gereint felt the effort it cost her to maintain that semblance of calm. "I don't know," she said. "I need time to think."

"Not too much time," said Bernardin.

"Tomorrow," she said. "No later than that. I promise."

Bernardin was not satisfied, that was clear, but it was also clear that he understood. His tone was gentle as he said, "Go and rest if you can. I'll do what must be done."

20

Long before morning, Averil knew what she had to do. In truth she had known when she spoke to Bernardin. Her father was alive, and she intended to keep him that way.

But how to do that—there was a dilemma. If the duke's heir seemed to be dead with no hope of his begetting another, the king's arrogance could not help but grow. He would think himself invincible and believe that no one could stand against him. He would leave her father alone, let him die of his own age and weakness, and be assured that once the duke was gone, Quitaine would be his.

Then when he tried to take it, he would find Averil in the way, alive, well and in full and trained strength. She would use the time; she would gather allies in secret, strengthen the duchy and face him with armies of mages as well as fighting men.

Or, she thought in an agony of indecision, the king might slit the duke's throat as soon as the funeral was over and claim the duchy as spoils of war. If Averil revealed herself and her deception, then chose one of the suitors and married him with all due haste, she might be able to turn the king aside. Surely the orders of mages and the Knights of the Rose would stand behind her, as little good as they had done in any of the other domains that the king had taken.

She had to decide tonight. There was no time left for maundering.

THE SUITORS CROWDED into the great hall in various states of undress, yowling with the loudest of them. Averil watched them from behind a pillar—the same one she had hidden behind when the duke was shot, if that meant anything but that it was the best vantage. Not one of them drew her eye, let alone her interest.

They were all shallow fools. Some had magic, but for them it was a toy and its practice a game, not the high and terrible calling that she knew it to be. None of them was weeping honest tears.

Already their numbers were diminished, gone to find the next likely heiress. By the time the funeral was over and the feast consumed, the last of them would have vanished. None cared for the welfare of Quitaine or its duke, only for the wealth its heir could bring to the marriage.

Someone else was watching them as well. Gereint was out in the open: hiding in plain sight. He could have been one of them, though rather too plainly dressed, or he could have been a servant. They took no notice of him.

Averil had all she could do not to fix on him like light in a burning glass. It was unexpected and powerful and not particularly unwelcome to realize how strongly he drew her. She would rather marry him than any other man here.

Of course that was impossible. Even if he had not been a Postulant of the Rose, he was the godborn son of a farmer. She was bound to marry among the children of Paladins. She should not even be thinking of him.

It was difficult not to, with such magic as he had. Maybe a god really had begotten him; or ancient blood had passed by countless generations of honest folk to wake full force in this distant descendant. However common his ancestry, there was nothing at all common about him.

He was not so ill to look at, either. Youth made him awkward, and he was terribly overgrown, but time would mend that. He would be a strong man, with grace to go with it. If he had been a son of Paladins, she would have done her best to lure him away from the Rose and into her arms.

She wrenched her mind away from that most unsuitable thought. The truth, as hard and cold as it was, was glaringly obvious. There was no man here whom she could legitimately marry, who could stand up to the king. She was better off dead than bound to one of them.

She wrapped herself in her servant's mantle and withdrew into the shadows. Her choice was made for her. She would let this game of her father's play out. Then, no doubt, God or the duke's scrying glass would show her the way.

THE KING CROSSED the border the second morning after Averil's supposed death, when he could—just—have been presumed to have received the news. There were a thousand men in his escort when the Knights of the southern marches rode to meet him. He greeted them with an expression of carefully wrought sorrow, though he stopped short of an artful tear. "My poor niece," he said, "and my poor kinsman. He must be inconsolable."

The Knight Commander of the South was a man of no little age and experience. Some of his younger companions bristled at that royal mockery, but he bowed gravely and said, "We accept your condolences, sire, in the spirit in which they are given."

GEREINT, COMING BACK from one of his many errands, found Bernardin in his workroom. The Lord Protector's eyes were shut and his hands were folded. He looked as if he might be snatching a nap, except for the scent of magic that was on him. It was so strong, Gereint had to fight back a sneeze.

The focus of it was on Bernardin's finger. He wore a ring of gold inlaid with colored glass in a pattern that reminded Gereint somewhat of the pendant he wore still, hidden under his shirt. When Gereint looked more closely at the ring, the pattern came clear: two men in battle armor standing face to face, speaking words that he heard as clearly as if they had been spoken beside him.

He knew of scrying with glass and crystal, but this was different. It seemed as if the Lord Protector's ring was a part of something much larger, like a shard of glass in a cathedral's window. And there, on that field of not-quite-battle, was another shard, connected by a matrix of magic. By bending his mind on it, Bernardin could see and hear all that passed around his fellow Knight.

This must be another Mystery. Gereint was almost startled into pulling back, but he was too fascinated. Once he realized what he was seeing, he began to understand the shape and extent of it.

Every Knight—and probably Squire and maybe Novice—shared in this vast mosaic of magic. They could speak to one another through it and pass knowledge from mind to mind. It was beautiful, intricately and finely wrought, and yet so practical that even Gereint's mother might have been forced to admit that it had its uses.

Gereint brought himself sharply to order. He could still see the field, and the Knight and the king standing face to face.

The king's face was starkly furious at the words the Knight had said to him. Above the golden curls of his beard, his cheeks were crimson. His lip curled; his voice was vicious in its softness. "Well then, messire. Have I your leave to continue to Fontevrai for the late and lamented lady's funeral?"

The Knight bowed with no apparent irony. "I can hardly stop you, majesty."

BERNARDIN'S SIGH BROUGHT Gereint back into focus. The vision went on behind Gereint's eyes, but he could see the outer world again and hear the Lord Protector as he said, "The king is coming. He'll be here in three days—less if he presses the pace."

"Can we bury the lady sooner?" Gereint asked. Maybe he should not have, but there was no one else there for Bernardin to be talking to.

Bernardin sighed again and shook his head. "It would be tempting," he said. "Unfortunately, state funerals are bound by ironclad tradition, and both priests and court would reckon it a monstrous insult to the lady's memory and their own dignity. We have no choice but to lay her in the crypt on the day after the king arrives."

Gereint bit his lip. Questions were crowding in his mind, but as usual when that happened, none of them seemed to want to come out. He settled for silence instead, and a new errand made urgent by the king's imminent arrival.

SOMEWHAT AFTER NOON he had an hour's freedom. His raid on the kitchens found Averil there before him, nibbling at a plateful of bread and cheese. There was roast meat to be had, too, and a stew of roots and onions and herbs that was remarkably savory.

Gereint worked his way methodically through all of it. Even when it was gone, a slight edge of hunger stayed to taunt him. He was growing out of his clothes again; there was a little too much wrist at the end of each sleeve, and his cotte strained at the shoulders.

Amid the constant tumult of the kitchens, he and Averil in their corner by the scullery were as private as if they had met at the top of a tower. He asked his most pressing question then, in between bites of the bread that she had left unfinished. "What happens when the king comes?"

Her eyes were shadowed; he wondered if she had even heard, or wanted to. Then she said, "You're asking me?"

"It comes back to you, doesn't it?"

"Does it?"

He clenched his fists to keep from shaking her. "Are you going to have Bernardin call out the army? Will you drive the king out before he comes any closer to Fontevrai?"

"You are so young," she said, "and so very much a boy."

He bristled. "You're going to just sit and wait for him to take you?"

"No," she said.

While she spoke, she had been grinding the last bit of bread to crumbs and then to powder. She stared at it as if she had never seen its like before.

He swept it away and thrust his face into hers. "What are you doing to do?"

She never blinked. Her eyes met his, clear and yet remote. Eyes like stars—he had thought that was a poet's fantasy. Now he saw how poets could say such a thing. "My father has laid a trap," she said. "The king is walking into it."

"What kind of trap? Magical? Do your mages understand what the king is? Do they know how to fight him?"

"Do you?"

Gereint sat back. "I know that whatever the princes and counts and barons around Quitaine have done, they've all lost their lives or their places or both. Where were their mages and their armies? Why didn't they see what was happening to them? Why hasn't a single one of them succeeded in stopping the king?"

Averil bit her lip. Her eyes lowered; her shoulders hunched. "I don't know," she said. Her voice was small. "It's as if some spell has paralyzed them all. We're forewarned at least. The orders have raised protections. The Knights are ready to defend us, and the army is on guard. The king won't find us easy prey."

"I hope not," Gereint said.

"So do I," said Averil. She pushed herself to her feet.

Gereint caught her hand. "Isn't there anything we can do? What we did with the mirror—there must be something—"

She paused. Hope dawned, then died in her face. "I don't know what we did. I've never heard of such a thing before."

"Still, can we try?"

"What can we try? We don't know where to start."

"We start here," he said, tightening his fingers on hers.

For an instant he thought he felt a response. Then she pulled away. "No! There's nothing we can do that all the Knights and the orders of mages haven't already done."

"But—" he began.

"Don't you have something useful to do? Go and do it. And so," she said, "shall I."

Her anger bade fair to singe his eyebrows. He backed off. She left him in confusion and his own rising temper.

"You're afraid," he said. His voice was deliberately quiet,

but he had no doubt that she could hear. "You don't dare do anything new—and it's the old ways that are killing you all."

She did not answer, except to shut the door rather too firmly behind her.

AVERIL'S ANGER COOLED as soon as she was out of sight and sound of the kitchen. She stopped and leaned against the wall of the passage, pressing her forehead to the cool stone.

Gereint was right, damn him. Ever since the Young God fell, magic had gone in a particular way and according to particular rules and limitations. The old way of the Serpent was so long gone and so completely suppressed that no mage of the newer orders now remembered it.

That was the king's best weapon. Wherever and however he had found his way to the ancient powers, he was using them to destroy his own vassals and raise himself to greater power than any king had held in Lys.

Had the Ladies known? They must have suspected. Surely Duke Urien could not be the only mage in the world who had foreseen it.

Averil's anger *was* born of fear. Not only fear of what the king might do and the mages might not, but of the thing that had awakened between her and Gereint. It had seemed so natural and so simple while they did it, but the longer she thought about it, the more she realized that it was like nothing she had ever heard of.

What if it was old magic, too? Or wild magic? For all she knew, those were one and the same.

She was beginning to understand how the world seemed to Gereint. Everything was new and unknown. She could trust nothing, least of all herself, because she had no knowledge. Whatever she did could be either eminently right or deadly dangerous. And if it was both . . .

She pushed herself away from the wall. She had to confront Gereint, and soon. They had to find out if any mage knew what this thing was.

But not yet. She needed time—not too much, with the king coming, but a little.

A day and a night. No more. She had to face herself and try to understand what had happened to her; then she could face Gereint. Then, God help them, the rest of the world.

21

T he king bent over a cage of glass. The serpent in it was vivid and shimmering green. It lay in apparent torpor, but its tongue flicked restlessly, tasting the air of its prison.

He slipped his hand into the covered basket beside him and lifted a mouse by the tail. The creature struggled and twisted. He dangled it over the serpent until the narrow head lifted and the long supple body began to coil.

He let the mouse fall. It came to ground running, but the snake was blindingly swift. Its fangs sank into the mouse's neck.

The mouse went rigid. Its eyes glazed. The serpent's body pulsed, its jaws opening wide. It began to swallow its prey.

The king smiled. "Such beauty," he said. "Such purity. Such mercy. Swift death; no pain. Would we were so blessed."

The commander of his escort smiled uneasily. He was already as far away from the snake in its cage as the king's tent would allow. If he backed another step, he would fall through the flap. "Yes, sire. I can see that, sire. Majesty, everything's ready. We only need your word to begin."

It was a pity, the king thought, that men in this age were so horrified by their own God's most beautiful creation. That was the fault of the Church that had turned lies into dogma and poisoned men's hearts against the truth. Even the king's loyal knights were bound by the delusion.

Still, they were loyal, and few more so than this man. Clodovec smiled at him. "Good," he said. "Excellently done, messire. When darkness falls, give the order."

The knight bowed and backed out of the tent—gratefully.

Clodovec sighed. There was much to do if the world was to see as he saw.

Soon. He lifted the flap that the knight had let fall, looking out across the camp.

The sun was sinking, the sky turning to blood and fire. There had been rain and lightning earlier, but it had blown away eastward, leaving the world washed clean. He breathed deep of the sweet damp air, finding even the stink of the camp oddly pleasant.

His men were done with their evening rations. As the king watched, the first trumpet rang. Its notes were as familiar as the beating of the king's own heart, calling his troops to arm and mount.

His squires were waiting to do the same for him. He paused a fraction longer, savoring the moment, before he let the flap fall again and surrendered himself to their ministrations.

GEREINT COULD NOT sleep. His mind spun and wheeled. It kept coming back to Averil's damnable, inbred stubbornness—then it veered off toward the warmth of her fingers in his and the wonder of the magic that somehow, by some alchemy he might never understand, ran freely between them both.

It meant something. It could do something. But what, he did not know.

There was so much he did not know.

After the midnight bell found him still tossing in his bed, he slipped out to the library. There at least he might put these hours to use.

Once his books were in front of him and his lessons spread out on the table, the letters blurred into one another. He folded his arms and laid his head on them, just for a moment.

His dreams were full of fire and shouting. People screamed; blood ran scarlet. Rivers of it flowed down the walls of the houses of the Rose and poured from the gates.

Gereint started upright. His back was stiff; the outline of a book was imprinted on his cheek.

The night was as silent as it should be. It was a long way yet until dawn. Somewhere far off, a night bird called.

He had had a nightmare, that was all. His nights had been full of them since he came to Fontevrai. He rose and stretched, groaning as his body protested. The pendant the ancient Knight had given him was so warm it burned.

Somewhere in the night, something shifted. Gereint froze in mid-stretch. It had felt like something vast stirring in its sleep.

The pendant seemed to move with it, then stilled—inert once more. It was no more magical than it had ever been.

The first screams were far away, barely to be heard. They drew nearer in waves, rising and falling. Beneath them ran a deep rumbling, a mingled sound of hooves thundering and men's voices chanting a war cry.

Gereint began to run.

HE COLLIDED WITH Averil in the passage to the hall. She looked as wild as he felt.

They whirled around each other. When they stopped, it seemed the world kept on spinning. "What—" Gereint said, or tried to say.

Her grip was strong enough to grind his bones together. "The king," she said. "The Knights. Every house—every man—I dreamed—"

"It's not a dream," he said with terrible knowledge. "Go on. Find Bernardin. I'll come back when I can."

"No," she said. "Stay with me. You'll get killed."

"I won't," he said with more confidence than he felt. "I have to see—for all of us. To be sure. Go to Bernardin. I'll find you there."

He did not wait for her to call him back again. She was right, of course—it was insane for him to leave the palace tonight. But there were times when a person had to do the mad thing, the thing that did not yield to order or control.

The order of the world was breaking. He felt it in the city, in those streets that were as truly inside him as the fretwork of veins beneath the skin. Old things and cold things were crawling in through broken walls and breached gates. Wherever they touched magic, it shattered.

Gereint was sick at the heart. Fear had not taken hold of him, not yet. He was too shocked for that.

The streets of Fontevrai were dark. Even footpads were hiding in their beds; drunkards and night wanderers had fled the miasma that crept down alleys and coiled in doorways.

Gereint had no defense but his untaught magic and the knowledge of the city that Riquier had set in him. He breathed as shallowly and moved as softly as he could, gliding along walls and darting around corners.

The night's silence pressed like a weight on his skull. When it shattered, it flung him to his knees.

Flames erupted in the night. Out of nowhere—as if out of the earth itself—men in armor swarmed like ants, streaming toward the mother house of the Rose. Its roofs were burning; fire arrows rose and then fell like a shower of sparks. The sudden light flashed off the metal of helmet and spear.

There must have been a thousand men marching in close ranks past the lesser street in which Gereint crouched. The first of them were already at the great gate, breaking it down as if it had been made of woven wicker and not oak bound with iron.

No one defended the house. There was no sign of life in it at all. In the torchlight the windows were black and empty like toothless mouths. Their glass was gone—shattered, like the protections that had lain on the house and the web of magic that bound the Knights together. It was all gone as if it had never been.

Tears streamed down Gereint's face. When the screams began, he felt them in his belly, stabbing like steel.

The army vanished into the house, leaving the gate in splinters behind them. Every scrap of sanity that Gereint had left bade him stay where he was, wait, watch and remember. But he had left that behind when he ran out of the palace. He abandoned his hiding place and bolted toward the gate.

As he ran, he felt a strange, twofold awareness. In the body he was struggling through magic as thick as running water, forcing his way toward the mother house. In the spirit he fled through the halls he had known so briefly, swept up in a blind tide of panic.

Many of those who still lived there were caught in their beds, pierced through with swords and spears and drowned in their own blood. Those few who by grace or strength had fought the spell were hunted down and killed.

There was no mercy for them or for any work of hands or magic that was in that place. They were all broken and despoiled. Blood ran over mosaics as old as Romagna and pavements wrought as much of magic as of stone. Bodies fell, hacked in pieces where they lay.

Gereint stumbled and went down. Body and mind came together with a dizzying rush. There was blood under him, and a man's body flung on its back. It was one of the Novices, a gangling young man whose name burned itself in his memory. Lucas: he had been shy and scholarly but enviably adept with the sword.

He had never had the chance to use that skill. He was unarmed, in his shirt, as he had run from his bed. His throat was cut through to the backbone.

Long after Gereint's stomach was empty, the convulsions went on. Somehow he got to his feet and managed not to turn and bolt into the night.

This house was so big that a thousand men could rampage through it and never find the one who stumbled after them. The fires leaped from roof to roof. The chapel was burning.

Hooves thundered away from the stables. The horses had got out—or someone had let them out. Gereint could not believe that was the enemy's mercy.

He went on because he was long past any hope of sense. He marked the face of each of the dead—such as had faces left to mark—and let the thing inside him, the magic that was so much stronger than either his knowledge or his will, rise to a deadly pitch.

He would die, too. He knew that. He was perfectly calm

about it. No one would mourn him or take particular notice
that he was gone—not after so many had died.

But he had to find the enemy first. That was harder than he
might have thought. The mother house was a maze, and the
enemy moved in a shifting fog of magic. There were no
screams to follow: the men of the Rose died in silence,
whether willing or magically enforced.

He followed the fog, then, and the trail of blood and ruin.
Fear was gone, drowned in blood. Anger had risen in its place.
He was glad of it, because it fed the magic.

He was running now as he used to do on a hunt, not particularly fast but steady. The dead were more numerous the
deeper he went, dispatched more hastily, without the bloody
relish of the outer reaches.

None of them was a Knight. They were all Squires and
Novices and Postulants. The Knights' rooms were empty, the
beds often torn apart and sometimes stained with blood, but
there were no bodies.

Gereint quickened his pace. He could feel the enemy now, a
coldly hostile presence not far ahead. They had divided to
wreak their slaughter, but they were coming back toward one
another.

If they went on as they were doing, they would gather in the
sandy court beyond the burning chapel, where the Knights
had held their mounted exercises and practiced the arts of battle. It was wide enough to hold them all.

Gereint's magic was straining against such bonds as he
knew how to set on it. Somehow he managed not to let it go.
Not yet. Not until all the enemy had come together.

Patience was by no means his signal virtue. He practiced it
because he must.

He rounded a corner and stopped short. A knot of men
moved just ahead of him. They were guarding something: a
tall figure, stooped now and stumbling.

It was one of the Knights, bruised and beaten but alive. His
arms were bound with iron that gleamed strangely—darkly,
like living scales.

Gereint's magic could not hold itself in any longer. It erupted from him in a torrent of heat and light.

It blasted the enemy—and, dear God, the Knight, too. He tried desperately, futilely, to shield the man, but the magic had had enough of obedience. It roared down the corridor into the open court.

Men died. Not enough—and too many, because some of them were Knights. Gereint smote them with the full force of his rage and despair.

The king's men screamed. The sound would haunt him until he died. But he did not stop. He would not, even if he could.

He drew up strength from the earth and from the fire in the chapel and from the enemy's own magic. He lashed out again and again. It did not matter what it cost.

The scent of jasmine wreathed about him. It lured him out of his trance of fury and brought him somewhat back to himself. The corridor was scorched with fire; but of the men who had died there was nothing left, even a drift of ash.

Outside in the courtyard was pandemonium: men shouting and screaming. Weapons clashed.

If they were fighting one another, so much the better. Gereint reached for such magic as he had left. One more stroke, and please God, they would all fall.

He was dizzy with the sweetness of jasmine, rising so strong he could hardly breathe. When he tried to move forward, his legs would not obey him.

There was a wall in front of him that had not been there before. It was stone and solid, and it was nowhere near the mother house of the Rose. When he looked up, he saw the white tower of the duke's palace.

He spun in a circle. The stench of smoke was still on him under the fading scent of flowers. There was blood on his hands and clothes. But there could be no doubt as to where he was.

He staggered, dizzy. For a moment it seemed he was in, of all places, the herbalist's room with its wonderful windows and its clear light. Messire Perrin's face was as vivid as if he stood in the court beside Gereint. "Go to your lady," Gereint thought he said. "Now more than ever, she needs you."

"Why would the likes of her need the likes of me?" Gereint asked bitterly.

The vision of Messire Perrin paid no attention. "Go," he said. "It's not your place to die tonight."

That was a rather odd way of putting it. Gereint found himself on his feet and if not running, at least staggering back through the gate. He could feel the compulsion on him, but it was infinitely stronger than his will to resist it.

BERNARDIN SLEPT AS if drugged. All the glass of the room in which he lay—window, ornament or working of magic—was broken. The memory of its breaking drummed in Averil's skull, a deep tone too low to hear.

She could barely walk, so strong was the shock of it. Somehow she made her way through the unguarded door and across the room to stand over the Lord Protector. Her hand moved of its own accord to rest over Bernardin's heart.

She called on no magic and attempted no working, but Bernardin gasped and convulsed. Averil started; Bernardin's hand clamped over hers, holding it fast. The Knight's eyes were open, staring. "The web—the Knights—it's gone. I can't—"

Averil could find no words to comfort him. As he spoke the words, she felt them in herself, so sharp they made her gasp. The Knights were all divided from one another, their magic sundered and their powers broken beyond any hope of mending.

The splendid fabric of their unity was gone. Some had died of it. Others were crippled beyond repair.

Bernardin at least was alive and conscious. He spoke clearly, though his voice sounded somewhat thick. "Go. See to the others. I'll rouse the guard."

Averil wasted no time in shock or foolish questions. He was well enough, now he was awake. She ran to do as he bade.

GEREINT FOUND AVERIL in the barracks, surrounded by dazed and staggering men. At sight of Gereint, she straightened. Her gladness almost made him burst into tears.

She took in the tale his body told, stains of blood and reek of smoke and, he had no doubt, a face that had seen horrors. None of it seemed to either surprise or dismay her.

When he reached for her hand, she did not push him away. She seemed to draw strength from him as he drew it from her. The world was not so terrible a place then, and the memories of what he had seen and done retreated far enough that he could do what had to be done.

The spell that gripped the city had fallen on every man of the Rose in the white tower: a dozen Knights counting Bernardin, three dozen Squires, sixty Novices, and one Postulant battling a throbbing headache. But the enemy had not come this far—nor would he, if Gereint had damaged him badly enough.

The Knights were staring at one another as if the wits had been scoured out of them. Gereint could see the magic inside each man, pulsing dark with confusion, but it was encased as if in glass.

He did not try to free it. That much wisdom he found in himself, too little and too late, but it would have to do.

He turned to Averil. She was already turning to face him. Once again as their eyes met, the world shifted. The light was clearer, the earth more solid underfoot.

Then Gereint dared to reach through the wall of glass and touch the magic that burned in each man of the Rose. He gathered it all together, making it stronger where it needed strength, and clearer where it was mired in confusion.

Some gasped and started; others shivered. Gereint bolstered them with his voice and the commingled magic that was still inside him, binding him to each of them. "The king is after us all. Wake and move! Where is your armor? Your weapons? Is anyone defending the duke?"

Gereint could feel the change in the air. The spell was broken. What was left was simple human shock, from which even these warriors of God were hard put to recover.

Half a dozen men sprinted toward the duke's chambers. In remarkably short order, one of the Novices came back, breathless, with Bernardin close behind him. He brought news that swayed them all with the intensity of their relief. "He's untouched. Mauritius has doubled the guard."

"He's not the target, for once," said Riquier. "We are."

"I think we always were," said Bernardin. He drew himself erect, waving Averil away when she would have supported him.

The Novice who had brought word of the duke was staring at her as if he had only just seen her. "Lady," he said. "His grace said—he asked—will you come?"

Averil's answer was to stride toward the door. The Novice half-ran after her. So did Gereint and, somewhat to Gereint's surprise, Bernardin. One of the other Knights was snapping out orders as Gereint passed the door: sending men to fetch armor and weapons.

Gereint should have told them where the enemy was and why he was unlikely to invade the tower tonight. But his tongue refused to obey him. He did not know that there was not another army waiting to invade the duke's palace. He could not even be sure that he had succeeded in shattering the force that had taken the mother house.

Better that the Knights be on guard and armed than that they be caught and ensorcelled again. He could still feel them behind his eyes, with fear and bravery together and a deep and growing anger.

Not in all the years of its existence had the order suffered such a blow. Never had king or lord turned against them so completely or taken them so utterly by surprise.

He left them to it. Averil was running with speed he had already learned to respect; he sprinted after her. Bernardin's feet thudded behind him.

DUKE URIEN SAT in the chair beside his bed, where Averil had spent more hours than anyone could count. He was sipping honeyed wine from a silver cup and eating sops of bread dipped in the wine.

Averil could have wept to see him so strong, but this was no time for tears or maundering. She knelt by his chair and took his hands in hers.

His smile was warm but fleeting. "You have to go," he said. "Now, tonight. Before the king comes here."

"No," she said. "I won't leave you. The king doesn't know I'm alive. I'm safe."

"You are not," the duke said. "However much terror I foresaw, this far exceeds it. You must go. Take as many Knights as survive, and escape."

"Why?" she demanded. Her voice felt raw in her throat. "If he's taken down the Knights in the whole duchy, or even the kingdom, how safe will it be for me to run away with them?"

"Safer than to stay here," said the duke. "Aim for the Isle. The Ladies will protect you."

"You're coming with us," Averil said. She did not mean it to be a question.

He shook his head. "This is my country. I'll not leave it."

"Then I won't, either."

They glared at one another. Averil was not about to give way. Neither, it was clear, was her father.

It was Bernardin who said, "I'll stay with him, lady, and guard him as I can."

"As you guarded him tonight?" Averil said with ominous gentleness.

Bernardin's lips tightened, but his response was mild. "We were all taken by surprise. That won't happen again."

"Can you be sure?"

"Daughter," said the duke, "we'll keep each other safe. Now go. The king will be here by morning. By then you must be as far away as horses can carry you."

Averil opened her mouth to object, but Gereint said, "Lady, he's right. The king won't touch a pair of old men—he'll think they're feeble and their powers are broken, and they'll do their best to foster the impression. But if he finds you, he'll try to make you his acolyte, or worse, his slave."

Averil whirled on him. However bloodied and scorched he might be, he seemed as ordinary as ever: a big, open-faced, overgrown boy with wide earnest eyes and an innocent face.

But those eyes could see farther than most. How far, she was beginning to understand.

"I don't want to go," she said. She sounded like a petulant child, and she knew it.

None of them, even Gereint, remarked on it. He said, "I'll go with you."

She opened her mouth to mock him, but even her temper could not do that, not after what they had done tonight. She settled for a growl and a glare.

"Go," her father said. "Go quickly."

She meant to do that, but in her own time. She kissed his hands. He pressed hers, trembling slightly, but his grasp was firm nonetheless. "Go with God," he said.

22

The Knights heard the duke's orders with expressionless faces. Most were still in shock, but they could do as they were told.

Mauritius had taken command. He bowed to his lord's will and began with remarkable calm to rouse his men and make them ready to ride.

Gereint was numb. As long as he had had to think and act, he had been well enough, but once he was mounted on one of the horses close behind Averil, his wits seemed to slide away.

It was pitch dark in the courtyard of the tower, with no moon or stars. The air was warm and thick and very still. He might have thought that there was nothing to be afraid of— that he had dreamed it all—except for the deep awareness of fire and slaughter. It rode in him like a nightmare, and like an ill dream it would not leave him.

His wild stroke of magic had destroyed a fragment of a fragment of a vast army. It might have discomfited the enemy for a moment, but it had made little difference. The tide of destruction had rolled over the whole of Quitaine and taken the Rose with it.

All the Squires and Novices who had been in the houses of the order were dead. The Knights were captured, their magic imprisoned, their minds bound with spells that owed nothing to any art or power they had known. Their great workings, their treasures, their wealth of gold and magic, were broken or seized. Even the Mysteries, the relics of the Young God's death and transfiguration, lay in the king's hands.

It was all gone. In one night, twice a thousand years of

power and magic had fallen. God knew when or how it could rise again.

What it meant and what would come of it, Gereint could not bring himself to contemplate. If the Rose was destroyed and the Mysteries were taken, then the king had the means to undo all that the Young God and his followers had done. He could free the Serpent and unleash chaos.

Gereint clung to the saddle of a horse he could not see in the darkness and tried to keep his eyes focused on the light of Averil's presence. It was the only bright thing in a world gone as dark as clotted blood and as dull as cold ashes.

THEY RODE OUT of the duke's castle by secret ways, through passages that had been built ages ago for just such escapes as this. All of those ways were wide and high enough for a mounted man, but some of them were steep and all were light-less. They dared not call attention to their passing, whether with torches or magic.

When at last they came to the end of those tortuous tunnels, the first light of dawn glimmered along the horizon. The walls of the city were behind them, rising sheer above the river.

They had emerged from a cavern under the cliff, onto a road that wound down to the river and then ran along it, hidden in a thick growth of trees. It was nearly as dark on that road as it had been in the tunnels, but the air that whispered in Gereint's ears was fresh and clean, with a taste of morning.

The king had entered Fontevrai. Gereint could feel him like a crawling over the skin. He prayed that the king could not feel Gereint in turn.

That lofty eminence would hardly notice a farmer's son. But if he discovered that that farmer's son had blasted a battalion of royal troops with magical fire, he would come hunting. Gereint crouched down over the horse's neck, as if anyone could see him in the gloom, and made his inner self as small and inoffensive as he could manage.

He could not stop seeing what went on in the city. He saw the procession through the streets in the first light, the king in sky blue and silver as if to mock the midnight blue and silver of Quitaine, and his thousand men in bright armor before and behind him. The people of Fontevrai came out to blink and stare, but none of them cheered. They watched in silence as the king rode by.

Gereint had half expected to see a train of Knights in chains behind the army, but the king was not so blatant about that—yet. He was keeping them hidden away, to bring forth when it served his purpose.

This morning he had another errand. He rode up to the citadel and paused in front of the gate. The guards made no move to help or hinder him. He, in return, deigned to ignore them.

The gate was barred, but a lift of his hand shattered the bolt. His vanguard swung back the heavy panels, laying open the courts within.

AVERIL'S HAND CLOSED over Gereint's. He fell out of the vision into dim green light and the glimmer of her face. Her eyes were shadowed. "Don't follow," she said. "You'll lose yourself."

"You saw, too?"

She nodded. "It's a trap. My father is the bait."

"For us?"

"For anyone who comes looking for the Knights' destroyer." She almost laughed, but there was nothing mirthful about it. "You would be a terrible insult to his sense of consequence."

"I would, wouldn't I?" Gereint sighed in something like regret. "I know he's your uncle, but I don't like him at all."

"Nor do I," said Averil. "Nor did my mother, though from all I've heard of her, I'm sure she pitied him."

"He would have hated her for that."

"He hated her for everything," she said, "just as he hates the Knights who turned him away and the God who made him less than perfect."

"Then do you think . . . ?"

"I think the Rose is only the beginning," she said. "What he's taken from them, what he can do with it . . ."

She could not go on, nor could Gereint bring himself to do it for her. They rode on hand in hand until the road narrowed and forced Averil to ride ahead.

AVERIL ENDURED THAT ride through sheer obstinacy. She refused to weaken in front of anyone, least of all herself.

When toward midday the trees thinned and the track turned away from the river, the Knights debated among themselves. Some of them wanted to be sure that the king had indeed attacked every house of the order in Quitaine. A few even dared allude to secrets, things that the uninitiate should not be allowed to hear.

The Knight Mauritius let them babble on for a while, until he said in a tone that cut across all the other voices, "If the web is gone, we have to assume that every house is taken. Let us hope we can find a clear way to the Isle. He won't have taken that. He's not that strong, yet."

"And if he is?" one of the other Knights wanted to know. "What then?"

The Isle was safe. Averil knew that in her center, as she knew Mauritius was telling the truth. She would have said as much, but her tongue would not obey her.

Mauritius spoke for her. "If the Isle had fallen, we would know."

The rumbles of doubt made her strangely angry, but Mauritius had overcome them without raising his voice or losing his temper. She clung to the saddle, trying not to stiffen against the jolting of her horse's stride. A thought was trying to be born in her. A flash of understanding. A plan, taking shape slowly.

Fontevrai was closed to her. When she tried to see it behind her eyes or catch a glimpse of it in the metal of bit or bridle-buckle, she saw nothing but brightness. She could not tell if her father and Bernardin were alive; she had no power to see.

She tried to approach Mauritius, but there were Knights all

around her, fancying that they protected her. When she rode faster, so did they.

They had closed Gereint out of their circle. He was riding in the rear. His shoulders were bowed; she could feel his exhaustion. There was a shadow on him that woke a flicker of alarm.

He had none of the training that she had had. All the magic he had worked had been born of nature and instinct. Small wonder he was worn out.

Mauritius needed to know what she and Gereint could do together. Maybe he had a name for it, or a recollection of a book somewhere, a word or a passage that explained it.

But she was being guarded all too well, and she could not come near the Knight Commander. He was riding toward the sea. He had won that argument.

They skirted a handful of villages and rode wide around a walled town—not without resistance from Knights who were still determined to believe that their order was alive and somehow holding its own. The sun sank toward the horizon. For long stretches they rode straight into it, blinded by it.

At nightfall they made camp in a wood, startling a herd of deer. One fat buck with his antlers in velvet fell to a Squire's arrow. In himself he was little enough to feed a hundred of them, but stewed in a broth of herbs and barley, with a ration of the hard dry bread that they had brought with them, he filled their bellies rather well.

AVERIL WAS BONE-WEARY, but she clung grimly to wakefulness. The Knights drew rosters of sentries, in none of which either she or Gereint was included. She was their charge and Gereint, as always, was given the care of the horses.

A nobleman would have been insulted, but he welcomed the labor. It distracted her mind as well as his, when she lent him a hand.

That made her watchdogs roll their eyes, but she stared them down. She needed to make herself useful.

They were still at it when the stew was cooked. A supercilious

Novice tried to call Averil away then, but she refused. He had to bring a bowl to her—and to Gereint when she insisted—and they ate in bites while they fed each horse its ration of barley.

Those men who could, or whose duty rosters gave them late watches, bedded down as soon as their supper was eaten. The rest did not stay awake long. By full dark, the only people awake were those on guard, Gereint seeing to the last of the horses, and Averil dragging out her tasks for as long as she could.

She had hoped that Gereint would finish before her and fall over like the rest, but he was dawdling, too. Finally she looked him in the face. "Go and sleep," she said. "I'll finish."

"I'm going with you," he said.

"I'm not going anywhere!" she snapped.

"You're a terrible liar," he said. "The horses are as tired as we are. If we give them another hour or two, at least they'll be fresher than they were."

She glared at him. "Where do you think I'm going?"

"Back," he said. "You've been trying all day."

She could keep trying to lie, or she could give in to the inevitable. "Yes, I'm going back. I don't know what we'll find or what we can do, but going on isn't helping at all. The king knows where we'll run to. If he hasn't blockaded the coast, he'll set guards on all the roads that lead to it. He's not going to let any of us escape from his kingdom."

Gereint nodded. "I see that. Your father must have seen it, too. He still sent you away. Maybe he knows something we don't."

"He doesn't know anything," she said. "No one does, except the king. My father hid me in plain sight; then he panicked. I'm going back where the king will never think to look: right under his nose. If there's anything we can do, any ruse we can try, we'll find it there. Not out here with his armies waiting for us."

"Maybe," said Gereint. "Maybe not. Either way, I'll go with you. I'm not much good in a fight unless it's with fists and staves, but I'm big enough to look alarming, and this thing we have between us—who knows? It might help us."

Sometimes, Averil thought, she could not make up her mind whether she wanted to hit him or kiss him. "Help me saddle the black and the brown. They've rested the longest and they're the farthest out of sight."

He was already slipping off toward them. They were nearly invisible in the gloom, which was why she had chosen them: neither had a white marking. As quickly and quietly as she could, she saddled the black. She heard rather than saw Gereint do the same for the brown.

She dared not trust to magic in a camp of mages, even as diminished as these were without their talismans and their works of power. As quietly as she could, she led the horse away from the camp. Soft breathing and the whisper of a large body passing through trees assured her that Gereint was following.

23

Mauritius waited for them in a clearing well past the sentries' line. He sat on a stone, clasping his knees, face turned to the fitful stars.

A circle of Knights and Squires closed in. They wielded no magic, but they had the strength of their bodies and the weapons in their hands.

Gereint stood to be bound. His captors were polite but unbending.

Averil did not suffer the same indignity, but it was understood that she would ride back to camp with Mauritius' hand on her horse's reins and no hope of escaping again. "We have our orders," the Knight said.

"Those orders will get us all killed," she said.

"Whereas your disobedience will merely get *you* killed," said Mauritius. "Your life has been entrusted to us. We will protect it, and therefore ours. You have my word on it."

"And still you think you can escape the king's net."

"If we ride fast enough," he said, "yes. The king has more than enough to do with the prizes he's taken. With God's grace, he won't come after us until it's too late."

"And if God withholds his grace?"

"We'll fight," Mauritius said.

There was nothing she could say to that. She was as much a captive as any of the Knights in the king's prisons, with as little hope of getting out alive.

They were all blind. The Knights with their magic broken, the king with his ambition and his hate, none of them could see what lay ahead of them. Prescience was one gift that mages had never been able to control.

Even foresight was a feeble thing in the face of human folly. Averil locked her anger inside, composed her face, and steeled herself to wait.

THEY WENT ON as best they could, traveling by night when they had to cross open country, and keeping to the shadows and the thickets when those were to be had. The straight way to the sea was too well populated and too well guarded. They hoped to find more open roads to the northwest, where the land turned harsh and the towns grew few and far between.

There were other reasons why they hoped to find no armies on that road, but no one spoke of that. No one spoke at all of the lands beyond the last town, or wanted to think of them.

After the second day, Gereint was let out of his bonds and set once more to looking after the horses. He kept his head down and his mouth shut and did not try to go near Averil. It was hard, being so close and yet too far to touch her or smell her or feel her warmth, but he could see no way to change it.

She was under guard always. Knights and elder Squires watched her. They had learned a lesson from her attempted escape, and would not underestimate her, or trust her, again.

Gereint could feel the anger smoldering in her. It deepened as they began to meet fugitives, escapees from the chapter houses who had taken to the same roads as they. Many were wounded and some were dying, lying on the backs of horses or mules or carried by their brothers.

They were gathering as if they could not help themselves. Gereint was still too numb for anger, but he could see what Averil was seeing. The king or his sorcerers must know what the Knights would do.

There was no pursuit because there was no need. The king had only to bid his armies watch and wait. When the Knights were all gathered, no matter where they chose to do it, he would find them there. Then the last of them would fall.

Ademar caught up with them the day after Averil tried to

escape, riding an exhausted and nearly foundered horse and leading a tiny company of Novices from half a dozen houses. They all told the same story.

"Every house," Ademar said. His world-weary air was gone, pounded out of him by days of running and hiding. "Every place where Knights have ever gathered in the whole of Lys, from one end to the other. Even the hermitage of Sainte-Eremite, where there was a single Knight and a Novice who looked after him, is gone. There's no refuge anywhere."

"And outside of Lys?" Mauritius asked. "Is there any word?"

"I don't know, messire," Ademar said. "We can't send or receive word. All the borders are guarded. We're rats in a trap, and the royal cats are closing in."

"What of Fontevrai?" Averil demanded. "How bad was it there?"

"Bad," said Ademar, and his eyes were haunted. "The mother house is the king's now. He's taken it all, and burned or broken everything he hasn't seen fit to use. I got out because I was on my way to yet another chapter house on yet another errand, and I wanted to make an early start. I was saddling a horse when the spell struck. I started to fall over, and the horse kicked me—you should see the bruise," he said with a shadow of his old insouciance. "Bless that nasty beast. I tried to go back into the house, for whatever good that might do, but it was already full of king's men. They must have been creeping into the city for days—God, what we could do with the spell that hid them! It's not wrought with glass at all. It—"

"We want to know about that," Mauritius said, "but first tell us how you escaped."

Ademar's face went somber again. "They were all inside, killing and capturing. Then something happened. They had set the chapel on fire, and the barracks were burning. A wall must have come down, or the wind must have caught the fire and flung it wide. I heard men screaming. They were burning. Half a thousand men were killed or burned so badly they died, or so I heard—but that was later. Just then, all I could see was a way open to escape.

"I went out through the gardens. There were no king's men

by the rose gate, but after I went through it, before the road carried me out of sight, I saw the roses wither. Then a troop of men in the king's colors ran out of the gate. That was when I knew the mother house was lost."

He sounded as numb as they all felt, his grief shut away until he had time for it. One or two of his fellow Novices carried him off to eat and sleep as best he could.

Gereint stayed where he was, as close to Averil as her ring of guards would allow. Ademar's story was already a market tale, it seemed—but no one was hunting the mage who had smitten the army with fire. Was it possible they did not know?

Far too likely they did know, and blamed it on the Knights. That hardly made matters worse; the order was already destroyed and every man in it was under sentence of death.

Gereint had struck such a blow as he could. Half a thousand men. He stared at his hands. They had never taken a human life. And yet he had more lives on his soul's account than many a soldier.

He should confess it. It was not a sin, the Church would say: he had struck in defense of his order. But the thing that laired in him was worse than guilt. He would never in this life be free of it.

THEY PRESSED ON because they had no choice. Even if Averil could go back, the Knights could not. Nowhere under this king's rule was safe for them.

They were ten days on the road past the camp in which Ademar had found them, riding west and north. They would have crossed that distance in half the time if they could have taken the direct way, but here at last, when they had hoped to find the way open, the king's armies made their presence felt.

Companies of men in sky blue and silver traversed the country and garrisoned the towns. They were guarding the border and watching the roads out of the duchy, whether to the wild lands of the north and west or to the sea and, across it, the island kingdom of Prydain and the Ladies' Isle.

The nearer the riders drew to the sea, the more numerous the king's troops became. Towns and villages spread farther apart, and the land between grew rough and stony. It rose in sudden crags and dropped steeply into deep valleys, where farmsteads clung to the slopes and herds of hardy sheep and cattle grazed the grass that grew among the outcroppings.

There were armed men camped at every crossroad. They surrounded the shrines and the country churches and occupied the farmsteads. Scouts who went out, too often did not come back. Those who did, each time had the same word.

"It looks as if they're retreating from us," Riquier said. He had gone out in the early morning with a pair of Novices and come back toward noon with an expression that reassured none of them. "They're the same distance in front as they were yesterday and the day before."

"Can we turn back?" Averil asked.

He shook his head. "They're behind us, too. They're all around us. We found a track or two that seemed to be free of them, but those are fewer every time we go out."

"We're going to have to run for it," Mauritius said, "and quickly, before the noose tightens around our necks."

"It's brutal country in the daylight, let alone in the dark," Riquier said.

"We have no choice," said Mauritius.

Riquier sighed and spread his hands. Even if he had had the rank to argue, it was clear he would not. Mauritius spoke the truth.

The only way they could go was forward. They broke the camp they had so recently made, saddled their weary horses and mounted once more.

Hope kept them going. They were close to escape. They would reach the sea and find a ship there to take them across.

Gereint wished he could believe that. There was cold all around him, like the strong clasp of a snake.

He rode because he could see no other way, and because Averil was doing the same. This game had to play to the end, whatever that end might be.

THE HORSES COULD make no speed in the moonless dark. They picked their way by feel and instinct, following a leader who must be praying that he did not lead them astray. Those who still had magic to wield, dared not wield it: they had no way of knowing what the king's men could do or what they could see.

For Gereint the night was not nearly as black as he had expected. There was a sheen over the earth, as if magic within it imparted the faintest suggestion of light. It was just enough to see where he was going.

It was brightest if he held to a certain direction, which happened to be the one in which they were riding. There was a track, as straight as the tumbled landscape would allow. It led them below the summits of the ridges and through hidden valleys, across streams that ran shallow before them and roared into flood behind.

The land was their ally. Gereint still did not dare to hope, but he was a little less close to despair.

Something was creeping over the hills behind them. It was long and dark and glistening like a vast serpent. He wondered briefly, too startled for horror, if it was the Serpent itself.

The king had taken the Mysteries, but if he meant to free the Serpent, he had not done it yet. This was his army marching through the dark.

Gereint's horse could go no faster without breaking its neck. It slipped and scrambled down a suddenly steep slope, stumbling onto a dark level.

Water trickled close by: another of the countless streams that traversed these moors. The air smelled rich and green, with a distinct hint of rot beneath. There was a marsh ahead.

The Knights in the lead went on without pausing. The footing changed from rough grass and stony scree to soft earth and sucking mud.

Near Gereint, two of the Squires were whispering to one another. "Do they know where they're going?" one asked.

The other's whisper had the air of a shrug about it. "Who can tell? I know where they're leading us, and I don't like it."

"We can't be going that far, surely. We'll turn toward the sea long before we come there."

"Let's hope so."

"There's a ban," the first Squire said. "No one can pass. Even the king's men won't be able to defy it."

"How do you know?" said the second. "We know nothing of this power that's struck us down."

"Nor do we know anything of the lands beyond the ban," the first pointed out. "It's all rumors and old stories. I'll wager it's no more than a stretch of barren country and a cold seashore. No evil things stalking mortal blood; no wild magic bubbling out of the earth. There's nothing there, and nothing to fear."

"You don't think so? We all grew up on those stories. *Beware the Wildlands. Wherever you go, choose any way but west. Watch out for the wild magic; it lives beyond the sunset.*"

"Nursery tales and old wives' nonsense," the Squire said.

"Old wives are wiser than you would think," said his friend.

They fell silent after that. Gereint half wished they would go on, but he was glad they did not. He had heard the stories, too, though it had not occurred to him that they told of a real country. They were just stories, he had thought, meant to frighten small children into behaving themselves. *Watch out for the wild magic or it will come and get you.*

Now, it seemed, he was riding toward it. Was that what he saw in the earth, that was slowly but surely growing brighter? It was even beginning to shimmer in the air.

It was not terrifying at all. It felt as warm as sunlight. He could tell that, as with sunlight, if he basked too long in it he could burn, but that was true of all magic.

They picked their way through the marsh, following the glimmer of the track. The brightness ahead grew steadily. The darkness behind closed in.

They were being herded away from the sea and into the

Wildlands. Gereint worked his way up the line, slipping around exhausted men and stumbling horses. He was tired but not terribly so; there was strength in the earth here, and it fed him and the horse he rode.

Riquier rode close to the front. His head was down, but it lifted when Gereint came up beside him. His face was a pale blur; his eyes were hollow.

Gereint gave the Squire what strength he could. It was not much without Averil to guide him, but it straightened Riquier's back. "Can you tell me where we're going?" Gereint asked.

"We're aiming for the Isle," Riquier said, "and praying there's still a way to get there. You know that."

"I thought I knew," said Gereint, "but we turned away from the sea hours ago. We're headed inland."

"We're not," Riquier said so quickly he could not have thought before he spoke. "It's the dark and the rough road. You're turned around in your head."

"*I* am not," Gereint said, for once not caring how it sounded. "Look and see."

"I have—" Riquier began, but then he stopped. His eyes went wide, staring into the glimmering dark.

Once again Gereint fed a trickle of strength into him, enough to make him see clearly. It worked: he hissed through his teeth. "God's bones! Another spell." He raised his voice as high as he dared. "Messire! Mauritius!"

The company staggered to a halt. Most were perceptibly glad to stop and rest. Mauritius turned to wait.

The Knight huddled with Riquier and Gereint on the narrow track, not trying to be secret, but the dark and the strangeness of that country took the strength out of their voices. "Messire, we're being led astray," Riquier said.

Mauritius raised his brows. "You know this? How?"

Riquier tilted his head toward Gereint.

The Knight's brows rose even farther. "You see it, messire?"

"You can't?" Gereint asked.

Mauritius shook his head. "I feel the sea in front of us. I smell it."

THE SERPENT AND THE ROSE   🌹   165

"We've turned northward toward the Wildlands," Gereint said. "The sea is west and south. It's a spell, I think. I don't know why it doesn't work on me. Maybe because I haven't taken vows yet?"

"Maybe so," Mauritius said. "Maybe it's you who's deluded. Can you show me?"

"I can show you."

Gereint started. He had felt Averil behind him like a fire on the skin, but he had not known she was so close.

She left her horse standing and came up beside him. He shivered with her closeness. Something about this country made it stronger.

It was almost too much for him to bear; and yet he could not make himself move away. The force that had drawn them together since they first met was so strong he could hardly breathe.

She seemed no more perturbed by his presence than she ever was. Something glinted in her hand. It was a silver mirror.

It caught the light of this country and shone softly. In its reflection, the Knight and the Novice were wide-eyed and visibly startled.

"I know what you think you see," Averil said. "Here's the truth."

She held the mirror so that they could see it. Gereint, leaning in from the side, saw nothing he had not seen already. There was the dark land, the army's noose closing around them, and the track that led into the wild lands and away from the swell and sigh of the sea. Its only virtue was that the enemy did not block it.

Other Knights had come as close as they could. One of them struck his horse's neck and spat. "Delusion and deception," he said. "Why is your magic intact when all of ours is destroyed?"

"I'm not of the Rose," Averil said coolly. "This is the truth, messire. If we go on, we'll be lost."

"In more ways than one," Riquier said. He sounded much less troubled than he must feel. He bent closer to the mirror,

peering at the northern edge. "You see that? It's an army waiting for us. Right on the border—there, almost too dark to see.
None of us will live to see the Wildlands. We'll all die on the
edge of them."

"They've herded us here," said Mauritius. He did not sound
troubled, either. "We can turn back and choose such ground as
we can. Or make a stand here. Or go where we're meant to
go."

"Go on into the Wildlands?" Ademar asked from the crowd
that had drawn in around them. He sounded appalled.

"It's death wherever we go," Mauritius said. "They're offering us a field to fight in."

"You know what field that is," Ademar said.

Mauritius bowed his head. He looked ready, suddenly, to
drop. "The Field of the Binding. Where the Young God—
where the Serpent—"

"Where the Young God cast down the Serpent." Averil said
it with clarity that steadied them all. "This is a game, and he
plays it to the hilt."

No one needed to ask whom she meant. They never forgot
who had driven them to this place.

"We'll go on," Mauritius said. The others murmured assent.
If any chose to differ, he kept it to himself.

24

The Knights used what was left of the night to prepare for what lay ahead. They stopped and ate from their dwindling store of provisions. Those who could sleep did. The rest found such rest as they could.

Gereint was not tired enough to sleep or warrior enough to know how to get ready for a fight. He choked down a little bread and dried meat and drank a sip or two from his flask.

Food and water sat heavy in his stomach. He was not a fighting man. He was useless with weapons. The one weapon he did have, the magic that had flattened half a thousand men in the mother house, was too dangerous to trust. There was nothing useful he could do, except look after the horses.

He had to stop thinking like that. If they expected to be beaten, they would be. Not that it was likely the bare twelve score of them could overcome ten thousand of the king's men, but armies had faced worse odds and got out alive.

He opened himself to the magic that was in the earth. It seeped into him, filling him with warmth and a sense of calm.

His fears receded. He gathered all the courage he had and reached out through the earth to the other part of himself, the bright magic that was Averil, then through her to the dimmer lights of the last remnant of the Rose.

They lay in a circle like panes of a rose window, transcribing a shape of power that made Gereint's lips stretch in a smile. When they mounted and rode, they would fall into a column, since the road demanded it. But he could bind them now with the power he had found, and it would protect them no matter where they were.

It was a peaceful thing, that working on the brink of battle. There was beauty in it, just as there was in works of more familiar magic.

That beauty startled Gereint. He had been seeing magic as a thing of terror. That it should be beautiful, and that he should be glad of it, seemed deeply strange.

He opened his eyes. Averil was kneeling beside him, sitting on her heels, hands folded in her lap. Her face was as quiet as he felt.

She said, "You're getting better at this."

"It's you," he said. "When you're with me, I can control it."

"You make me stronger," she said. Then: "You're not afraid."

"Are you?"

She shook her head in a kind of wonder. "I know I should be, but my heart is so light it scares me. What is it? Is it a spell?"

"It's the land," Gereint said. "It's welcoming us. It may save us."

"How?"

"I don't know," he said. "I just know it can."

"So do I," she said, "and that scares me worse than ever."

"I used to be terrified," Gereint said. "Everything I did was dangerous. Here, it's still dangerous, but it doesn't matter. If I die, the earth will take me. It won't let me destroy anything that isn't myself."

"It's wild magic," she said. He could tell her voice was trying not to shake. "That's what it is. No order, no restraint, no—"

"It has its own order," he said, "and its own shape and beauty. It's not captured in glass, but it's not raw confusion, either. We can use it, lady. We can turn it against our enemies."

"Can we? Dare we?"

He met her eyes. "Look inside yourself and see."

Her eyes closed. She shuddered.

He tried to understand how she must be feeling, with her world crumbling around her. It had never been his world; he had known little of it until he ran away to the Knights. The pain that he felt was personal pain, for people he had known and a dream he had had, and a thing he had done that would haunt him until he died.

It was not so different for her. He took her hands and held them to his heart, letting her feel how it beat, strong and steady. That was life. There was no clearer order and no greater magic.

She shuddered again, deeply, and looked again into his face. Whatever she saw there made her shivering stop. Her hands had been cold; they warmed in his clasp.

He heard the slight catch of her breath; then she slipped them free. He let them go, though it was hard. The camp was stirring around them, waking and readying to ride.

DAWN WAS COMING. The wind had shifted, turning from west to east. It had a faint taste of rain.

They skirted the edge of the marshes and followed the track to a wide rolling moor. A stark and barren ridge bordered it to the north and east. The west looked out over a dim country that, as the light rose, showed itself misty green.

There was no green here. Gereint had heard that the grass grew thick on battlefields, fed by the blood and bones of the dead. Blood had been shed here, rivers of it, and bodies buried in the low mounds that curved along its western edge; but warring magics had so blasted the land that nothing could grow on it. The earth was naked, bare and stony, swirled with dust that heaped in hollows like dusky snow.

Some of the dead were still here, wandering lost even in daylight. And yet Gereint could not see any image of the Serpent or the Young God who had destroyed it. That had sunk beneath the surface, buried as if in deep water.

The Knights' advance slowed. An army stood in ranks, waiting. Sunrise glinted on helmet and spearpoint.

They did not wear the colors of Lys, the innocence of sky blue and clear silver. Their armor was black, with a subtle shimmer like oil on water. It looked like the scales that Gereint had seen on Duke Urien's coverlet. Their shields were made of the same dark metal, and coiled on them was the image of a serpent poised to strike.

"The gloves are off," Mauritius said. "The truth is out. And only we are here to see it."

He was smiling. Most of them were. They were Knights of the Rose; they were born to do battle against the Serpent.

Here on the ancient battlefield, where their order had begun, almost surely it would end. But it would be a brave ending.

THERE WAS AN order in battle, as precise as a dance. First the armies chose their field. Then they drew up on it, face to face, and exchanged challenges. Often those challenges led to negotiation and sometimes to surrender; then there was no bloodshed, and no battle, either. Or a champion would come forward and call for single combat, and whoever won, won for them all.

No herald rode out from the ranks of the enemy, though a Squire and a pair of Novices advanced onto the field and waited. They had a banner, black with a silver rose, that fluttered uneasily in the wind; they had bound to it the scarlet streamers of the call to parley.

The sun had shifted visibly when the Squire raised a voice like the blare of a trumpet. "Messires! Have you nothing to say?"

The only response was silence.

"We have no intention of surrender," the Squire said. "We will fight. You, messires, will die."

The enemy was a wall of shimmering black, motionless and speechless. "Are you shriven?" the Squire demanded of them. "Have you entrusted your souls to God? Pray while you can, messires—before we send you all to hell."

Then at last a voice boomed out from the ranks. There was no telling which man spoke, or if it was a man at all. It might have come out of the earth: a deep voice, echoing faintly, with an even fainter but still distinct suggestion of a hiss.

"Your God is dead. There is no mercy. Your blood will feed our lord, and your souls will serve him for eternity. You are an offering, men of the withered and forgotten Rose. Through your sacrifice the world shall be set free."

All around Gereint, the Knights stiffened perceptibly. The Squire-herald's back was perfectly straight and his voice perfectly steady. "God defends us. The Young God watches over us. They are our shield and our deliverance."

"They are dead," said the voice out of the army, "and damned."

The Squire took the banner from the Novice who held it. Its staff was a spear. He held it up so that the wind caught the banner and unfurled it.

The Rose was dull, its silver tarnished. Nevertheless the Squire kept his head high. He wheeled his horse and sent it back toward the rest in a lofty, cadenced, almost painfully slow canter.

The outer guard of Knights opened to let him in. Once his fellows had passed through, the wall closed again.

The Knights paused, waiting for God and their commander knew what. Weapons were loose in sheaths, lances poised, arrows nocked to strings.

Riquier came up beside Gereint and pressed a scabbarded sword into his hand. It was a plain thing, short and thick-bladed: a short sword in the old Romagnan style, little enough like the great swords of the Knights.

"Take this," the Squire said. "You'll need it."

Gereint resisted the urge to fling it away. The short sword was a stabbing weapon, a defense in close quarters. He knew too well what it meant. He had no armor and no protection but his uncertain magic. His coat was leather, but a blade could pierce it with one sharp thrust.

He and Averil were the only ones without armor, the only ones who were not trained fighting men. She had a weapon at least: a bow and a quiver of hunting arrows. The bow was in her hand, out of its case but not yet strung.

A triple wall of Knights and Squires surrounded her. When they parted to let Gereint through, none eyed him with pity or scorn. Ademar even smiled, though it came out as a tight, pained grimace.

They did not know what else Gereint was doing. He brought his gelding to a halt beside Averil's mare.

His magic yearned toward her. Soon enough he would let it have its way, but for now he kept it under control. Averil's eyes were fixed on the field ahead, whatever of it she could see through so many armored men.

The power of the place was rising with the sun. The king's men seemed unaware of it. They stood like a wall of steel, with no movement in them but the flutter of pennants in the freshening wind.

The Knights fell into the formation that seemed ingrained in them: wheels within wheels, like the full-blown petals of a rose. Its center, that in a rose was living gold, was Averil.

It was time, Gereint thought. He reached for the power that had been so strong only an hour before. In the heart of the rose, it should be stronger than it had ever been.

It was not there. He groped like a man who had lost a limb.

There was power everywhere around him, power in the earth and the air and the sky. But within the rose, it could not reach him. Even through Averil he could not touch it.

Their protectors guarded them too well. Gereint opened his mouth to protest, but no one heard. He tried to push his way back out, but a wall of steel surrounded him.

The Knights had begun to move, carrying him with them. He was going to die because none of them knew what he could do.

He tried to speak to Averil, but she had gone away inside herself. Her bow was strung now, an arrow in her hand.

He had suffered in dreams like this. As in dreams, he found himself mute and helpless. All he could do was cling to his horse's saddle and pray.

They were moving faster now. The army behind them had shown itself, barring any hope of escape.

They had no thought of running away. Along the edges of the rose, lances lowered and locked. They were all facing forward, riding against the army ahead.

Gereint drew his pig-sticker of a sword. It weighed heavy in his hand. The wooden swords he had trained with were longer and much lighter; their balance was altogether different. Nothing he had learned among the Knights would serve him here.

He had slaughtered pigs. Calves, too, and spring lambs. He knew what to do with a blade like this.

Riquier was a wise man. Gereint looked for him, to wish him well, but they were all anonymous in armor and helmets. He let the well-wishing spread among them all. Maybe it would do them some good.

THE ENEMY LOOKED ready to let the Knights exhaust themselves with a long and fruitless charge. The Knights stopped just out of arrow range and lowered their lances.

If they had hoped to see confusion among the ranks, there was no sign of it. Even when Averil's arrow arced toward the king's men, catching fire as it flew, they did not move.

The arrow reached its zenith and plummeted. As it fell, it spawned a swarm of deadly darts, each tipped with flame. They fell on the enemy in a lethal rain.

Then there was movement, a convulsion across the whole of that line. Horses screamed and reared. Men toppled.

Gereint's mouth was hanging open. He nearly fell off his own horse for gaping at that improbable slaughter.

The two armies surged toward the Knights. Averil nocked another arrow. Her face was set; she bit her lip. It was costing her high to work this magic in this place.

Gereint tried to give her what he had, but as before, he was blocked and stymied. If he could have broken the wards, he could have drawn on the power of this earth, but that would have laid them all open to assault by magic as well as more mortal weapons.

There was nothing he could do but clutch his nameless and unlovely sword and watch the spell take shape again. This time the enemy was forewarned. They flung up shields, then from behind them unleashed their own hail of arrows.

The arrows veered and slid and rattled to the ground all around the circle of Knights. Their protections had risen into a dome as clear as glass. They stood inside it, poised and still.

There were armies on all sides. Every way was blocked and every path of escape barred.

Wave after wave of arrows fell upon them. The protections held, but with only the raw power of the Knights to sustain them, they could not hold for long. Already some of the Knights were wavering, losing their grip on the working.

Averil's power was nearly spent. A third time she drew an arrow from her quiver. Her hand shook. She bit her lip and stilled the shaking.

Gereint's jaw ached with clenching. Dear God, there must be something he could do.

For lack of better inspiration, he slid out of the saddle. As soon as his feet touched the ground, he knew he had made the right choice. The Knights' wall of magic was thinnest there. He could draw up a trickle of strength.

He laid his hand on the neck of Averil's horse. The skin twitched, but the horse held its ground. He heard the intake of Averil's breath, sharp and short beneath the screams of the wounded.

This arrow did not fly so far or give birth to so many offspring. And yet it wielded more power than either of the others. It stung the enemy into motion.

The bow slipped from Averil's hand. Gereint reached to catch her before she fell, but she held on to the saddle. Gereint pulled himself up behind her.

He no longer cared what anyone might say or think. Averil leaned back against him. Her gratitude was distinct inside him.

Gratitude was not what he was feeling. Even stronger than terror and almost as strong as their twofold magic was the heat that rose in him.

It fed the magic, drawing strength from her as well as the earth. The Knights' wall could not keep it out.

As if Gereint's distraction had brought it down, the wall fell. The Knights leaped to the charge. Averil's horse sprang with them, almost leaving its riders behind.

Averil clutched the pommel and Gereint clutched Averil. Power surged up in him—straight through his body and into her.

It took him by surprise. He reeled. With a ringing crash, charge met charge.

25

The battle raged all around the circle. Averil in the middle had only a quiver of unmagical arrows to offer, and the bow that Gereint had brought with him when he mounted behind her. When the quiver was empty, she drew the knife she wore at her belt. It was meant for cutting meat, but it was sharp.

She had stopped being afraid long ago. She was going to die today. That seemed certain. The Knights were fighting as if they had no care for life or limb—only to take with them as many of the Serpent's servants as they could.

They began with lances and spears. When those broke or fell, they turned to maces and axes and swords. Men began to fall. Most were king's men, but too many were men of the Rose, men whose names and faces she knew.

It seemed she could do nothing, now her arrows were spent, but stand and wait for death to come to her. She counted the dead obsessively, even while she watched for the weapon that would penetrate the wall of guards and take her life.

Far down beneath her mortal consciousness, something else was rising. The strength of it was enormous. This country fed Gereint's power and therefore hers.

It fed something else, too—something older and deeper than magic. Something she should not be thinking of, not here or anywhere, if it was Gereint she thought of.

He was the other half of her.

In one hand she held the knife. The other found Gereint's. He was reaching for her as he always did—as he always would.

Twelve Knights and Squires and Novices had fallen. Thirteen: a Novice took a spear in the throat, defending the Knight who had been its target. She wrenched her eyes from his body. There were so many now, so much blood soaking into earth that had been parched of it for twice a thousand years.

Gereint was losing his grip on his temper. His frustration knotted in her middle. He knew too little. He always knew too little. And people were hurt and died, because he was too ignorant to help them or himself.

He was going to fling himself into the fight. She flung herself into him instead, with all the power she had left.

He was a bottomless well of magic, so deep she could find no end to him. When she was inside him, his ignorance vanished. Her knowledge, her long years of training and study, filled his empty places.

He made her strong. She had great power of her own, but with him she was stronger than she had known a mortal creature could be.

She did not feel like a god. She felt like nothing that she had heard of.

Everything outside her was still the same. Battle raged; men died. Souls fled, curling like mist above fallen bodies, then blowing away in a wind no one of earth could feel.

The circle was breaking. The sheer weight of bodies crushed it, driving the Knights back upon one another. There was barely room to raise a weapon.

Gereint's sword glinted in the corner of Averil's eye. His fingers flexed on the hilt. His breathing quickened, then went deliberately slow and deep.

Armed men jostled the horse they both sat on. It braced its feet. A pair of bodies rolled under it, locked in combat. It staggered but held its ground.

Averil braced inside. Gereint's strength filled her until she was like to burst.

She raised it like a sword. For the last time the enemy's army surged, rising to overwhelm them all.

She reached to the very bottom of her twofold power. There

she found an answer. She did not understand it—not yet. She only knew that it was there.

She gave them all to it, lives and souls alike. It lifted them up and out and away.

"THE EARTH GAPED and swallowed them."

The messenger had found the king in the ruins of the mother house of the Rose, standing where the chapel had been. Shards of glass lay thick on the floor. All the windows were broken, letting in the wind and the rain.

He was wet and muddy and worn with long travel, but his message was burned in his skull. He recited it in a half-chant: how the armies herded the last of the Knights onto the ancient field, how the battle went precisely as the king had ordered it—and then, just as the deathblow fell, the Knights vanished.

"The earth opened," he said, "and closed over their heads. There is nothing left of them. Our sorcerers, my lord, could find no sign, not even a glimmer of magic. They're gone, taken from the world."

"Gone?" said the king. "Completely?"

"Utterly, majesty," the messenger said.

"And nothing came of it? Their blood raised no powers? Nothing came in response to the sacrifice?"

"There was only silence, sire," said the messenger, "and the bodies of the dead and dying."

The king turned his face to a sudden spray of rain from the tall narrow window above him. Drops of it ran down his cheeks and dripped from his beard.

He believed with all his heart that hot anger was, in the end, less satisfying than cold revenge. He let the surge of rage flare and die. In every house of Knights but here, his assault had not cost him a single man. Here, he had lost half a thousand.

But he had won that fight and taken the spoils—all but the one thing he wanted most. If it had ever been in this house, it was no longer. He had gambled that the key to it was with the remnant who escaped, whom he had allowed to find the Field of the Binding.

Somehow they had escaped again. He was not willing yet to see a pattern, but he would allow that there might be one. They had something—some power that protected them. None of the rest of their order had been able to claim as much.

"Bring me the Grand Master of the Knights," he said to the servants who were always present, waiting on his will.

They had to carry the man in: his legs and feet were broken and he could no longer stand. His arms hung useless; his fingers were seared stumps. He still had his tongue, as little good as that had done his captors before now.

The king's men propped him in the chair that they had also, at the king's command, brought to this place. They strapped him into it with leather bands.

The dark eyes in the bruised and beaten face were quiet. There was no more fear in them than there had ever been. If his split and swollen lips had allowed it, he would have smiled.

It did no good to rage at that overweening arrogance. The king schooled himself to ignore it. Some of the Knights had gone mad before their bodies broke beyond repair, but this one was not going to break.

He was alive because there were other ways than torture to extract the truth, and the king had sworn to find the one that succeeded. Clodovec answered the Knight's smile with one that had no warmth in it. "The last of your kind are gone," he said. "We gave them the gift of death on the Field of the Binding."

Nothing changed in the Knight's face, nor did his eyes flicker. "That was a great honor," he said. "I trust they died well."

"One could ask if they had to die at all," the king said.

"Indeed," said the Knight. "Was there a question you wished to ask me, or did you bring me here to gloat?"

"Why," said the king sweetly, "both. You know what we want of you. We have all your treasures except one. That one will come to us—it is inevitable. Tell me where it is and I'll give you a clean death."

"Death is death," said the Knight, "whatever the manner of it."

"You think so?" the king asked. "A soul can die, too. Did you know that?"

"No one has such power," the Knight said.

"No one in this age of the world," said the king, "except those who remember the old magic. It was a mistake, messire, to suppress it so completely. Now no one knows how to oppose us, or even where to begin."

"Courage is always a fair beginning," the Knight said.

"Death for you will be oblivion," the king said. "No ascent to heaven. No passage through purgatory. Your soul will be eaten and pass into nothingness."

"If that must be," the Knight said steadily, "then so be it."

The king's teeth ground together. "One of you," he said, "one of all of you will tell me what I need to know."

"None of them knows," the Knight said. "That is the truth, sire. This Mystery was hidden from all but our eldest and strongest. Those are dead."

"All but you," said the king. "I can keep you alive, messire, in such pain that you pray to die—but death will never be given you. You say you're not afraid of death, even of the soul. What of life? Can you endure that?"

"My hope is in my God," the Knight said, "my rock and my deliverance."

"You may quote scripture," the king said, "but scripture will not save you."

"No," said the Knight, "but it's a great comfort."

The king's fist rose. He drew a sharp and hurting breath. With an effort that made his body tremble, he lowered his hand. "Take him away," he said to his servants. "Bury him deep. Let him live—but let it be in anguish, until he breaks and tells the truth."

They bore the Knight away. The king stood in the broken chapel, alone but for his ring of guards, and indulged in a moment of perfect ambivalence. The order of the Rose was broken, and all that had belonged to it was his—all but the one thing he wanted and needed most.

He had placed too much hope in that plan of his. Those Knights who could escape had gone straight to the Field of the

Binding as he had intended them to do. But they had performed no working there, nor had anything risen when their blood poured out on the earth. Their sacrifice had done nothing to free the Serpent from its prison.

He would find that prison. He would break it and unbind the prisoner. He had sworn a solemn oath, and he meant to keep it.

26

The remnants of the Rose stood in a green silence. A broad expanse of downs stretched away before them. An even broader expanse stretched behind.

There was no sign of the Field of the Binding. The enemy's armies were gone; the barren moor had vanished. The sky was soft overhead, misted blue, with a thin drift of cloud veiling the sun.

The Knights lowered their weapons. Wounded or hale, those who were afoot swayed in shock; those who were mounted wheeled their horses about, looking in vain for an enemy that had winked from sight.

Averil was still bound to Gereint's power. The strength of it kept her upright. She had thought of nothing but getting them away from certain death to some place, any place, that would offer them safety. Now that the magic had given her what she prayed for, she could not imagine where they were.

"We're in the Wildlands," Gereint said. He slid from her horse's rump to the ground and dropped to one knee, pressing his palm against the close-woven grass. "Here. Feel it."

She could hardly avoid it while her magic was still tangled with his. Part of her wanted desperately to pull away, but the rest knew that if she did, she would collapse. She could not afford to do that. Not yet.

He was barely perturbed by the sudden shift or the power that had wrought it. Through him she knew where they must be: deep in the empty lands, far away from the moor and the battle. She had brought them many days' journey, transported them in one leap of magic from the border of the Wildlands to their heart.

She twisted in the saddle. The downs behind her were blank and featureless, unmarked by path or track. But when she turned back, a road stretched ahead, a wide green track edged with an almost imperceptible glimmer of light.

Nothing here was to be trusted. It was all wild magic, magic without restraint or order. The earth breathed softly, deeply, underfoot.

Maybe the Serpent was here, sleeping beneath her horses' hooves.

As soon as she thought it, she knew it was absurd. This earth was alive in ways she could not have foreseen, but there was no god or power of the old time imprisoned in it. Whatever slept there was much smaller and less potent than the Serpent.

The Knights were close to the edge of endurance. This after so much loss and destruction was more than they could bear. She had to take them in hand quickly or she would lose them.

"Messires," she said. She had no need to raise her voice. Her murmur was as loud as a shout in this preternatural silence. "We'd best go on while the day allows. We're well past the enemy's pursuit, but we need water and shelter. My heart tells me we'll find it ahead."

"Your heart tells you?" the Novice Ademar said. "There must be powerful magic in it, then, because all I see around us is wasteland."

"It's good grass for horses," Gereint said. His matter-of-fact tone and his broad country accent were remarkably reassuring. "We can graze them as we go and water them when we can. We'll find refuge by sundown—it's waiting for us."

"It is?" said the Novice. "How do you know?"

"I know," said Gereint. For once since Averil had known him, he did not act as if he expected to be slapped for saying such a thing. "Here, I'll go in front. Then if anything comes to eat us, I'll choke it with my body, and the rest of you can get away."

Ademar hissed in annoyance, but the edge was off his terror. There was a little color in his face, and his eyes were not so wild. "You had better be right," he said darkly.

"Try and see," said Gereint.

When he moved away from Averil, she almost cried out, begging him not to leave her. But she was still inside him. That did not change as he left the straggling circle and walked out alone onto the path that she could see.

His head was up and his shoulders straight. He walked easily, with more grace than one might have expected in such a hulking boy. He was learning to carry himself like a fighting man.

Averil hardly needed to touch her horse's sides with her heels. It was already in motion, following the others.

They fell into a column, three abreast, which happened to be the width of the road. Gereint walked alone in front of them. He was tireless: the earth was feeding him as he walked, and the sunlight filled him as if with sweet water.

Through him Averil also was fed, then more dimly the rest. They were not aware; they moved in a half-trance, stunned with the shock of all that had happened on that day.

That was well enough for now. When they woke, there would be difficulties. Averil hoped that would not happen until she was stronger and surer of herself and more able to answer their objections.

THEY FOLLOWED THE track westward into the setting sun. No bird or beast stirred. There was only the grass and the rolling hills, and once a stream that ran, clean and empty of life, alongside the road. They were able to drink and water the horses without setting foot off the road.

It seemed very important that they do that. Averil was afraid that at least one of the Knights would rebel and venture the open downs, but none did.

As the sun sank lower, it dazzled them with its light. They went on half blind.

Gereint still led them. He was not using his eyes. Averil

could feel how he shut them and let the road guide him, leading his feet where they needed to go.

His feet knew when the land changed. His eyes opened. In the glare of the sunset, Averil saw through him how the downs ended like the shore of a sea. Stark hills rose out of it, clothed in trees.

The track ran up into the wood. Averil's horse raised its head and whickered, scenting water. It had been a long while since that stream beside the road.

On the wood's edge, sheltered by the trees but still in sight of the downs, they stopped and made camp. Those who were whole tended the wounded; those of the wounded who could walk looked after those in worse case than they.

Some were dying. Averil had known none of them except as faces in an army, but it seemed important that she learn the name of each, his rank and family and a little of what he had been. Every one of them had ridden without complaint; none held her or anyone to blame.

One of them, a Novice so young his cheeks were still as smooth as Averil's, was most insistent that she understand this. "It's no one's fault," he kept saying. "We thought all that magic was gone from the world. We didn't know. How could we? How could we have suspected?"

There was nothing she could do for him but let a little strength trickle into him from Gereint's seemingly inexhaustible store, and listen while he talked. He had taken an arrow in the gut; the pain must be appalling, but he showed no sign that he felt it.

His body burned with fever. She laid her hand on his brow, drawing such of the heat as she could. He closed his eyes and sighed. "Cool," he said. "So cool."

"Can you help him?"

She looked up into Gereint's face. There was only one answer the child wanted, and she could not give it.

Gereint's eyes darkened. He dropped to his knees. The boy frowned at him, puzzled. "Am I dead already?"

"Not yet," Gereint said. His voice was much gentler than his expression.

"You shine in the dark," said the Novice. "Will you show me where I need to go?"

Gereint bit his lip. "I'm not an angel, Nicholas."

The boy shook his head. "You're the light that guides us. Show me, please. It's so dark, and I don't know where to go."

Gereint's glance at Averil was rather wild, but he did not ask her to help. He took Nicholas' hands in his. Death had already sapped the life and color from them. "Your soul knows," he said.

"Help me," the boy said.

Gereint drew a deep breath. Averil laid her hands over his. She was not sure she knew what to do, either, but the Ladies taught that one soul might guide another through the working of great magic.

It was easier each time they did this, to bolster knowledge with strength and work magic with a single mind and will. The child's soul was a pure thing, as light as spun glass, clear and bright. It needed no guidance, but it was innocently glad of their presence.

It was a soft death, free of either fear or pain. When the body was empty, Gereint sank back on his heels.

Averil sighed and reclaimed her hands, folding them tightly in her lap. Other men were dying, and their deaths were much less gentle than this. She had to do what she could, if she could. But first she had to find the will to stand.

Camp was made, their few tents up and the wounded in them. Mauritius had chosen to risk a fire, for such comfort as it could offer. Since they had seen no walking or crawling or flying thing, not even an insect, he reckoned it was safe enough.

Averil was not so sure. But neither was she sure that it was dangerous. She held her tongue and thrust herself to her feet.

Gereint did not follow. Someone was calling him, reminding him that insofar as they had a master of horse, that was his office.

She would have welcomed the simplicity of looking after the horses, but care of the dying was a Lady's gift and a lady's duty. A handful of exhausted Knights and Novices were doing their best; she sent them to their supper and then to bed.

She hardly needed to insist. They were out on their feet.

THE SUN SET on her labor. The stars came out, but they were no stars that she knew. There was no moon, and yet she should have seen a thin curve of new moon.

She would not have said she was afraid. The dead were at peace and the living were sleeping as gently as they could in the aftermath of battle. The danger that had pursued them was far out of reach. If there was danger ahead, it was too far away for her to sense.

Still, she should have recognized the stars. It troubled her that she did not.

The Knights were all asleep. Even the sentries drowsed at their posts. An enemy could have slaughtered them before any woke to see him.

Gereint was awake. She found him on the camp's edge near the horses, sitting with his knees drawn up. His eyes glinted in the starlight.

She sat beside him. The grass was soft and cool under her. The stars, though strange, seemed oddly warm.

This was how Gereint saw and felt the land around them. He was godborn, he had told her. She had always thought that such children were simply spared the stigma of bastardy; there were no gods, not since the Young God was taken up to heaven. Now she wondered if after all it was the truth.

In Fontevrai he had never quite fit. Here he seemed as much a part of the land as the grass and the trees. Even his magic was clearer and stronger.

His hand rested on the grass with a peculiar tenderness. She slipped hers beneath it, lacing her fingers with his. It was a dangerous thing to do, but tonight she needed to feel his touch, to assure herself that she had not made a terrible and deadly mistake.

He kept his eyes on the stars, but he raised her hand to his heart and held it there. That strong rhythm, with the warmth of his touch, filled her with a deep calm. She laid her head on his shoulder and closed her eyes.

GEREINT HELD HIMSELF perfectly still. She did not know what she was doing to him. He did not want her to know.

For her he was a place to go for comfort. When she needed to be strong, he was there.

He was glad to give her that. But he was mortal, and his body was growing in ways he could not stop or change. It took every scrap of strength he had not to move or speak.

She thought he was calm, and in that calm she found peace. She would never know how much of it was despair.

27

When the sun rose, it rose in the east. It seemed to be the sun of earth, in spite of the stars that had been so strange. The endless roll of the downs and the green tangle of the wood were as they had been the day before. Nothing there had changed, and nothing walked or crawled or flew.

One thing was different. They had laid their dead side by side on the eastern edge of the camp, with spears around them and men to guard them. The men swore they had not closed their eyes, but the bodies of the slain were gone. The grass was green and thick where they had lain, and in each man's place grew a sapling of oak or ash or thorn.

AVERIL OPENED HER eyes on the morning. She was lying on a blanket in a circle of grazing horses. She could not see Gereint but she could feel him in the wood, fetching water from a stream that ran through the trees.

It was a peculiar sensation, this knowledge of where he was, but she did not find it unpleasant. She sat up, yawning, then rose. The horses slanted ears at her but did not leave their grazing.

The Knights were breaking their fast, with many glances toward the place where the dead had been. There was bread baking—nearly the last of their flour, said the Novice who handed her half a fresh-baked loaf.

They were coming out of their trance. She found Mauritius with the elder Knights, standing near the green barrows and the new grove that had sprung up in the night.

They welcomed her gladly enough, even bowed to her rank. "Lady, do you know anything of this?" Mauritius asked.

Averil spread her hands. "It's not my working. It's an honor, I think. The earth has been kind to us."

"So it seems," the Knight said. "We owe you thanks, lady. Without your intervention we would all have died on the Field of the Binding, and there would be no green grave for us here or anywhere."

It had not been Averil alone, but she was oddly reluctant to confess Gereint's part in it. That was his story to tell. She inclined her head and said, "I did what I could. With luck, the king will believe us dead and his troops won't try to follow us. We'll buy time to escape."

"Do you know where we are, lady?" one of the elder Knights asked.

"We're in the heart of the Wildlands," Gereint said behind her.

Mauritius' brow arched. "You know this country, then, messire?"

"I know a little," said Gereint. "The track we're on leads in time to the sea. But it's a long way, and strongly guarded. Some of those guards may be willing to help us, if we ask them properly."

"Help from the creatures of the Wildlands?" Mauritius asked with a visible shudder. "At best, by all accounts, they're tricksters and minor devils. At worst they loathe us and pray their dark gods to rid the world of us."

"Is that all you know of this country?" asked Gereint.

"It's all anyone knows," Mauritius said. "After the Binding, when the Young God's Church grew strong, old gods and creatures of the wild magic withdrew of their own accord, marked their boundary and retreated behind it. There was no pledge given or vow sworn, but it was understood that they would let our orders and magic be, and we would honor their borders and let their land be."

"Then we shouldn't be here at all," Ademar said.

"It's not forbidden," said Gereint. "We were allowed to come here. This land we're in was made for us, and the road we follow is ours. It will lead us where we're meant to go."

"I don't like this," said Ademar. "We've been driven out of Quitaine and destroyed in Lys, and there's nothing we can do but run and hide and try to stay alive. If this is where the wild magic went after the Binding, then in God's name, how can we trust it? It's the enemy of all that we are."

"Is it?" Gereint asked.

"Why do you know so much?" the Novice demanded. "Is this where you're really from? Have you been lying to us from the beginning?"

"No!" said Gereint, and that was his old self, visibly hurt that Ademar should say such a thing. "Everything I've said is true."

"He never knew his father," said Averil. "Maybe he really is godborn, and this is his inheritance."

Gereint's expression was as outraged as Ademar's. "I'm as human as anyone else. It's just . . . the land is telling me what it wants of us. Maybe because I have the least training: I don't know enough to shut it out."

"That is possible," Mauritius said. His calm voice silenced Ademar and seemed to bring others in the circle to heel as well. "It's a lesson to us. We relied on our works of magic, our talismans and our intricate devices. We lost the arts that we called lesser, but which were more truly a part of us. Our enemy understood this and exploited it. And now we run through the Wildlands because nowhere else will have us."

"The Wildlands may not, either," Ademar muttered.

"We can ask," said Gereint. "I think we're meant to."

"So they can refuse and then destroy us?"

"They will if you keep talking like that," Averil said sharply. It brought the boy to attention, with a flash of fury before he recalled who she was. She favored him with her sweetest smile. "There is help ahead of us, I do believe that. I set my magic to find it, and it is doing so. Whether it's help we can or will accept . . . that's for time to tell. I would rather die pursuing hope than wither away for fear the hope is false."

"Considering the alternatives," Riquier said from the edge of the circle, "I'm willing to risk it. Death is nothing to fear, the priests say, but I'd rather be alive."

"We could be worse than dead if we stay on this road," Ademar said.

"We'll be dead if we wander off it," said Gereint. "We're bound to this way. We have to follow it to its end."

"And whose fault is that?"

"Mine," said Averil. "I beg your pardon if I prevented you from becoming a blood sacrifice to the Serpent's cult. I don't think we're facing anything worse than that."

"You hope we're not," said Ademar.

He was not alone in his naysaying. She stared them all down. "I am sorry that I did not leave you to die," she said, "and sorry that I brought you here. I will do my best to keep you alive and bring you home. That's all I can promise, and all I can do. Will you stay with me at least until I prove that my choice was the right one?"

Rank had its privileges. They were not happy, but they subsided.

She was no longer their prisoner whom they guarded but their lady whom they followed. The shift was subtle but deep. Something inside Averil unlocked, even while her shoulders bent with the weight of duty.

She was meant for this. She glanced at Gereint. He had a peculiar expression, as if he were feeling the same intermingling of burden and relief.

He turned abruptly and strode toward the horses. No one moved to stop him.

THE TRACK LED straight through the wood. The Knights strained to see and hear, but no bird sang and no beast stirred in the undergrowth. Their stores were dwindling fast; in a day or two they would have to conjure up a village to trade in or game to hunt, or they would starve.

Gereint had no words to say to them. Whatever was ahead was calling him with a clear strong voice.

Even under Averil's command, the Knights were restless. When at evening they found a clearing, conveniently placed with water to drink and grass for the horses to eat, a few gave thanks, but most made camp in silence.

Gereint performed his duties in equal silence. Dinner that night was frugal: a strip of dried meat and a wedge of the morning's bread. He ate it out of habit, but his body took more sustenance from the water that he drank.

He was trying not to think of what he might be besides a farmer's son of Rémy. Mostly when a child was godborn, people knew who must have fathered it. There had never even been a rumor about Enid, and she had never said a word.

He had always supposed that she was ashamed to confess the one and only indiscretion of her supremely practical life. He had had dreams, of course, that his father was a Knight or a lord or even a priest: someone who could not claim his son without dishonoring his position. But a god? That was not possible.

These lands were open to him because he had no training to blind or shield him. That was all it was. That was all it could be.

AVERIL WAS ASLEEP already in the midst of the Knights. He bedded down near the horses. As he lay on his blanket, the pendant swung under his shirt. It was warm against his skin.

He drew it out. It gleamed in the long twilight, with its intricate enamelwork outlined in threads of gold. There was nothing magical about it. If there had been, it would have broken with all the rest of the Knights' works.

It was a lovely thing in this light, and it had a solid weight in his hand. He turned it, peering close. The back was as elaborate as the front, a pattern of branches and vines, twining in sinuous curves.

There were layers within layers, worlds within worlds in that seemingly simple thing. Gereint frowned. Might it be magical after all? Not all magic was the orders' magic, as the Knights had learned at terrible cost.

Still, even if it was a work of power, what use was it? It did not invite him to work any spells with it. It simply and purely was.

He closed his fingers over it. It was no warmer than his skin after all.

He slipped it back under his shirt and shrugged. It was a remembrance of a mage who must by now be dead. He would cherish it for that.

And yet as he lay on his blanket and tried to sleep, the pendant seemed more irresistibly present than it had been before. Maybe this land was changing it or waking it or making it aware of a purpose it had long forgotten.

Whatever the truth might be, he sensed no danger in it—not to him and not tonight. Sleep found him finally and buried him deep.

ON THE THIRD morning of their journey, a Squire named Odilon went missing. His fellows from the chapter house of Arlais begged to go in search of him, but both Averil and Mauritius refused.

"If he's on the road, we'll find him," Averil said. "If he left it, there's nothing any of us can do. I won't risk any more of you."

Even with the Knight at her back, staring them down, these Squires and Novices were close to revolt. Gereint bit his lip before he said anything that might tip them over the edge.

Averil looked each one of them in the face. Some blushed and looked away. Others met her gaze with unconcealed defiance. To them she said, "Give it a day, messires. If by morning you still mistrust me, I'll let a pair of you go hunting."

"Why not today?" the most defiant asked with a lift of the chin that dared her to smite him.

"One day," she said levelly. "Tomorrow you may do as you please, if it still pleases you."

They gave way. Once they had broken camp and mounted to ride, the mood in the company set Gereint's teeth on edge. It was as if something was feeding it, some darkness inside of them.

They had to have brought it with them. It was not in this earth, though there was peril enough here. It might be the Serpent's poison in them, or the burden of defeat grown too heavy to bear.

Whatever it was, it was dangerous. Gereint could only hope this road would end before their patience did.

No MORE THAN an hour past the camp, they found Odilon. At first they thought it was a rough-hewn stone beside the road; then as they drew nearer it seemed a heap of empty clothing. Only when they were nearly upon it did they realize that it was a body lying on its face. By the silver mail and the deep blue mantle, they knew it for a Squire of the Rose.

It was just within reach of the road. The one surviving Knight of Arlais turned it onto its back.

Men's breath caught. Gereint swallowed bile. The face was shrunken and emptied of life or color, the skin stretched tight over the skull. The lips were drawn back from long yellowed teeth and gums as white as bone.

"There's no blood in him," the Knight said. "He's sucked dry."

Off behind Gereint, someone was retching. He hoped uncharitably that it was one of the men who had stood against Averil.

She said nothing, nor did she gloat over her victory. She looked as sick as Gereint felt, but she kept her scanty breakfast down. It was Mauritius who said, "No one leaves camp or track for any reason. Is that understood?"

There was no defiance now. The men of Arlais moved to take the body, but it had somehow moved beyond their reach. As they stood staring, the grass grew over it, taking it into the earth.

28

N o more," said a Knight from the south of Quitaine in the lilting accent of Proensa. "We're turning back. Not even God knows where this road leads, except to death or worse."

"We can't turn back," Averil said. "We can only go forward."

"To what?" the Knight cried. "What will become of us?"

"It is said," Mauritius said when Averil did not answer at once, "that deep in the Wildlands dwell Powers that once were gods. Whether they are well or ill disposed, no one knows, but they may be willing to hear our plea."

"If those are old Powers," the elder Knight said, "they have no reason to love us."

"They never loved the Serpent, either," said Mauritius. "They were crushed or enslaved while it held sway. Under us at least, they were free to find their own country. We've never troubled them."

"Except to make our world too narrow and constrained a place for them," said the elder Knight. "My great-grandfather used to tell tales of the beings who lived in wood and water and flitted through the air on summer nights. How many of us have ever seen one? They're gone, fled from the world we've made."

"Our world may be the smallest part of the worlds they know," Averil said. "Remember, messires, what they taught us when we were children. Much of magic is belief. If we believe in their ill will, we may bring it on us. The more we trust them, the more they may be trusted."

"The wild magic can never be trusted," the Knight said.

"We have nothing else to trust," said Mauritius.

As if the land had been listening to them, toward noon of that cloudless, featureless day, the track began to ascend ever more steeply. Just below the summit of the highest ridge, they found themselves in a broad green bowl. Its heart was a pool that reflected the sky. Around the pool grew trees heavy with fruit: apples and pears, plums and peaches, and cherries so red they glowed in the soft sunlight.

The Knights recoiled from what they judged to be a trap. But Gereint plucked an apple from a bough that overhung the track. The sky did not fall; flocks of harpies did not descend upon them.

He turned to the rest. "These are for us," he said. "Take enough to blunt your hunger, then enough to dine on tonight. Let the rest be."

They glanced at one another. Riquier rode forward boldly. If his face was somewhat pale and his hand shook slightly, that was to be expected.

When he had filled his helmet with fruit and lived to tell of it, the others ventured where he had gone. They were very careful not to succumb to greed.

Gereint dismounted and loosened girth and bit and tied up the reins. His horse dropped its head at once and began to crop the grass beneath the trees.

He sat with his back to a sun-warmed trunk. The apple he ate slowly, bite by bite, tasted of that same sunlight. Like the water of this country, it nourished him more completely than any fruit of mortal earth. It was like meat and drink together, filling him full.

The Knights' muttering had dropped below the threshold of hearing, but he heard it nonetheless. Averil seemed not to hear it or else not to care. She appeared asleep, sitting in a circle of Knights with her face turned to the sky.

Her eyes were shut, her hands turned palm up in her

lap. The earth was rooted deep inside her. Its magic was un-furling.

Gereint's heart contracted. For the first time since she had brought them all to this country, he was afraid.

He slid through her guards, not caring if they stared, and dropped to his knees in front of her. It was dangerous to dis-turb a mage in the middle of a working, but he seized her hands and glared into her eyes. "Stop that. Whatever you're doing, stop it."

She blinked, gasped, shuddered. Her eyes opened; she stared at him as if she had never seen him before.

He flung her name at her with all the force he had. "*Averil!*"

Recognition dawned. Her body shook. Her breath hissed. "I—have to—"

"Not alone," he said fiercely. "Not without me."

"It's wild magic," she said. "I can't let you—"

"Why are you letting yourself?"

Her lips tightened. "I have to do this. I brought us here. I have to get us out alive."

"You are the one who matters," he said. "You can't sacrifice yourself."

"There is no one else," she said. "No one else can—"

"I can," said Gereint. "We can."

"This is not the magic we know," she said. "It's dangerous."

"It's the magic I know," he said. He gripped her hands tightly. "Don't fight it. Remember what we've done. It has to be both of us, lady. Neither can do it alone."

She had reached the edge of endurance. All he could do was hold on. What she had been doing, what she had thought to do, was mad without Gereint. He did not know why or much of the how, but of that he was certain.

He looked around him. The Knights were either out on their feet or staring without comprehension. It was as if they lacked some vital sense that would allow them to see what Gereint and Averil saw.

Even the younger ones met his stare blankly. Riquier swayed where he stood. Mauritius might have had a glimmer, but he recoiled from it. It was bred in him to turn his back resolutely on anything that did not bind itself to the orders of mages.

They had to change. If they failed, they would die. The land would kill them if the king of Lys did not.

Gereint bit his lip. The fruit of this country had done nothing to open their eyes. They were bound too tightly to ways and powers that could not help them here.

Even Averil could not free herself from those bonds, though she fought them as best she knew how. From childhood she had been taught one way. That teaching trammeled her.

"Give it to me," said Gereint. "Let it go."

Her head tossed from side to side. He made himself as steady as the mountain beneath them. "Release," he said. "Let go."

When she let go, she took him by surprise. He was braced for further resistance; the surge of power nearly flung him flat.

Now she held him and kept him from falling. They hung poised. It was a blessed relief to let go, to fall headlong into her magic as she fell into his.

Hand in hand they walked through the ring of armed men and out of the grove. The ridge rose steeply again, but not so steep they could not walk upright.

At the summit they halted and looked down.

The mountain was made of glass. It fell away below, black and gleaming, with edges as keen as steel. Mist shrouded its foot; the track plunged into it, as straight as ever.

No grass, no tree or flower grew there. No water ran. This was pure earth, its bones annealed with fire.

"The First Magic." Mauritius spoke beside Gereint. His voice was soft with awe. "I did not know—I could not have imagined—that it would be here."

"It's wild magic," Averil said. "Wilder than anything mortals have known. Nothing veils it. Nothing softens it. We can protect you, but if even one man missteps, we can't answer for his life or soul."

"I understand," Mauritius said. He was much calmer than Gereint would have expected. His tone was coolly practical.

"We'll have to leave the horses behind. They can't walk on this, even if the slope would allow it."

"They'll be safe here," said Gereint.

"We have to hope so," Mauritius said.

THEY LEFT TWO Novices to tend the horses—with a prayer that either party would see the other again—and took with them what they could carry. Water, fruit, weapons. Armor was too heavy for walking. Those who had it kept their helmets and left the rest.

Not one of them refused to go. Whatever they might think of this course that Averil had chosen, they chose to follow her.

Their courage came near to breaking her heart. She did not shame them by saying so. She saw them drawn up in file with Gereint foremost, then took her place just behind him.

The way down the mountain was steep but not quite impossible. They learned quickly not to slip and catch themselves against a jut of rock: those who tried left blood in their wake.

The mountain accepted the offering. The mist below seemed to grow no closer, though when they looked back, they could see how far they had come. There was no green in the world, no life, only black glass and glimmering track.

Here at last the Knights could feed on magic as Gereint had done since he came into the Wildlands. This was their kind of power, power locked with the crystalline lattice of glass. They bathed in it as in a fall of blessed rain.

The descent was no easier for that. The farther down they went, the steeper the track became. It began to double on itself, sidling along the cliff.

It was slow and slippery going. Before too long, Averil's legs began to ache. The mist was no closer than it had been an hour ago. The sky was blank and cloudless, but its blue was dulled, as if obscured by . . .

Mist? She paused long enough to peer at it. She could see nothing but sky.

While she was distracted, her foot slipped on the glassy

smoothness of the path. She skidded; her efforts to catch herself only made her slip the more.

Strong hands caught her. She fell against Gereint. Whatever power he had to keep his feet on this track, she was grateful for it.

He held her for a moment longer than he strictly needed. She let the moment lengthen again, until with a wrenching effort she drew away.

He let her go just a fraction quickly. Her feet, thank the good God, were steady on the path. She was not going to think about the warmth of his body against hers, or the strength of his hands, or the way she felt profoundly safe in his arms. Those thoughts were not proper for either of them.

BY A MIRACLE or by the land's grace, none of the Knights fell or died on that descent. They paid for it in blood, even so; hardly a man escaped without a wound.

The mist that had seemed so distant for so long was suddenly all around them. It was full of whispers and strange flutterings. After days in a land completely empty of aught but grass and trees, these invisible presences were subtly disturbing.

The track went on before them, not as steep but even narrower. There was no telling what it fell away to or how far down it went. It was hardly broader than a sword's blade.

Behind Gereint, Ademar muttered that this errantry did not need Knights, it needed a troupe of rope-dancers. Gereint caught himself smiling. His heart was in his throat; he dared not think about where he placed his feet, for fear he would think too much and feel too little and fall. And yet his spirits were astonishingly light.

As suddenly as it had taken hold of them, the mist vanished. More than one man gasped.

The fall was not so very far after all: half a dozen times the height of a man, maybe. But not even a madman would have wanted to lose his footing on that blade of a bridge.

A river flowed below: a river of fire. The mist had protected them from it. Now its heat seared them. Those who still had armor hissed and cursed. It must be scorching them through shirt and padding.

They could not stop to get rid of it: any shift in balance could fling them from the track. They had to suffer, not always in silence.

Gereint quickened the pace as much as he dared. Mist rose again before him, obscuring the end of that road as it had the other. Maybe it was a passage between worlds, or the boundary of a spell.

Whatever it was, it taxed the Knights to their limit. They were not raised to see magic as a mystery. They could not even rebel: there was no turning back on this road, more than any they had traveled since this eerie journey began.

Once again Gereint gave them what strength he could. It was harder here; his element was earth, not fire. But the glass on which they stood gave him the opening he needed.

As the magic left him, he came near to stumbling. He caught himself just short of it.

He could not afford another misstep. He gritted his teeth and fought the urge to run toward the mist. Speed was his enemy. He had to go on as he had begun, firm and steady.

It was the hardest thing he had ever done, and harder with every step. He was not just carrying himself. He was carrying them all. Any shadow of doubt, any hint of wavering, would destroy every one of them.

He needed every scrap of discipline he had learned as both farmer's son and Postulant of the Rose—and then as much again. He lost sight of everything but the thin black strip of road ahead of him. Even the mist receded from his vision; the fire he would not look at at all.

Again, as before, the mist swallowed him without warning. He was very careful to feel the others behind him, to know where each one was.

The river of fire was gone—that was a mercy. The old gods knew what lay ahead. He set his teeth and firmed his mind and pressed on toward it.

29

The mist rolled back like a curtain. Light flooded over them. Scents came with it, and sounds that they had almost forgotten the name of.

Birdsong. The chirping of insects. Not too far off, the yipping of a fox.

They stood in a green meadow on the edge of a wood. That was not so uncommon of late; but there were rabbits feeding in the grass and jackdaws quarreling in the trees, and a squirrel scolding in rare fury.

Up against the trees, beside the trill and sparkle of a brook, stood a cottage. It looked as if it had grown there, with its plastered walls and its thatched roof.

Its door was painted green. Roses rambled up over its sides and wreathed the door in white and scarlet and pink—strikingly and rather painfully like the rose gate of the mother house in Fontevrai.

This was no house of Knights. Behind a woven wicker fence Gereint caught sight of a garden: beans on tall poles and a grapevine on a trellis. No doubt there were rows of cabbages, too, and onions and leeks, if it was anything like his mother's kitchen garden.

It was the homeliest place imaginable, as ordinary as the farm where Gereint had been born—but after so many extraordinary things, that very ordinariness was frightening.

The track led straight to it. Gereint dared not hesitate too long. If he lost the others' trust, they could all lose everything.

There was nothing for it but to carry on. The grass seemed

real enough. The birds and animals had no fear of them, which was odd but not overtly dangerous. The earth was quiet.

There were eyes in the wood. When Gereint tried to focus on them, they slipped out of sight, but the corner of his eye caught them. They were not mortal eyes; they hovered at odd heights and gleamed strangely.

His hand touched the door of the cottage. It was solid and well made, bound with wooden pegs rather than iron nails. He lifted the latch.

It seemed much larger inside than out, but it was no faerie palace. It was dug into the earth so that he had to descend steps into it, and it was round and peaked high. A hearth stood in the middle under the opening of the roof. All around it were boxes and barrels that proved to be full of wheat and barley, nuts and apples, wine and mead, raisins and dried currants and spices both familiar and strange. Hams hung from the beams, with herbs drying in bunches between. A dozen fat fowl lay on a wooden table, plucked and spitted and ready for the fire.

There was enough provender here to feed all of them with a little effort. Through the door in the rear Gereint found the garden, planted as he had expected, and past it a long house with room for them all to sleep. There were even privies, which looked freshly dug, but there was no sign of the hands that had dug them.

Like all the rest of this land, this was made for them. They had little choice but to take it. Those who blessed their food did so with an air of defiance, but suffered no calamity for invoking the name of the good God in this place.

Gereint did not intend to sleep once he had eaten. The others went to bed in the long house, with men set on guard at the doors. He stayed in the cottage.

The fire was banked. Night had fallen under stars that were, at least, familiar; he glimpsed a scattering of them through the opening above the hearth. He sat on the tamped earth of the floor, with his cloak offering such cushion as it could, and clasped his knees to his chest.

He had thought Averil had gone to bed in the long house, well and thoroughly guarded, but when he looked across the fire, she was sitting there in much the same position as he was. Her hair was the same color as the embers.

A sigh escaped him. He was not afraid to be alone here, but he did not like to be apart from her, either. It was good that she was with him, though she might have been safer among the Knights.

For the first time in days, his stomach was comfortably full. He rested his mind on that. The rest could wait for the morning.

A small part of him dreaded the night, but he saw no enmity in the starlight. The earth was as glad of him as it had always been. He was in no danger. He would have wagered his life on it.

SUNLIGHT DAZZLED GEREINT'S eyes. He blinked and squinted, peering out of the fog of sleep.

He was in the long house, lying on a pallet near the door. Beside him, just out of his hand's reach, he saw Averil sitting up, looking as confused as he felt. The Knights were still snoring.

There were people standing all around them. Few if any of them were human. One near Gereint looked like a young birch tree, with dark eyes and long leafy hair. Another wore a man's face and body and a stag's antlers. Yet another seemed to be a voluptuous woman, but below the waist her body gleamed with scales; she stood upright on a snake's coils.

Her smile was fanged, her eyes yellow and slitted and inhuman. He did not doubt that her bite would carry poison. And yet he sensed no evil in her.

She was not altogether benevolent, either. She was biding her time and reserving her judgment.

So were they all. The long house was full of them. They were the wild magic in flesh and spirit, weighing and measuring these invaders from the mortal world.

Gereint sat upright. "You invited us," he said. "You brought us here. How are we an invasion?"

His voice sounded unnaturally loud. The Knights did not

stir. A spell was on them; it looked like the one that had laid them open to the king's attack, but it did not feel the same. That had been serpent magic. This was magic of earth and air.

He pushed himself unsteadily to his feet. The wildfolk watched him with interest. He stared back, determined to wait until one of them condescended to speak.

That could be a long time. His bladder twinged. He set himself to ignore it.

Averil rose from her bed and stood straight, steadier than Gereint. Her head was high; she looked like the child of kings that she was. "Tell us if you will," she said, clear but soft, "what you wish of us. Your hospitality is without fault; your help has been beyond price. But why? What do you gain from preserving us alive and whole?"

"Dinner," said a great hulking creature with a bear's pelt and a man's eyes. Its teeth were as long as Averil's fingers, bared and gleaming as it laughed.

The being beside it, which might have been human if it had not been so nearly transparent, slapped it hard enough that it let out a startled grunt. Gereint braced for a battle, but the bear-creature gave way, grumbling under its breath.

The Knights were stirring. The wildfolk's eyes sharpened. Those with wings fluttered close; those on hooves or paws or serpents' bellies leaned toward the waking men. Their curiosity was so strong that Gereint could taste it: like rosewater and bile.

He fought the urge to gag. At the other end of the hall, a Squire opened his eyes to find a flock of fey creatures hovering over him. He cried out and lunged with a sword in his hand.

The feys shrieked. Cold iron tore their fragile substance and dissipated it into the aether.

The bear-creature roared. The man-stag bellowed. Knights leaped from their beds and sprang into a circle. Those with weapons raised them. Those without stood armed with fists and defiance.

Gereint tried to stop them, but his voice went unheard. Averil caught at the nearest Knight's sword hand and found herself thrust into the middle of the circle, guarded as overzealously as always.

At least Gereint did not have to suffer that. He did his best to throw himself between the Knights and the wildfolk. The stench of fear and anger was so strong that it almost overwhelmed him.

He pushed it back. The wildfolk actually withdrew: not far, just to the walls, but if they had been poised to attack, now they were merely watching again, waiting for he did not know what.

The moment hung in the balance. The Knights shifted from foot to foot. If one of them lost his head, they would all be lost.

Gereint turned to tell them so, but the air had changed. The door was open; sunlight streamed in. A man stood in it.

He truly was a man, tall and broad in the shoulders, with hair as bright as the sunlight and a face hidden for the moment in shadow.

The edge of danger dulled. The Knights lowered their weapons. The wildfolk did not bow; not exactly. But their respect was deep and distinct.

The man spoke in a voice that struck Gereint with familiarity. "Messires. Welcome. Did my friends disturb you? I beg your pardon for that. They're curious, no more; it's been a long age since they looked on the sons of the Rose."

"Fierce curiosity," Mauritius said, "and faces such as we have never seen in living memory." He stepped forward from the circle, daring the wildfolk to stop him; but they made no move to stand in his way. "This is your house, messire?"

"I do live in it on occasion," the stranger said. He stepped forward out of the dazzle of light.

Gereint sucked in a breath. No wonder the voice had been familiar. Messire Perrin, whom he had known as an herbalist in Fontevrai, was a great deal more than that here.

He took no notice of Gereint—if he could have deigned to remember a mere Postulant running errands for his betters. All his attention was on the Knight. "You are my guests here," he said, "and under my protection, insofar as you may think to need it. Don't be afraid; you'll come to no harm."

"What assurance do we have that we can trust you?" Mauritius asked.

"My word and my honor," said the stranger whose name, maybe, was Perrin.

"I trust you," Gereint said. He had not meant to say it, but it refused to stay unsaid. "I believe you mean us well. I thank you for that; if I can ever return the favor, you have only to ask."

The silence that followed his words was complete, until one of the Knights hissed between his teeth. Even Averil was staring as if appalled.

Messire Perrin was not appalled, but he did look surprised. Gereint met his eyes steadily. They were grey as he remembered, but there was a light inside them, a hint of power that was neither human nor mortal.

"Messire," the tall man said, "I thank you for your kindness. Gods grant you will not regret the gift you give me."

"I don't expect I will," Gereint said.

Messire Perrin smiled suddenly, as dazzling as the sunlight that still slanted through the door. "You have courage, messire. For that I give you my hand."

He held it out. But before Gereint could take it, Averil stepped between.

The force of her presence was like edged glass. Her voice was so sharp it cut. "*I* don't trust you. This innocent may believe in you, but I see how the wild magic bows to you. Wild magic serves nothing but itself—but I can make it serve me. Touch a hair of any man's head, threaten my people in any way, and I will raise whatever power I may. Am I understood?"

Messire Perrin bowed without evident mockery. "Perfectly, lady."

"Good," she said. "Then I thank you for what help you've given us, for whatever reason you've given it."

"From you, lady," he said, "that's as great a gift as any I can give."

She drew back, but she kept her eyes level on him. He bowed again and smiled. "You're free of this country," he said to them all. "You've passed the tests of earth and magic; the land has accepted you and the people of air have granted you passage. The road to the sea is open if you wish to take it—or any other road you may choose."

The Knights glanced at one another. They were daring to hope, but expecting that hope to be dashed.

Averil said it for them. "Why? What do you gain from this?"

"Hope," Perrin said. "And maybe freedom."

She raised a brow.

Messire Perrin smiled, but his eyes were somber. "What your king would do to this world will destroy us even more quickly than it will enslave you. We release you to do battle against him—to defend us as well as your own people."

"Why should we defend the wild magic?"

"Because, lady," he said, "without it, the world's balance cannot be preserved."

"I don't understand," she said.

"I think you do, lady," he said.

She shook her head. Her brows were drawn together; her lips were set. If she did understand, she did not want to.

Gereint could not reach within her to bring comfort. She was closed to him, deliberately and strongly.

"Rest here today," their host said, "and tomorrow if you will. On the day after, you may go, with our blessing and the blessing of all who live free in the world."

Averil clearly did not believe it. But she refrained from saying anything more.

Their host had to step around her to leave the long house. He did so with no visible sign of annoyance. If anything he seemed amused.

He took his leave with a bow and a smile and left them to do as they would.

30

W hat's got into you?"

It had taken Gereint most of the morning to track Averil down. After Messire Perrin left the long house, the Knights had erupted in a clamor of questions and argument. Gereint was trapped in it; when at last he extricated himself, Averil had disappeared.

He found her beside the track that had brought them here, sitting on the stump of a tree, scowling at the glimmer of the road. At the sharp sound of his question she did not move, but he saw her shoulders tighten.

He stood in front of her, not quite on the track, and glared down at her. "You brought us here. You let the land lead you. And now that we've come where we were supposed to go, you've gone all contrary."

"*You* led us," she said. "I followed."

"It was your magic that opened the way." He dropped to one knee, the better to see her face. "What is it? Why are you afraid?"

"I'm not!" she said so angrily that he knew she was terrified. "I used the wild magic because it was close to hand. That doesn't mean I want any part of it."

"It's just magic," he said.

"It's not *just* anything!" she flashed back at him. "It undoes everything that we are."

"That's the king's magic," he said. "This *is* what we are—deep down where all true things live. Don't you feel it? Can't you see it for what it is? *He* can. He knows."

"He is a Power of this land," she said, "and deadly dangerous."

"I met him in Fontevrai," Gereint said. "He made a potion that helped your father a little."

She blinked. In the middle of her eruption of temper, his words could have made no sense to her at all. "What—how—"

"He's an herbalist in your city," said Gereint, "among other things. I'm sure he's human—or part of him is."

"Part of him most surely is not," she said. "Did you see how the wildfolk were when he came? They're in awe of him."

"Aren't you?"

"I trust nothing about him."

"You should," said Gereint. "He told us the truth. We're of more use to him and his people alive and strong than dead at the king's hands. He'll help us in any way he can."

"That's why I don't trust him," she said. "What happens when we stop being useful? He knows everything about us. He can swallow our magic and destroy our souls. Then the world will be given up to wildness."

"That's your teaching speaking through you," he said. "You know it's not true. Look in your heart. What do you see?"

Her lips set. She shook her head. "I can't see."

"You won't."

He took her hands. They were cold in his and stiff, but they did not pull away. Maybe they could not.

He poured warmth into her. She resisted like a child who, when forced to drink, sets its lips tight and twists it head away. But he was persistent. He would not stop until she opened to him.

Her fears were dark and strong. Everything she had done since Fontevrai, all she had been, struck her with a fierce revulsion.

It was like a disease, a sickness she had brought with her from the Field of the Binding. Messire Perrin had raised it to the surface, but it had been in her through all the long journey—even while she worked magic that no master had taught her.

It was not that she feared the sin, or that she had any dread of working evil with these powers she had discovered. It was the magic itself, the nature of it: because it was not part of any order or learned rule.

Gereint could only give her himself: his strength and surety and his trust in her.

"You trust too much," she said.

"Better than not trusting at all," he answered.

She shook her head. "I don't know what to do. I don't know what I am. I thought I could be a Lady of the Isle—but that wasn't meant for me. I was—I am—a child of Paladins. Quitaine was meant to be mine. But now the world is broken and the Rose is withered, and what is coming is so black in my dreams . . ."

Her voice trailed off. It was a while before she could go on. "There is no order for prescience," she said. "No mage trusts it. But I keep seeing what lies ahead of us, and it makes my blood run cold."

"You don't see danger here," Gereint said. "Admit it. It's all in the world without."

"Everywhere is danger," she said. "There's death for us wherever we go."

"Not here," Gereint said.

"Not for our bodies, no. Our souls are a different matter."

"Maybe our souls need to change. The Rose is gone in Lys because we turned our backs on every other kind of magic. If we're to restore it, we have to find another way."

"Not this one," she said.

"Why?"

She shook her head. Her face was closed and her mind with it.

She had been so strong for so long and done so much that it was all the more shocking to see how near she was to breaking. He took that tight, locked face in his hands. It was stiff and cold.

He should not be doing this. It was worse than improper; it was dangerous for both of them. She was a daughter of Paladins; he was a godborn nobody. She was bound by law

and duty to marry only her own kind. Even a touch was sac-
rilege.

Here in this country, where magic filled everything that
was, none of it mattered. When he bent his head, she did not
stiffen or pull away. He did what he had dreamed of since that
long afternoon in the duke's stable. He kissed her.

Her lips were cold. Her body shuddered. She needed every
bit of warmth he had, and every grain of strength.

He had to make her see. Her mind was clouded with shock
and fear and long exhaustion. He made himself a burning
glass and turned it to the sun.

She gasped. Heat flooded into her; her lips burned.

Gereint started to draw back, but her hands stopped him.
The kiss was long and deep.

It ended because they had to breathe. Gereint sank back on
his heels. His face was flaming.

Her own cheeks were pink. He looked for anger but found
none. Her hand rose to her lips; she drew a breath.

He watched her take refuge in composure. It was a remarkable, almost terrifying thing.

"I still don't trust him," she said.

That was the way it would be, then. She would not flay him
with outrage, and they would not speak of this again. He had
done what he set out to do: he had brought her back to herself.

He had to do the same for himself. Somewhere he found the
words. His voice was steady, though his breath came somewhat
more quickly than it should. "At least will you think about it?"

"I will try."

Gereint nodded. That was all he needed from her.

He stood up, drawing her with him. "Come and eat," he
said. "You need your strength."

She did not argue with that. As soon as she was walking, he
let go her hand—a little hastily, maybe. She hardly seemed to
notice. She had far more on her mind than a boy's foolishness.

THE KNIGHTS RESTED all that day. Most of them dozed in
the sun in front of the cottage, waking to eat or drink from the

inexhaustible stores, then falling back into sleep again. They seemed to be of Gereint's mind: inclined to trust their host and do as he bade them.

Averil knew she was being contrary. After all she had done to bring them here, she found she could not simply accept what the stranger had said. It seemed too easy; too simple. There had to be more to it.

As the sun sank over the long downs and the deep wood, she was careful to show them all—especially Gereint—a calm and peaceful face. That was not always easy; wild magic overflowed in that place, and its creatures came and went in increasing numbers as the day waned toward night.

Too large a part of her found them fascinating, even exhilarating. There were so many and so varied. The scholar in her wanted to study each one and come to know it. But she could not let herself indulge in such flights of fancy.

Days were shorter now, the long summer fading. At night and in the early morning, autumn's scent touched the air.

After the sun had gone down and the Knights had gone once again to their beds in the long house, Averil lingered by the fire in the cottage. Gereint tried to sit up with her, but sleep took him as soon as darkness fell.

She sat in the firelight, watching the beings that danced in it, with Gereint's soft snore for company. It seemed a long while but could hardly have been more than an hour before she heard the footstep she had been waiting for. She turned her head to meet the stranger's gaze.

He looked less human in this light than he had in the morning. His face was too sharply carved, his skin too pale; his hair had a moonlight sheen. A white light of magic burned in him.

She rose. It might be mad of her to face this Power of the wild magic alone, but the others would only have impeded her.

He regarded her with calm interest. He might have seemed benevolent, but the power that was in him was purely of the wild magic.

Her own heart was drawn powerfully toward him. The

magic in her wanted to rise and encompass his—not exactly as it did with Gereint's, but in a way too similar for comfort.

This, all too easily, could be her world; this could be the magic that she chose. She who had been bred for a hundred generations to the orders of the mortal world, somehow had harked back in blood and spirit to older ways.

She had to fight it. She of all people could not give way to this. It would change her too much, and through her, change her world.

Gereint's voice echoed unwanted in her mind. "Maybe it needs to be changed."

She shut it out. Her chin lifted; she said, "Messire, it's time for the truth. This isn't a free gift we're given, is it? What do you really want of us?"

"One might ask rather," the stranger said with every appearance of goodwill, "what you want of us. The others hold their fears and their old misunderstandings at bay, but you let them rule you. Why?"

She had not expected such directness; it left her briefly speechless. When she could find words, they seemed feeble and foolish. "Because I've let myself be led too long. I'm in revolt. Yes, I'm afraid. Should I not be? You have no reason to love me or mine. We drove you from our country long ago. Surely we're no better in your mind than the powers that would supplant us."

The stranger's head tilted as if he gave careful thought to her words. When she was done, he said, "You are more like us than you want to know. Will you come with me?"

"To what? Death or worse?"

His smile managed not to verge on mockery. He stooped and touched Gereint's shoulder.

Gereint woke all at once. His eyes flicked from the stranger to Averil; he stood, setting himself between them. Which of them he was defending, she could not tell.

The stranger bowed slightly; Gereint bowed back. "Come with us," the stranger said.

Gereint nodded once. His expression was alert; his eyes were clear. Averil could find no sign of a spell on him.

If this was a trap, she had set it herself. She took a deep breath. It steadied her a little, but it made her dizzy, too.

The others were already in motion toward the door. She could refuse to follow. For a moment she wavered, but she had not come this far only to retreat. She strode after them.

31

There was still light in the sky. Averil took the count of familiar stars above the breathing darkness of the wood. Spirits of air were dancing in their light, gossamer shapes flitting in patterns that she could almost make sense of.

The wild magic was rising strong in her. Her heart wanted to give way to it. Her mind did not dare.

She had to make a choice. There was no running from it, not any longer. Not in this country.

For a little while still she could evade it. The stranger led her into the wood, following a path that ran straight and smooth through the thickets of trees.

If she had been wise at all she would have turned back and hidden among the Knights. Tonight was not a night for wisdom. Gereint had taken station behind her, walking softly in her wake.

His presence comforted her more than she had expected. She had not wanted him to go at all, but she found she was glad. The world was a safer place with him in it.

Even this world. She glanced back. His face was a blur in the gloom. His shoulders were as wide as the stranger's.

He had grown again. He was going to be a very big man. She found that comforting, too, in its way, even though she knew he was still awkward with weapons. He would not always be so.

He was not the ignorant boy he had been. There was a confidence in him that had not been there before. He set his feet lightly but solidly; he cast about with eyes and magic, searching for danger as deftly as a master mage.

She could sense no threat, but this was not a safe place. Away from the track, the wood was perilous. Things moved in it that were kin to the airy spirits she had seen above the cottage as the lion of the plains is kin to the housecat on the hearth.

Between the track and her guide, she was protected. Gereint had her back. She was in no danger—except what she brought on herself.

THERE WAS NO reckoning distance in the starlit wood, but they walked long enough for the stars to shift overhead. Averil was all but asleep on her feet. The men ahead and behind seemed as fresh as ever, breathing easily, but her legs ached and there was a stitch in her side.

She was shamefully glad when the stranger stopped. At first there seemed to be no reason; then she realized that a wall had appeared in front of him. Maybe it had been there all the while and she had been too blind in the darkness to see.

There was no telling what it was made of. She thought stone, thickly overgrown with greenery. There was a door in it: the stranger's hand traced the outline, waking a glimmer like silver faintly touched with moonlight.

He was careful to trace the full line of it, from earth to lintel and back to earth again. It was as tall as his hand could reach, and somewhat wider than the breadth of his shoulders. He set his hand to the center of it and leaned.

For a moment it resisted. His breath left him in a sharp hiss. Abruptly it swung open.

He was not so lacking in dignity as to stumble, but his step forward was somewhat quicker than it might have been. The air beyond was no different than what they breathed here: night air, rich with leaves and damp earth. The stars were clearer, the trees thinner—thinning fast beyond the gate.

Beyond the trees was an all too familiar landscape of rolling downs. Far off but still within sight, something rose out of them: a low round tower or a dance of stones. At that distance, Averil could not tell which.

Before she passed the gate, she had wondered what need there was for a wall, if there was nothing beyond it but more of the same wilderness. As she stepped through, she understood.

Her eyes kept telling her that this landscape was the same as all the rest that she had seen in the Wildlands. Her magic insisted that this familiarity was a deception. She was not in the world she had thought she knew.

The wall was a barrier between worlds. Without were the Wildlands. Within was a country for which she had no name.

On the other side, the wild magic was strong. Here, it was in the air she breathed and the grass she trod. Everything was magic: grass and stone, tree and flower and the flocks of creatures that filled earth and sky even more thickly than they did in the Wildlands.

They were everywhere, dancing like fireflies over the downs, swarming in the starlight, and swirling about the three who had ventured into their country. All three fascinated them, but Gereint could hardly move, so thickly did they crowd around him.

He waded through them, trying visibly not to harm them. They peered into his face and plucked at his hair and brushed his hands with wings and webby fingers. None of it seemed to hurt him: their touch was like the brush of moth's wings.

When he held up his hand, a flock of them settled on it, chittering in minute voices. It sounded like an exhortation, but it was in no language Averil knew.

He laughed with delight. They flew up in a cloud, sparking silver and blue and palest green.

It was strange, Averil thought, that he who had had such horror of magic had come to be so much at ease with it, and she had lost all ease or comfort. Somehow she had to find her way back—through him, maybe, but above all, through herself.

He had been raised to shun all magic. Wild magic was no more to be feared than any other. The affinity he felt for it did not trouble him. Here in the heart of the wild magic, he walked light and sure, like a king in his own country.

The thought made Averil stumble. And yet she could not unthink it. This was his country, and he belonged in it.

She could belong here—if she let herself. She stumbled again. His hand steadied her, warm and solid as it had always been, giving her strength where she needed it most.

She was lost in confusion. The wildfolk danced over and around them, singing a sweet eerie song.

He met her eyes. His own in the starlight were level, dark and quiet. "You're stronger than you know," he said.

"Or than I want to be?"

"Than you dare to be." He wove his fingers with hers and walked down the long straight road. She had to follow or be dragged.

The stranger was well ahead, not looking back. Averil could turn and run, break free and escape, but she could not bring herself to do it. She had demanded this journey. She had to see it through.

TIME WAS STRANGE in this place. It stretched forever, but the stars barely moved. Step by step the circle of stones drew nearer.

It was a giants' dance as she had first thought. The stones were as old as the earth; whatever had raised them was beyond mortal understanding of time.

The wildfolk were even more numerous there than elsewhere in this country. They were larger, too, and stronger. Some wore faces that Averil could have sworn she knew: images of gods and daimons, strong spirits of the old magic.

The Church called them demons, but she sensed no evil in them. They were made of magic, shaped by mortal faith and their own desire. The greater ones had beauty to break the heart.

They hovered in the air, winged or borne up by magic, or stood straight and still along the track like a guard of honor. Their eyes glittered as the mortals passed, but not with malice. Averil would almost have said they were amused.

Even when mortals worshipped them, the gods had been incalculable. Now, as diminished and forgotten as they were, they were still outside of human understanding.

She would remember those faces like marble images and those bottomless eyes. Of all the strange things in that strange country, so far they were the strangest; and yet in them she found a focus. They were not evil, no more than the stars were. They were as much a part of the world as any other being under the moon.

She felt as if the world had shifted, only to grow more solid underfoot. What exactly she understood, she was not sure yet. That needed time and solitude, neither of which she was about to get.

She could wait. The hanging stones were full in front of them now, crowned with stars.

The stones were alive. Their roots were in the earth; they drew up magic as trees draw up nourishment. Their thoughts were deeper and infinitely slower than the thoughts of trees.

Beside these unimaginably ancient Powers, the old gods were as slight as the wildfolk that flocked around Gereint. Averil bowed to the ground.

The stones were far beyond taking notice of mortal homage. Still, she had to do it. It was a matter of honor.

The stranger led them between a pair of stones, under a lintel that rose three times Gereint's height above their heads. This was yet another gate and yet another world within the world: a circle of starlit grass watched over by the oldest of old things.

Its center was another stone, but low and squat, barely rising above the grass. At first it seemed shapeless, but as they approached, Averil realized that it had a head, rising neckless out of sloping shoulders, and massive haunches, and pendulous breasts drooping over a vast round belly.

It had the most rudimentary of faces: straight line of nose, pits of eyes. There was no mouth that she could see. There was nothing human about it, and yet it was rawly, powerfully female.

The stranger bowed to the ground before it—before Her. "Mother," he said. Only the one word, but it was all he needed to say.

Averil bowed as he did, with the dim awareness that Gereint

had done the same. The Mother did not move, but the force of Her attention was like a blast of wind.

She was deep inside of Averil, far down in the utmost depths of her heart. Had She always been there? Averil had never gone down so far.

This was the source of all magic—wild or tamed, of any order or none. From this deep spring it all came. And Averil was part of it. She was the Mother; the Mother was in her.

Two thousand years of order and breeding were a blink of the eye to the Mother. Long before either Ladies or Paladins, She had been. Long after they were all gone, She would remain.

Averil was Hers as every creature was—female even more than male. Out of Her, they had all come.

Gereint knew. His knowledge was bright and whole inside her. He found it exhilarating.

Averil was not sure what she thought of it. It was profoundly and incontestably pagan. And yet it was also true.

The priests' dogma, their bearded God and his warrior son, had no more strength—and no less—than any other faith of lesser gods. Averil had seen them in their ranks without, standing guard over Her from Whom they all came. They were gods in truth; their powers had swayed mortal hearts as the good God's did in this age of the world. But She would still be long after the good God was as thoroughly forgotten as the gods of Hellas or Romagna.

This was a mighty heresy and an even mightier truth. But Averil still had a question, and she dared to ask it.

"Why?"

The Mother did not speak. Words were too feeble to contain the thoughts within that mind. Even vision could hardly hold them.

The answer came as a deep understanding. There was no Power greater than the Mother, but She was the earth, and the earth was not invulnerable. Some of the Powers that had grown out of Her were inimical to Her, as the disease that physicians called the crab could devour the body from which it grew.

One such had been hatched in the morning of the world. It

had been a small cold thing then, one of many that burrowed through the Mother's flesh. But it had learned to feed on Powers and take them into itself.

Its appetite was insatiable. The more it ate, the more it craved. It grew into sentience and learned to wield the magic from which it was made. It took slaves from among the wildfolk and then from humankind, compelled them to serve its will, and when they grew weary or rebellious, it devoured them, body and soul together.

At last a small band of slaves rebelled. Some few of the gods and daimons allied with them, and one god, who was stronger than the rest, sent his son to lead them. So the Serpent was conquered and bound, but no one had the power to destroy it. Some feared that if they succeeded, the fabric of the world would weaken—so deeply woven was the Serpent into every part of it.

When the Serpent was bound, that fear receded. In too many, it vanished altogether. But there was real danger, both in freeing the Serpent and in destroying it.

The order of the Rose was the Serpent's most potent enemy. When the king destroyed it, he opened the way for his allies. Those, no one had seen yet; nor should anyone wish to see them. They were wildfolk once, but the Serpent had given them strength. They were beyond terrible.

Not only mortals were in danger. This land was threatened, too. The Rose still survived elsewhere in the world; the Isle was still safe. They would not long remain so if the Serpent was freed, but until that happened—and please all the gods, it would not—they could stand against the Serpent's followers.

That, the Mother made clear to Averil, was why She had opened this road to the Knights. She could not or would not spare them the tests and dangers of this country, nor would She tame its magic for their comfort. It was as Gereint had said: they had to change or die.

Averil did not want to die. That thought was clear in her. If it made her a coward, so be it.

The Mother bent Her rough sketch of a face toward Averil. The full force of Her attention was almost more than Averil could withstand. The Mother took in the whole of her: every thought, every fear.

There was no contempt in that regard; no sense that Averil was beneath Her notice. Averil was trained in the most powerful of the orders yet deeply imbued with wild magic; she shared a strange and hitherto unmatched bond with a godborn mage. She was something new in the world.

For that she had been allowed to come to this place, and for that she was alive and free to return to her own world. The Mother laid no command on her and forced no choice— though if Averil chose the Mother's way, there was one thing she must give in return.

It was not a complicated thing. When Averil came to her inheritance, she would relax the bonds on the duchy. She would make its air free for the wildfolk and allow the spirits of earth and air and water to enter as they had in the old time.

Simple, but not easy. The Church and the orders of mages would object. The strength of their magic and the power of their prayers would unravel the airy substance of the wildfolk.

As she looked into those pits of eyes and felt that careful lack of compulsion, Averil made her decision.

The Mother turned away. Averil reeled in a world gone briefly empty of life and light, until her senses recovered themselves and she could see once more.

Gereint and the stranger waited in silence. The stranger offered nothing, but Gereint was there as always to make her stronger and lighten her heart.

He had never failed her. She knew he never would. She hoped—prayed—that she could do the same for him.

32

Averil was profoundly quiet as she walked back down the long road from the Mother's dwelling place. Gereint made no effort to break the silence. He had his own thoughts to keep him company, and his own decisions to make.

It seemed obvious that the Knights would take their freedom and run for the Isle. They had already spoken of moving on to Prydain, where their order must still be alive: its queen was no friend to the king in Lys. It was expected that Gereint would go with them. He was a Postulant; he went where the order commanded.

He wanted more than ever to be a Knight of the Rose. But he was also meant for something else. The Mother had not spoken to him as She had to Averil, and yet he had felt Her touch on his spirit. If words could be put to it, they would have been, *Go where your heart leads.*

His heart led him through the Wildlands behind Averil. As he walked, he was potently aware of the worlds through which they passed. But even more than those, he was aware of Averil.

He had lost despair somewhere between the Field of the Binding and the Mother's circle. Maybe he could never have her in the way his body wanted—but he already had more.

So he told himself. Maybe he even believed it.

Her back was straight. He could feel her exhaustion; it had sunk to the bone. And yet she was strangely refreshed.

The Mother's circle was long gone. If they looked back, they would only see the track through the ancient wood.

The dangers that had stalked them on the way to the Mother

were as strong as ever, but some light of Her clung to them still. It kept the dark things at bay.

Gereint made sure to remember that: how it felt, what he did. It might prove useful.

It was some time before it dawned on him that Messire Perrin had vanished. He had been in the stone circle with the Mother. Gereint remembered that distinctly. They had followed him out of the circle—or had they?

Gereint had followed Averil. She had known the way—they both had. It was perfectly straight and impossible to mistake.

Unless they had been led astray. Unless . . .

Doubt was a sickness. In this wood it could be deadly. Gereint made himself focus on the road and the lady and the place to which they were going: the cottage by the wood, where the Knights slept.

Once he thought of them, he could feel them. The pendant that was always around his neck was warm. He could almost have said that it guided him: warmer as he drew near the Knights, cooler if he turned to one side or the other.

There was a spell on the Knights, but it was nothing to be afraid of. It was a working of healing and peace. It soothed the raw edges of their grief and made their hearts stronger.

Gereint followed the track of it until the trees thinned and he stood once more in front of the cottage. Messire Perrin sat on the doorstep, watching the dawn brighten above the wood.

He smiled as they approached, and rose and bowed. "Welcome," he said.

Gereint thought Averil might tax him with where he had been and how he had come here, but she held her tongue. She walked past him as if he had not been there at all.

Messire Perrin was impossible to offend. He did not seem to move, but when Gereint moved to follow Averil, he filled the doorway. "Guard her well," Messire Perrin said.

"Always," said Gereint. His eyes sharpened. "Is there something I need to be aware of?"

"No more than you have been," said Messire Perrin. "She's more valuable even than her people understand. And so," he added, "are you."

"Because of what we are when we work magic?"

Messire Perrin's eyes glinted. "That, and other things. You should tell the Knight—the dark one, Mauritius. It's something he should know."

"I'll tell him," Gereint said, "though I don't know if he'll believe me."

"That one will," Messire Perrin said.

Gereint had to admit that it was likely. Mauritius was a man who listened, and he had always treated Gereint fairly.

Messire Perrin nodded as if he had spoken. "A fair morning to you, messire, and a fair journey. We'll meet again."

Gereint opened his mouth. By the time the words came, the doorstep had flooded with the first sunlight, and Messire Perrin melted into it. The Knights were waking within. In the meadow beyond, Gereint heard the snorting of horses.

They were there, all the horses and mules that had survived the battle. The two Novices who had been guarding them sat in the grass, blinking and staring. It could not have been clearer that it was time to depart from this place; nor could they have been more glad to do it. This was an uncomfortable country for their kind.

Gereint refused to think the thought that followed it, that he was comfortable here. He felt at ease among the crowds of spirits; the magic that ran through everything, living and otherwise, sang clear harmony with his own. If he could feel as if he truly belonged anywhere, it was here.

And yet he had to go. His heart called him away from comfort to trouble and pain—but she would be there, and the Knights. They were his heart's home, however ill a fit he was for the world they lived in.

WHEN THE SUN was fully above the horizon, the horses were saddled and ready. The Knights had eaten one last breakfast of barley bread and summer berries with curds and cream. The taste of it lingered on Gereint's tongue as he rode away from the cottage.

He was the last to go. Averil was among the first. She had not spoken a word since she came back. He might have thought her spellbound, but she was thinking. The choice the Mother had offered her was made, but she needed time to absorb it.

It was a short road: much shorter than the way in. By noon they were in sight of familiar barren hills. By midafternoon they skirted the edge of the Field of the Binding.

The king's armies were gone. Of the battle there was no sign. The sky was clean; the hawk that wheeled in it was no spy for any enemy.

And yet they slipped warily around the edge, seeking out what cover they could find. Few of them could look directly at that bleak plain. Memories, ancient and recent, lay heavy on them all.

Nightfall found them on the road to the sea. They camped well out of sight of the town of Deauville, where had been a chapter house of the Rose.

That was gone. They could feel its loss from leagues away. The king's men had razed it and sown its gardens with salt.

It was Riquier who said what they were all thinking. "The web. It's in us again. But how—"

Mauritius reached into the purse at his belt and drew out a shard of crystal. It glinted in the firelight. He turned it slowly, eyes half closed as he sought in it for the paths of magic that had been closed for so many days.

They all searched in purse or saddlebag. In each was the same: an oblong of faceted glass, no longer than the last joint of the smallest finger.

"This is a great gift," Mauritius said.

"Or bribe," said one of the elder Knights. "What do they expect in return?"

It was Averil who answered, "Salvation. If the king succeeds, they'll be as dead as the rest of us."

That made sense to them, though not all were happy about it. It was a quiet camp that night, with no murmur of conversation and no laughter or singing. Many went early to their blankets and curled around the crystals in their hands, cherishing the magic that had returned to them by the wildfolk's gift.

GEREINT WAS POWERFULLY tempted to evade the task that Messire Perrin had laid on him. There would be time enough in the morning. Or he could wait until they had come to the sea. Or—

He dragged himself up from his blanket and forced his feet to carry him to the other side of the camp.

Averil was there before him. She sat facing Mauritius, hands knotted in her lap. The silence between them was thick enough to cut.

Gereint almost retreated, but Averil's eye flashed toward him. Although he could not exactly say it was welcoming, he judged it best to stay.

It seemed a long time before Mauritius sighed and said, "Suppose you tell me what brings you here. We all need sleep. It's a long road tomorrow, but it will finally bring us to the sea. There's a ship waiting; we have to hope the king doesn't find it before us."

Averil frowned at her hands. "He won't," she said.

Mauritius raised a brow. "Indeed?"

"Indeed," she said. "In the Wildlands, they promised. The king will be well away from the port."

"You trust them," he said. It was not a question.

"I believe they have no reason to betray us," she said. She drew a breath, then another. Finally she said, "I can't go with you."

"You must," said Mauritius.

She shook her head. "With all respect, messire, I'm done with letting you carry me like baggage. I'm going back to Fontevrai."

"Your father has given me orders," he said. "I intend to obey them."

"My father doesn't know everything that we've come to know," said Averil. "Quitaine is my inheritance. I'm bound to protect it."

"Your father and his Lord Protector—"

"They are worthy men and strong mages," she said, "but the king has found the weakness in their magic. He has not found mine."

Mauritius' brows met. "All the more reason not to risk losing you. On the Isle, surrounded by strong protections, you can labor on Quitaine's behalf."

"I have to be in Fontevrai," she said. "What I need to do is there."

"If that is the truth," Mauritius said heavily, "I hope you can protect all of us—because we are commanded to follow wherever you go."

"No," she said. "You'll go to the Isle and then to Prydain. Raise what powers you can and strengthen the order across the sea. I'll wage war in the enemy's own heart."

"You can't go alone," Mauritius said. "I can send a company to guard you, but—"

"I'll go," Gereint said.

Mauritius rounded on him. For once the Knight lost his grip on his temper; he lashed out with all the force of grief and sorrow and loss. "You? What can you do? Your talent is considerable but completely untrained. You have no skill in weapons. Your magic—"

"His magic binds to mine," Averil said. "He makes me stronger; I teach him control."

Mauritius stopped short. That had caught him off guard. It gave Gereint the opening he needed to say what he had to say.

"It's a new thing," he said, "but it's real. It's saved our lives more than once. That's why we'll be safe. The king doesn't know about us. He'll think her magic is as broken as everyone else's. As for me, what am I but a stablehand?"

"That is mad," Mauritius said. "The risk—if you have miscalculated, if you underestimate your enemy—"

"It's a risk we have to take," Averil said. "You have your fight, messire. I have mine."

Mauritius was not listening. "I can't allow it," he said. "Not only the danger but the sheer impropriety of it: a young man, a young woman—"

"A ducal heir and a Knight in training," she said. "We never forget, messire. Not for a moment."

Mauritius shook his head. "No. You can't. I'll bind you if I have to. You are going to the Isle."

She lifted her chin. Her face was calm, her voice serene. "You won't be doing that again."

Her magic reached inside Gereint—so fast and so strong that he was taken by surprise. But he had no thought of resisting her. What she demanded, he gave of his free will.

With delicacy that needed both skill and strength, she wrought a web of starlight and darkness. In it she set a jewel like the moon and minute sparks that were the souls of the Knights.

The working hung between Averil and Mauritius. For all its appearance of fragility, it was a shield, strong enough to widen his eyes.

They flicked from Averil to Gereint, then back to Averil. Mauritius had the sight to see what was between them, and the magic to comprehend what they had done.

Gereint held his breath. Mauritius was a knight of God, sworn to uphold the laws of the Church. He might denounce them as heretics or forbid them to wield this magic that owed nothing to the proper and prescribed ways.

The silence sank under its own weight. Averil did not try to break it, nor did Gereint. She let the shield fade, but the memory of it lingered.

At last Mauritius said, "I see I cannot stop you. Will you at least let me send men to guard you?"

"It's too dangerous," she said. "I'm dressed like a servant. Gereint is very good at looking like one. We'll be riding better horses than servants can usually find, but we need the speed—and if we have to, we'll invent a master who's sent us to the city on an errand."

"That would be the truth," Gereint said, "in its way."

There was nothing Mauritius could say that would sway them. With great reluctance, he gave way. "In the morning," he said, "we'll supply you with whatever we can. Then may God protect you."

"God and our magic will do their best," Gereint said.

33

It was harder to ride away from the Knights in the morning than Gereint had expected. Once Mauritius had given leave, the rest were bound by their vows to accept it, but Riquier and then, somewhat to Gereint's surprise, Ademar made it clear they were not happy.

"You had better come back to us," Ademar said, "preferably alive."

"Dead will do," said Riquier, "as long as you do come back. I've a great deal more to teach you. I won't release you from that."

"I don't want you to," Gereint said. "When I've done what I can for the lady, I'll find you again. That's a promise."

"Be sure you keep it," said Ademar. "You're the only truly interesting thing I've seen in a year."

Gereint bit his tongue. Ademar was putting a bold face on it, but his eyes were suspiciously bright.

It struck Gereint that this was a friend. Riquier was a teacher, which was different—but that was its own kind of friendship.

He had never had friends before. Between his being godborn and his being so full of magic he was a danger to everything around him, he had never had occasion to become familiar with anyone but his mother.

These mages had no fear of him or his magic, and it did not matter to them who his father had been. For whatever reason, they cared what became of him.

"I will come back," Gereint said. His throat was so tight he could hardly speak.

He mounted hastily before he broke down and blubbered in front of them all. Averil was already astride and conspicuously cultivating patience.

The Knights had their own riding ahead, half a day to the sea and, pray God, the ship that would take them across it. They parted with few words spoken but with such a weight of emotion that it was almost unbearable. So much hung in the balance and so little was certain. It was terribly likely that they all would fail.

That did not bear thinking of. Gereint fixed his eyes forward. The distance that separated him from the Knights felt like a bandage tearing from a half-healed wound.

It would not stop hurting until he was with them again. But the other half of him had to be here with Averil, magic bound with magic and fate with fate.

AS THEY RODE, the veil lifted from the world. Skeins of wild-folk swirled and streamed around them. While they stayed on the straight track to Fontevrai, they were well and thoroughly escorted.

The land felt no different than it had when Gereint first rode across it. There was no darkness on it, no subtle slither on the edge of perception. The king's men who had been so numerous after the fall of the Rose seemed to have gone to ground.

None of them was hunting a pair of servants on carefully nondescript horses. Averil chose to ride in daylight and without stealth, taking the open road.

The provisions that they had brought from Messire Perrin's cottage proved to be enchanted. They did not decay or grow stale, and there was always a full loaf, as fresh as if it had been baked that morning, and a bag of fruit, and a jar of soft herbed cheese.

Mauritius had reckoned it a week's ride from the edge of the Wildlands to Fontevrai. There was no need to pause in town or village, but Averil insisted on it. "I have to know," she said the morning of the second day, "what the people are saying, what rumors are flying in the markets. Do they know what threatens them? Does it matter to them?"

"Probably not," Gereint said, "unless it touches them or their livelihood. If the taxes don't go up and the soldiers don't trample through their barley fields, they'll reckon life is good enough."

"They'll care if they find their children taken as sacrifices and their fields stripped bare to feed the Serpent's followers."

"How do you plan to convince them of that?" Gereint asked. "I don't know what they do to the mad in these parts, but in Rémy they tie them up and call for the priest to drive the demon out."

"Is it mad to ask questions and listen to the answers?"

"If they're the wrong questions," he said, "yes."

Averil's frown did not bode well, but for a good three days she consented to stay on the road and pass by the towns and villages. People labored in the fields as they rode by, bringing in the harvest; the apples were ripe in the orchards.

By the morning of the fifth day, the road that had been deserted began to thicken with travelers. Pilgrims on foot trudged toward the shrine of a saint Gereint had never heard of, who was celebrated in these parts. A farmer's cart, full to overflowing with cabbages for the market, slowed them to a crawl; the road was too narrow just there to pass, overhung with hedges and running on a bridge over a small but rapid river.

This was an excellent place for an ambush. The skin tightened between Gereint's shoulderblades, but when he cast his magic abroad, he found nothing that should not be there.

Still, he was glad to come over the bridge and through the hedges to the open fields again. The sun had dimmed; clouds were gathering, driven by a chill wind. Gereint caught the scent of rain.

The storm closed in near the gates of the town to which the farmer was hauling his wares. Averil refrained from dwelling on her victory. When the road turned away from the town, she turned from the road, riding through the gate into a cobbled square.

It was a town of fair size, with a covered market—most useful in this weather—and a handful of inns. As little as Gereint knew of such things, he knew to look for the cleanest rather than the most opulent.

The one he chose was neither the nearest to the gate nor the farthest. Its stable was clean and well kept, the horses bedded on fresh straw; the common room was remarkably like it, with woven rushes in place of straw. The innkeeper was a woman of imposing girth who took their measure and packed them off to separate rooms: Averil in a private parlor in the back, Gereint in a sort of barracks above the common room.

That was appropriate, but Gereint disliked it intensely. So did Averil. "My servant will sleep across my door," she said.

So much, he thought, for any pretense of being a servant herself. The innkeeper bridled, but Averil's gaze was steady. The woman gave way, even bowed slightly. "As you wish, lady," she said.

Averil did not choose to correct her, either, on the matter of a title. "We'll dine downstairs," she said. "Be sure to bring double portions for the boy. He eats like a starving wolf."

That won a wintry smile from the innkeeper. She sat them down at a table in the best and brightest corner and plied them with food until Gereint was ready to cry for mercy.

He did his best to eat it all, with Averil's willing help. Between them they disposed of a roast capon, a venison pasty, a sallet of herbs and late-summer greens, and a frumenty of barley and honey and dried figs, all washed down with a quite respectable brown ale.

Gereint sat back groaning. "This wolf won't hunt for a week," he said.

Averil smiled faintly. Her eyes were alert, taking in the slow increase of custom as people came in to get out of the rain. Most were locals—always a good sign in an inn—but there were a few pilgrims, disdaining meat and ale but falling with a willing appetite on fresh-baked bread and strong cheese, and one or two traveling peddlers, and a nondescript brown man whose magic was strong enough to make Gereint sit up and take notice.

It was not serpent magic. It felt a little like the arts of the Rose, but there were differences that Gereint had learned to detect. This must be a mage of the five Elements, Gereint thought, or maybe of Sainte-Cécile: a seer with a talent for healing and a lesser talent for weather-working. And yet there was more to him, some overriding sense that Gereint could not quite name. When he tried to put a face to it, he kept seeing the baron's huntsman from the woods near Rémy.

The storm was not this man's, Gereint did not think. He seemed as discommoded by it as the rest of them. He had taken shelter as they all had, and warmed himself with heated ale and a venison pasty.

Averil showed no interest in him. She was listening to the gossip of farmers and tradesmen. Gereint, who had heard its like since he was old enough to toddle through the market behind his mother, let it pass over him.

They did not talk about the king or magic or anything but each other, the weather and the harvest, the rise in taxes and the pain that caused. Gereint's ears sharpened slightly at that, but they cursed the duke for it. Of the king they said nothing.

The room was growing warmer as it filled with bodies. The reek of wet wool and crowded humanity made his nose twitch. He caught himself sliding into a doze.

When the soldiers came, they seemed a part of his dream. They wore leather cuirasses and the badge of a local barony, but there was something about them . . .

It might be the dream he had been sliding into that gave him, at last, the hiss of scales. There was nothing unusual about them. They were sturdy men, well fed, with a clear predilection for this inn's ale. Their language was as profane as soldiers' tended to be, barely restrained by Dame Aubin's grim stare.

They did not swear by the good God or his son. That might simply be the custom in this place, but Gereint found it odd. All their oaths had to do with bodily things. They made no mention of the spirit at all.

It was a kind of emptiness, as if that part of them were not there. Once Gereint understood that, he could not see them as human men. They were images of men that walked and talked, ate and drank and swore—but not by the good God.

He squeezed his eyes shut. He must be dreaming it. But when he opened them, the baron's men had even less substance than before.

As unobtrusively as he could, he peered at the others in the inn. There was nothing peculiar about them. The souls that animated them were as real and complex as they should be. It was only the men in armor who were strange.

He was not sure he knew what to think of that. Averil might, but he could hardly ask her here. Nor would it be proper—let alone safe—for him to get up and leave while she stayed alone in this crowd.

He tried to reach through the magic they shared, but she was closed to him. Her attention was on the flow of gossip. She knew as little of that as Gereint had once known of magic; she found significance where there was none, and failed to see what truly was important.

GEREINT SHOULD NOT have said it in quite that way. His patience was exhausted by the time she finally stopped pretending to sip from her cup. He kept his head down—barely—on their much interrupted, frequently obstructed way through the room. It was rather too satisfying to catch the hand that tried to pinch her behind and bend back the longest finger until its owner mewed in pain.

That was the only liberty anyone took. Gereint's size and glowering presence were enough for the rest.

Once they were in the box of a room, most of which was taken up by a heavy and scrupulously clean bed, Gereint let go his frustration. "Why are you refusing to see what's there and listening to what has no meaning at all?"

"I could ask the same of you," she said with the hint of a snap. "Maybe you're too used to tavern gossip to hear it."

"I heard it," he said. "There's nothing remarkable about it. But those soldiers—"

"What about the soldiers? All I saw was bluster and brag."

"You weren't looking," he said. "That was all there was to them. There was nothing under it. They were empty—as if something had taken their souls."

"That can't be true," she said. "They weren't king's men: they were wearing the badge of Baron Valéry. His youngest son was one of the suitors in Fontevrai. The boy is a fool, but his father is a loyal servant of my father. He would never—"

"How do you know what anyone will do once he's under a spell? We know how many dukes and counts and princes have fallen. Why not a baron? It's all fodder for the Serpent."

Averil's mind was closing again as it had in the Wildlands. Well aware he might do more harm than good, Gereint gripped her shoulders and shook her hard enough to rattle her teeth. "Stop that. If even you can lock your mind shut when the world doesn't look the way you expect, how do you think any other noble can survive? The king hardly needs magic. All he needs is denial."

"I am not—"

Gereint carefully kept his mouth shut.

Her glare had physical force, like a blast of heat. "I can't be that blind!"

"Maybe it's in the blood," he said. "You can open your eyes—though it hurts. Use mine if you have to."

"In the blood," she said, as if the words had caught in her mind and held. "Do you think—but the soldiers aren't nobles. They're as common as—as anyone else here."

Gereint knew what she had meant to say. He would not have been offended if she had said it.

"They're as common as I am," he said for her.

"Not you," she said. "Not with what's in you."

He shook that off. "Maybe that's why. Offspring of Paladins fall to their own overconfidence, but ordinary people have to have the souls sucked out of them."

"It's not overconfidence," she said, but not with anger. That had drained out of her. She sank to the bed as if her knees had given way.

Gereint sat beside her. He should not have done that, but she looked so forlorn that he could only think of comforting her. "Agelong surety, then, that the world is yours to rule. Whatever you call it, it's a curse of sorts. It lays you open to the Serpent's magic."

She turned her hands palm up in her lap. They were empty, like the soldiers in the room below.

Driven by an impulse he did not try to understand, Gereint slipped the pendant from around his neck and set it in her palm, folding the fingers over it.

She frowned. "What is this?"

"It was a gift," he said, "from a very old Knight when I left the mother house for your father's palace. I don't think it has any magic in it—or else it has so much it's beyond understanding. It's pretty; it's oddly comforting. I thought you could use a little of that."

"We're supposed to be quarreling," she said crossly, "not giving gifts." But she did not fling the pendant away. She opened her fingers instead.

The enamel glowed as it always had, a shimmer of intricate shapes and colors. Gereint knew more of the art now than he had when he first saw it; he could see that it was a masterwork in miniature.

His heart panged slightly at giving it up. But it felt right to see the pendant in Averil's hand. She traced one of its many curving lines with a finger.

She frowned, but not out of temper. That was forgotten. "A Knight gave you this?"

He nodded.

"Then it can't be just for pretty," she said. "Are you sure you want me to have it? He gave it to you."

"I'm sure," he said.

She turned it in her hand, studying the way the light caught it. "He didn't say what it was for?"

"Just that I should keep it by me always," Gereint said, "and something about bonds and breaking, and focus. And a cantrip." He paused, startled into memory. "Father Vincent gave it to me, and I forgot. 'From the mind to the heart and the heart to the hand: so is magic ruled and contained.' I had so much else to remember, it slipped away altogether. But it didn't matter, really, because I did learn to keep my magic under control. Because—because of you. I don't think they foresaw that."

"I don't think anyone did." Averil held out the pendant. "If the Knight said to keep it, then you should."

"He also said it would help me. I think you need it more than I do. Not because you need help with your magic, but because what you're going into is so dangerous."

Her fingers closed again over the pendant. He did not think she was aware that they had done that. A breath escaped her: half surrender, half exasperation. "Very well. I'll keep it for you. When all this is over, you can have it back."

Gereint started to shake his head, but then he shrugged. He was done with quarreling for tonight. "Well enough," he said.

34

With the pendant between them, their contention had dissipated. Averil slipped the chain over her head and let the pendant slide under her bodice. Gereint thought she sat a little straighter and seemed a little less taut about the shoulders.

Maybe he imagined it, but it raised his spirits. He spread the straw pallet across the door with a good enough heart, careful not to dwell on the fact that she was almost close enough to touch, and they were all alone. A Knight had to have that discipline, too, along with all the rest.

He had thought he would not be able to sleep, but as soon as he lay down, he fell as into deep water. As he slept, he realized that he was not dreaming his own dreams. They were odd, formless, now touching on a sense of dread without face or name, now brushing past a shiver of elation so strong it was almost unbearable. Through it he began to see images, but they were dim, blurred, as if he peered through rippled water.

Slowly he recognized them. They were sinuous, twining and curving: an intricate knot of serpents. Then he realized they were tendrils of gold and green and blue and red, winding through the circle of a pendant.

The tendrils had eyes and flickering tongues. The eyes were jewels; he could see through them to worlds of wonder and terror.

They were guarding something. What it was, he could not see. There was a spell of protection on them, and one of binding, woven so deep it was all but imperceptible.

Protection, he thought, clear in the dream. *That would explain—*

The dream rocked violently. The dreamer was shocked almost into wakefulness. The dream—her dream—came abruptly clear. He looked into Averil's wide and startled eyes.

The pendant had strengthened the bond between them. Binding as well as protection—that must be its power. It was like the web of the Knights, but it only seemed to need the single ornament between the two of them. Gereint's memory of it after its long tenure about his neck seemed to have been enough.

More strangeness; more magic that sprang from no source the orders would recognize. Averil's fear of it was close to instinct. So was Gereint's fearlessness. They met in the middle, clashed and then suddenly stilled.

Gereint stood in the dream, face to face with Averil. There was nothing else in this world but the shining thing she wore around her neck.

As he so often did in the waking world, he clasped her hands. Whatever they were standing on—earth, air, starlight—rocked distinctly but then steadied. The jeweled light between them blazed until it blinded him. Then there was nothing but white emptiness and deep peace.

WHEN GEREINT OPENED his eyes, morning light showed pale beyond the shutters. Averil was still asleep.

Her hair was tousled out of its plait. One hand cradled her cheek; the other clutched the pendant beneath her shift. Her face even in sleep was tight.

He wanted to smooth the tension out of it, but he did not dare. If he touched her now, he would not be able to stop. He would want all of her. And that he could not have—not now, not ever.

He got up as softly as he could, stretching the stiffness out of his body. He could go down and fetch breakfast, but he did not want to leave her alone.

She would never be alone while they were bound as they

were now. She was in the back of his mind, riding deep in his heart. When he touched his magic, she was there.

His stomach growled, so ordinary and humble a thing that it made him laugh—painfully, but with real mirth. He went to feed it before it woke Averil with its snarling.

PART OF AVERIL wished she could undo everything she had done since she laid eyes on Gereint. The rest of her would not have changed it for the world. She had stepped off a precipice into infinite space—and hence into infinite danger, but infinite possibility, too.

Gereint's pendant had completed, somehow, what had been between them since they met. It was still part of him; maybe even more now than it had been while he wore it around his own neck. It made him inextricably a part of her.

She was carefully not thinking of all that might mean. No one was thinking of it—or Mauritius would never have let the two of them go alone to Fontevrai, even against Averil's resistance. If she must marry, and a Knight could not marry, and a Paladin's heir could not marry a commoner in any case, where did that leave either of them?

They should not be, and yet, incontestably, they were. By law and custom they could never be more than Knight and lady. By the reality of their magic, they were more truly one than any wedded pair she knew of.

There was another reality beyond that: the one that took away everything but the simple bodily truth. He was a man and young. She was a woman—and however she tried to ignore it, she had a body, too.

She was fortunate that despite all the stories she had heard of peasant lads and their lasses, this one was still an innocent. He kept his hands to himself, and his eyes mostly. Sometimes she could feel him thinking of her, as clear as a touch, but even that was carefully chaste.

She caught herself wishing he were a little less the pure knight and a little more the lusty farmer's son. This exquisite restraint was maddening. He should master his magic as thoroughly as he mastered his body—they would all be safer for it.

She brought herself sharply to heel. These thoughts were not worthy of either of them. They had a duchy to save. All the rest, proper or improper or outright impossible, would have to wait.

WHEN THEY RODE out of the inn, the rain had stopped. The road was muddy but passable. The air was cool, almost cold: autumn air. Overnight, it seemed, the leaves had turned red and gold; they drifted underfoot, skittering away from the horses' hooves.

In the night while she slept, Averil had accepted what Gereint had said: that there was something strange about the baron's men. That strangeness, now she acknowledged it, crept under the surface of everything she looked at. Something besides summer's heat had gone out of this country.

The wildfolk that had trailed behind them were gone. She did not remember when the last of them had melted into mist, or whether she had thought then that they had simply retreated from the lethal order of these mortal places. Maybe it had been more than that. Maybe . . .

The common people were still safe—but that could not last. Nor did she like to think why they had not been touched. Snakes would only eat live prey.

She pressed the pace as best she could, aiming straight for Fontevrai. Neither Gereint nor the horses complained. They were slowed often enough by traffic on the road, and more of it the nearer they came to the ducal city.

There were more soldiers, too, marching or riding in companies. Whatever badges they wore, they suffered the same affliction: the souls had been sucked out of them. They did not trouble passersby; wherever they were going, evidently it had nothing to do with ordinary humanity.

She could not say she was becoming accustomed to them, but after a while the blow was not quite so strong. Then late in the day, she received a shock that nearly flung her from the saddle.

Outside of Morency, in sight of its broken chapter house, a lord bishop rode in his carriage, surrounded by his guards and clerks and holy monks. They were a vivid company, as bright as the grove of poplars in autumn finery through which they happened to be riding.

But they were not chanting psalms as such processions usually did, and not only the guards were empty inside. The clerks' eyes were flat and the monks' faces had lost some essence of expression. Behind his scarlet curtains, the bishop was as dull as a spent crystal.

If the Church had fallen victim to this spell, then no one was safe. She would not say there was no hope, but her courage was more shaken than she liked to admit. All she had to fight this was a pretty pendant on a silver chain, a godborn boy who had been raised a farmer and such magic as she could muster.

"You have more than that," Gereint said, riding in her thoughts as he had ridden in her dreams. "You have yourself."

"But what am I?" she asked. "I'm no prince of the Church."

"You're the descendant of Paladins, a child of kings. All your foremothers have been enchantresses of the Isle."

"Then maybe I'm more vulnerable than anyone," she said.

"You're forewarned," he said. "You're guarded. You can see past the order of the world."

"But is that enough?"

"It will be," he said.

He spoke as if he believed it. She found herself giving way to the purity of his faith. The greatest part of magic was belief: that was the first lesson a child learned on the Isle. It was time she stopped to remember it.

Her courage was coming back—sometimes in a trickle, but it was steady. The world had rocked so often underfoot that she was learning at least to keep her balance no matter what it did.

She would need that where she was going. She had to be stronger than she had ever dreamed of being, and surer of herself and her choices. There was no room for doubt or fear. She had to put them aside and hold to the straight path.

The Church and the barons' armies were corrupted. She had

to expect that the barons were as well. Quitaine was rotting from the top to the bottom.

Which meant that her father—

She cut off the thought before it turned into a shriek of panic. In a little more than a day, she would be in Fontevrai. Please God, she would see for herself then what had become of the duke.

She urged her gelding to a somewhat faster pace. The heart of it all was in Fontevrai. She would find it there and do what must be done.

35

They were being followed. Gereint was not sure at first, but after they passed the empty shell of a bishop, the dim sense he had had since they left the inn became clear. Someone or something was tracking them.

The bishop's company seemed oblivious to anyone around them. The rest of the travelers they met had their own preoccupations. And yet there was that prickle in the back of the neck.

There was nothing to be seen. The wildfolk were gone; Gereint could not ask them what they knew. And that troubled him, too.

Averil's back was tight. He moved his horse closer to her. The road was all but deserted here, winding through hedgerows toward the low roofs and sudden spire of a town with its church. A woodcutter trudged beside his laden mule; a peddler bent under the burden of his pack. Other than those, there was no one to be seen.

Neither woodcutter nor peddler showed any interest in a pair of riders. There was no hint of magic about them, either.

Whatever tracked them was out of sight beyond the turning of the road, and yet it was strongly aware of them. Gereint did not know how to track it in turn, or whether it was wise to try at all.

He slowed his horse to a stop. Averil rode on a few strides, then halted and turned. She did not ask what he had done or why. She was watching the road as he was.

He tossed the reins into her hand. "Ride on," he said softly, "but go slow."

She frowned, but then she nodded. The clarity of her awareness came to rest inside him.

The hedge here was not unlike the ones around Rémy. Here as there, gaps presented themselves, through which one could wriggle and squeeze. On the other side was a harvested field with bare furrows and stubble of barley.

Gereint ran lightly along the side of the field. With Averil riding quiet in him, he found the knowledge he needed to track with magic as well as eye and mind.

It was a strange sensation, as if there were three of him: the man in servant's clothes making his way along the hedge, the woman similarly dressed riding in a slow walk toward the town and someone else. There was magic there, like a flare of heat in front of him. It focused on the place where Averil was, marking her by the shape of her magic. Gereint it could not see at all, or else he did not have the power to see what it saw.

He had to pause to balance the disparate parts of himself. The hunter advanced at an easy pace, as if sure of his prey.

Gereint found another gap in the hedge. Through it he could see a narrow stretch of road. After a slow count of breaths, the hunter came into view.

Gereint's breath hissed through his teeth. It was the man from the inn, the nondescript person dressed in brown, whose magical order Gereint had not been able to decipher. He was alone—no royal troops behind him. He rode a mule as plain as he was, but built for rather more speed than mules were known for.

Averil was coming back down the road, but the sense of her was still riding ahead: even more strangeness, which made Gereint faintly dizzy. He shook off the dizziness. The hedge parted in front of him; he sprang down into the road and landed lightly behind the mule, just as Averil rounded the turn.

The mule halted. Its rider seemed more intrigued than disconcerted. "Such strong magic," he said, "and bound to no order. Were you ever tested?"

Gereint glanced at Averil. She was frowning. "You're a magefinder?" she asked. "But—"

The man's long mouth stretched in a wry smile. His hand

brushed down his plain and fusty gown. "Where are my vest-
ments and tabard, my clerks and escort? Let us say I choose to
cultivate caution."

"Why would you do that?" Gereint asked.

The brown eyes narrowed, but the smile persisted. "Why do
two mages of such power ride in servants' clothes and track
down anything that happens to follow them?"

"It's the times," Gereint said. "I hadn't heard that any of the
other orders were troubled by the king's purge. Only the
Rose."

"The Rose was both wealthy and heretical," the magefinder
said, "or so we're being told." He looked them up and down.
After a moment he seemed to make a decision. "My name is
Denis."

"Mine is Averil," she said, "and this is Gereint." She held
out her hand.

He kissed it promptly and with an air that said he had done
it often before. Gereint smoothed the frown from his forehead. Mages of the orders were nobles far more often than
not. He should hardly be surprised that this was another son
of Paladins.

"The Isle?" said Messire Denis, still holding lightly to
Averil's hand.

She nodded.

"And you," the magefinder said, peering at Gereint. "I'm
not sure—"

Gereint's smile was tight. "I was never tested. My mother
doesn't believe in it."

"That could be dangerous," the magefinder said.

"Yes," said Averil with perilous calm. "If you're only tracking us because it's your gift and your instinct, then I applaud
you for it, but it's time you went hunting elsewhere. We're
spoken for. But if there is another reason—"

Messire Denis spread his hands. "I can only do what I was
born to do."

"We'll ride together, then," Averil said. "There's always
safety in numbers."

Gereint watched the magefinder carefully, but he did not

seem disconcerted. Nor did he seem overeager. "These are uncomfortable days," he said, "and mages are in greater discomfort than any. I take it you're traveling to Fontevrai?"

Averil nodded. "And you?"

"I have business there," Denis said.

"As do we." She handed Gereint the reins of his horse. As he mounted, she turned her gelding's head back toward the city. With the man on the mule between them, they rode on.

MESSIRE DENIS WAS not a great talker. For the most part he rode with his head lowered, counting off the beads of a prayer-string.

They were stone beads, not glass, which was a little odd. The stones were subtly colored, moss agate and red amber and dark topaz. There was a peculiar fascination in them as they slid through the long thin fingers.

Gereint snapped awake. He had been about to fall into a trap, a spell set to bind his will. Even now that he had won free of it, he dared not look too long or closely at the beads or listen too carefully to the words that the magefinder murmured under his breath.

Averil did not seem to have seen or heard. Gereint had to hope—or fear—that the spell was set only for him. The beads in their pattern made him think of a cage, or a snare to trap a soul in.

He dared not speak to her aloud or any other way, not with a mage between them. He could not run, either, and leave her to God knew what fate. The magefinder might not be weaving a spell against her yet, but he would. Gereint had no doubt of that.

There was a great deal more to this trap than Gereint had thought. Even by hunting the hunter down, he had fallen into the snare—and now he could not get rid of the man without arousing suspicion.

He could only go on and pretend to be unconcerned and watch for any sign of treachery. At least, he thought, this was a mage and not a troop of soldiers. Magic, with Averil's help, he could use—unlike the weapons he lacked the rank or skill to carry.

While he rode, he gathered such magic as he could, as quietly as he knew how. The earth was oddly dulled and blunted, but there was still power in it. He drew as much as he dared and kept it inside him, sheathed like a sword.

He was dimly aware that this could be dangerous. If Averil's consciousness let go of him or he lost what control he had, all the hoarded magic would burst out in a blast of fire.

It was worth the risk. Averil might think she could ride undetected into Fontevrai, find her father and present herself to the king and carry on unharmed, but Gereint was not nearly so sanguine. However aware of it she might claim to be, this could be another case of that same blindness which made her kind such easy prey.

Who knew? Gereint might have his own broad swath of danger that he could not see. All he could do was watch and wait and keep his fears to himself, and hope they would prove baseless.

WITH THE COMING of noon, the clear sky clouded and the sun slowly dimmed. They followed the road around the town with its tall church spire and paused beyond to water and graze the horses. Messire Denis took the opportunity to doze with his back against a tree, so guileless that Gereint grew more suspicious than ever.

Under guise of dividing the bread and cheese from their enchanted store, Gereint leaned toward Averil and said just above a whisper, "Let's leave him here. He makes my skin crawl."

"He'll just follow us," she said in the same low tone, breaking off her half of the loaf. "I'd rather have him where I can see him."

"And where he can work spells on us?" said Gereint.

"We're on guard," she said. She bit into the rich brown bread.

"Will that be enough?"

She thrust a wedge of cheese into his hand. "It will have to be," she said. "Go on, eat. Keep your strength up."

There were times when Averil reminded Gereint rather too vividly of his mother. He surprised himself with homesickness: a malady he had suffered very little of. Just then he would rather have been on the farm in Rémy, dangerous ignorance and all, than on this road, riding to God knew what.

He brought himself sharply to order. He was riding to Fontevrai. If Averil was right, she was in no danger of her life, though her soul might be another matter. She knew what she had to do. With his help, she might succeed.

She *would* succeed. He had to believe that. He steadied his mind and body and choked down his share of their rations. She was right: he needed the strength.

WHEN THEY LEFT their stopping place, Messire Denis was still with them. He had not eaten and would not take food from them, but he did drink a little from the stream.

Fasting was a holy sacrifice. Saints practiced it. So did sinners in search of absolution.

Everything was suspicious these days. If Gereint was not careful, he would trust nothing at all; then he would start jousting with shadows.

Better mad than dead, some would say. Gereint was as much on his guard as he knew how to be. He rode behind and Averil rode ahead, and between them they kept watch over their companion.

After a little more than an hour's ride, the wind began to blow. They had passed yet another town, this one clustered tight around the ruins of a house of the Rose. Beyond the town was a shrine to the Twelve Paladins.

It was an odd place, peculiarly pagan. Twelve ancient and crumbling trees stood in a circle around a stone hut. It looked unimaginably old. Gereint could believe that the Paladins had stopped here on their way back from the Field of the Binding.

The strange, muffled sense that clouded the earth was even

stronger here. Centuries of faith on top of old power should have caused this place to sing, but it barely mumbled.

The soul was taken out of it as from the soldiers whom Gereint had seen in the towns. It was like a sickness through the whole of this region, a grey plague aimed at its heart.

Of all the emotions that had ridden Gereint since the Rose fell, anger had somehow failed to touch him. Not any longer. Seeing this ruined shrine, remembering the men whose souls and selves had been sucked out of them, he felt a blast of pure rage.

It almost undid him. His magic leaped for the opening. Even in that uprush of fury, he did not want to blast the shrine. He wrenched the opening shut so fast and hard his body felt bruised.

He clutched the pommel of his saddle, dizzy and reeling. The magefinder had ridden ahead into the circle of trees. As if to reflect the battle he had just fought with his magic, the door to the shrine was open, hanging off its antiquated hinges.

Some distant part of Gereint cried the alarm. His horse carried him forward, following Averil's.

The noose snapped shut.

36

The shrine disgorged soldiers in such numbers that it might have been a house of the Wildlands, notably larger inside than out. They swarmed around the riders—and it was a swarm, as empty of soul or spirit as an invasion of ants.

Averil sat quiet on her horse. She was not afraid, nor was she particularly surprised. Gereint judged it wise to follow her lead.

The magefinder had withdrawn to the wall of the shrine. There was someone else with him, dressed in a priest's black gown, an older man but of the same kind: neither tall nor short, lean and ascetic, with a deceptively nondescript face and long dark eyes. They could have been kin or countrymen, men of the same mind and magic.

Gereint felt the chill that ran down Averil's spine. She recognized the priest. He was the king's man—and maybe more.

She ignored the troops closing in around her and fixed her eyes on the priest's face. "Messire," she said. "Hunting souls to feed your master?"

The man's thin brows arched. "Yours is particularly choice, my lady. Are you offering it?"

"Not in this life," she said.

"You may not have a choice."

"I think I may," said Averil. "Take me to the king."

"Why should I do that?"

"Because," said Averil, "I was dead and I live again."

Gereint held his breath. This was a dangerous game. There were at least a hundred men around them, all heavily armed, and not one would flinch at taking their lives.

Averil kept her head high and her eyes steady. The priest studied her carefully. After some time he said, "Your name, lady?"

"Averil," she said, "Marguerite Emeraude Melusine de Gahmuret, whose mother was Alais, whose father is Urien, who descends from Longinus of the Spear and from the Young God's beloved. Blood of gods is in my veins. Take me to my uncle, and be quick. I have messages that will not wait."

"Indeed," said the priest. He seemed only slightly taken aback by her display of sudden and royal arrogance.

Gereint would never have expected it of her. Which only went to prove that there were still things he did not know.

"Father Gamelin," said Averil in a dangerous purr, "time is passing. Take me to the king."

The priest's head tilted. He shrugged. "As you wish, lady," he said.

Averil rode through the ranks to the priest's side. When Gereint tried to follow, a wall of armored men stood between.

The magic coiled inside him, raising its head to strike. Averil's lifted hand stilled it. "My servant rides with me."

"We are all your servants, lady," said Father Gamelin.

She leveled her eyes on him. The priest shrugged and gestured to his men.

The ranks opened like a gate of steel. Gereint's nape prickled as he rode through, but neither weapon nor spell threatened him: only the priest's eyes, measuring him, and the magefinder fixed on him with a kind of hunger.

It was hard to trust Averil's judgment, here in the spider's web. Gereint wavered on the brink of blasting them both out of there, but once more he stopped before he let his power go. This was Averil's plan; he had to let her carry it through to the end.

He took his place at her right hand as a guard should do. He was not sorry to leave the shrine, though his anger at its desecration was slow to fade.

These priests had done it. He had no proof, but his heart was sure. They had been working some magic that sapped the soul out of a sacred place, for a purpose he did not know. To free the Serpent, maybe; to bind the kingdom.

And Gereint was riding straight for the center of the blight. He tightened his grip on his magic and even more on his temper.

IT WAS A grim ride from the shrine of the Paladins to Fontevrai, in a grey rain that set in harder as the day wore on toward nightfall. In clear weather and on fresh horses they would have reached the city just before dark, but in the rain and mud and at foot-pace they still had half the distance yet to go.

Averil refused to regret her choice. It was the king she needed to see, and this would bring her to him quickly—even with the delay.

They spent the night in a monastery dedicated to Saint Etienne, the magefinders' patron. Its guesthouse at least was not altogether corrupted, though Averil was glad not to enter the monastery proper.

She had been aware of the smolder of Gereint's anger, so much so that she hardly noticed her own. This was her duchy. These were her people. Liege lord or no, the king had no right to corrupt her church, blind her barons and turn her soldiers into slaves.

She paced the bare chill room while rain hissed on the roof. "I should never have left," she said. "I should have stayed."

Gereint was outside the door, and yet he heard her. His presence was warm in her heart, his anger a match for hers.

She reached out for it, but paused. Something was watching. It waited, hoping to discover whatever secret they shared.

Snares within snares. Averil withdrew into herself, as cold and lonely as that was. She could, if she strained, hear Gereint's breathing, deep and deliberately steady.

She sat on the hard narrow bed, one of many along the wall. She was the only guest there tonight; the only one in some time, from the signs. Gereint could be in the room with her: it was big enough. He at one end, she at the other—who could take issue with that?

They could not risk it. She startled herself with the force of her wanting him—not only his magic and his presence but his arms around her and the warmth of his body.

She was perilously close to not being able to live without him. That would never do; but it was hard to care in the dank night, with enemies all around them and death or worse in front of them.

She felt as much as heard him get up from his pallet. He was still dreaming, but his body was moving as if someone else had taken control of it.

Maybe someone had. She glided toward the door, pausing only long enough to snatch up her cloak and wrap it around her.

He was already out of sight down the corridor. She had to pause again to quiet her breathing and force herself to focus. Panic would serve neither of them.

He was moving inward into the deadness of the monastery. Far off, she heard voices chanting. It must be time for one of the night offices. The chant was oddly empty, like the halls through which it echoed.

She was already cold; she could hardly be colder. But the warmth had drained from her heart.

Gereint was stronger than this. It must be the dream that led him, or a seed of despair that had sprouted in this barren soil. He would not leave her or the Rose for a mere spell—not after so many other spells had tried and failed.

Who knew when a man would break? She quickened her pace.

THE CHANTING GREW suddenly louder. Even in desperation, Averil slowed. The passage opened abruptly into the cold and echoing space of the chapel.

Candles flickered wanly in the gloom. Hooded figures lined the choir. The glass of the tall windows was dull, covered over with leaden paint. In the day no light would come in. At night it was blind dark.

The altar was empty. Where chalice and spear should have stood was blank stone.

Averil had more than half expected to find relics of the Serpent, but the enemy had not gone so far—yet. The good God was gone, but nothing overt had come to replace him.

Gereint swayed in front of the altar. By some trick of the light, his hair gleamed like burnished gold.

There were others with him, young men, broad and strong. They were all rapt, wavering on their feet, eyes full of sleep.

The priest who celebrated this perversion of a rite was not the one she had expected. He was a stranger, but she could feel Father Gamelin and the magefinder nearby, feeding the spell with their power. The one who stood proxy for them laid stark white hands on the head of the foremost young man and intoned, " 'Lord, he is not worthy to pass under thy roof. Speak but the word and his soul will be healed.' "

The man snapped erect. His eyes and the cords of his neck bulged. The chanting droned on.

It sucked the soul out of him. Its workings were bound in the patterns of words and the timbre of voices. There was something of the high magic in the regularity of its patterns, but there was no purity of glass to constrain it. This was old magic, forbidden magic, that should justly have been forgotten.

Averil shattered it with a high, fierce cry. She set no power in the sound, but it cut across the roll of chanting. The spell broke. The man in the lead dropped. She hoped he was dead.

The others behind him wavered. Their ranks broke. Gereint, in the rear, lashed out with the power he had kept sheathed like a sword.

The blinded windows burst into shards. Monks fled, shrieking like women. A spear of glass pierced the priest's eye. He fell, as dead as the man he would have ensorcelled.

Averil stood motionless amid the tumult. So, she noticed, did the priest Gamelin. "This is not your country," she said with ominous gentleness, "nor are these your servants." She beckoned.

Gereint, thank God, was conscious enough to understand. He came to her side and loomed there. He was wide awake; she could sense no sleep in him. No spell, either.

It seemed her first judgment had been right. He was as

strong as she had thought. As to what he had done and why—that would have to wait.

She kept her eyes fixed on Gamelin's face. It was blank. She hoped he was at least nonplussed. "No more of this," she said. "Go now and sleep, if you do any such thing. I will settle this with the king."

"Please do, lady," Gamelin said, as sweetly poisonous as ever.

She inclined her head the barest fraction: acknowledging his courtesy, however false. He bowed in return, a bare fraction more.

She elected to take that as an advantage. He was waiting for her to withdraw, but that would have conceded weakness. She stood pointedly still as the chapel emptied of people, waiting for him to accept the dismissal.

For a long while she did not think he would. But at last, when there was no one left but the dead man and Gereint and Averil, Gamelin gave way.

She did not celebrate it as a victory. This was far too subtle a war. He had yielded, but he might twist that yielding into an altogether new and deadly trap.

She could only hope to stay alert and keep her grip on both her temper and her magic. Gereint was safe; so were a dozen other young men. That safety might be illusion; they might all be soul-lost by morning. But for now, briefly, they could stop and breathe.

37

In the dubious safety of the guesthouse, Averil pulled Gereint in with her and flung him onto the nearest cot. He lay staring at her. "What was that for?" he asked.

"For being an absolute and utter, intransigent idiot," she said fiercely. "What in God's name were you thinking?"

"I was thinking that there was a spell set to summon the likes of me, and I had to know where it led," he answered with no evidence of either fear or gratitude. "You should have stayed where you were. Now there will be questions, and probably an inquiry. Can you afford any such thing?"

"I can't afford to lose you."

"You may not be able to afford to keep me." He scraped his hands across his face. "God. I could scrub for a week and not get rid of the stink of that spell."

"You could have been lost."

"I wasn't," he said. "I did find out what they want."

"Slaves," she said.

"Men whose loyalty is unshakable, bound to one another as well as their master, who can fight as one body and act as one man. They're all over the kingdom, and the mages are making more every moonless night."

"They're mages themselves, aren't they?" she said. "All of them. It's magic that's bound as well as hearts and souls."

He nodded. "Magefinders find them. It's been going on for years. Strong young men have been raised and trained and then bound. If my mother had believed in magic—if she had let the magefinders near me—I could be one of them. I could have—been—" He broke off, shuddering.

She had precious little comfort to give him. "All the orders are corrupt," she said. "And the Rose . . ."

"The Rose would never yield," he said. "So they broke it."

She sank down beside him, drew up her knees and clasped them tightly. She was shivering, but for once she hardly felt the cold. "It's going to stop," she said. "Right this moment. Now. It ends in Quitaine."

"That easily?"

She seared him with her glare. "I don't care what it takes. I'll get the king and his sorcerers and all his plotting out of my duchy. If I have to cut his heart out with my own hands and cast the spell that blasts the rest of them, I will do it."

"I'm sure you will."

That was not mockery. She met his clear grey stare. "Help me," she said.

"In any way I can."

Averil felt comforted out of all proportion to the gift. In the world's eyes she was all alone but for an untutored boy. In her own heart, she had everything she needed.

That might be absolute foolishness, but she clung to it. Willful ignorance and hopeless submission had failed the rest of her kind. She would see what came of boldness verging on insanity.

AVERIL WAS UP before dawn, with both horses saddled and breakfast eaten: the last of the bread that they had brought from the Wildlands. For the first time, once it was gone, none came to take its place. The spell had worn out or been broken; after this they would have to find their own way in the world.

The rain had lightened to a drizzle. The air was raw and damp, with a chill that cut to the bone.

She was warm with slow-burning anger. She regarded the troop of soldiers that barred the way out, knowing she should not look for any sign of intelligence in those flat eyes, but unable to help it. "Father Gamelin," she said, not caring where he was or how he heard her. "It's time to ride."

He emerged from the shadow of a doorway as if he had

materialized there. It did not matter to her if he had. She aimed her horse at the line of soldiers.

At the last possible instant it parted. The taste of freedom was vanishingly brief. There were more of them outside the monastery's wall, waiting in silence that knew nothing of cold or rain or the games of princes.

She made sure to remember as many faces as she could. These were mothers' sons, brothers and cousins and fathers. Somewhere in Lys, kin and friends waited for them.

She hoped none knew what had become of them. That was grief she would not wish on anyone.

Her anger had set deep. She nurtured it carefully. It had to sustain her for as long as it took to see the end of this—and that might be years.

She could not think too much of that or she would quail. She lifted her face to the kiss of the rain. But for the fog and mist, she would have been able to catch the first glimpse of Fontevrai. As it was, she would be lucky to see it when it was directly in front of her.

It was there. She felt it in her heart. She rode toward it with all the courage she could muster.

38

Like the rest of the duchy except for the houses of the Rose, Fontevrai looked exactly as it had when Averil left it. It took the eyes of magic to see the worm in its heart.

Even the camp outside the walls with its ordered ranks of tents under the king's banner was deceptively ordinary. Royal and lordly escorts camped in this way out of respect for the lord of the demesne. There were more of them than usual, but not nearly as many as the king had brought with him: Gereint's fault, though only Gereint and Averil knew it.

The guards at the city gate wore the duke's deep blue and silver, darkened to near-black and grey by the persistent drizzle of rain. They were not like the soldiers who surrounded Averil in voiceless ranks; they were still their full and mortal selves. They had a haunted look: the grim pallor of men fighting a long battle they could hardly hope to win.

Still, they were fighting. They were holding on, and so was the city. That gave her hope.

The duke's banner flew from the topmost turret of the citadel. Averil let go a breath she had not known she was holding. Her father was alive and in residence.

The king's banner flew below the duke's: blue sky and silver lilies; no serpent yet. His majesty was the duke's guest, that placement said.

Averil knew better than to trust anything she saw that had to do with the king. She made sure Gereint was close beside her and fully on his guard. She made sure, too, that she rode in not as a prisoner but as a noble lady surrounded by her escort. It was a subtle but critical distinction.

INSIDE THE GATE of the citadel, Averil turned to Father Gamelin. "I must visit my father. Then I intend to rest. Tell his majesty that I shall receive him tomorrow morning."

"Lady," said Gamelin, "the duke's heir is lately dead, and he had but the one. While it suited us to indulge your fancy, now that we are here, you have explanations to make. I fear we cannot permit you the free exercise of your will until we are certain that you are who you claim to be."

Averil studied him down the length of her nose. He was not a man to blanch or fidget, but he did seem a fraction stiffer about the shoulders. At length she said, "You may escort me to the duke. If he is indeed alive, well and in possession of his faculties, he will provide all the explanation that you require."

"He is ill and old," the priest said, "but by all accounts he is still sane. I will take his word if he swears that you are his."

Averil nodded briefly. She handed her horse's reins to the guard who stood nearest, swept up Gereint with her glance and turned toward her father's rooms.

LITTLE HAD CHANGED in the citadel, either, except the light seemed subtly dimmer and the packs of suitors were gone. Most of the court had dispersed to its own business; it would return as autumn advanced, but these days only the clerks and the standing guard and the determined layabouts lingered in the duke's hall. A thin strain of music wafted from their midst, a slow lament in a minor key.

Gamelin's arrival woke a flurry. People hastened to get out of his way. The song broke off on a painfully sour note.

That was another count against the king and his followers. Averil added it to the reckoning.

Her father's door was guarded by men who eyed Gamelin with no love at all. They recognized Averil and Gereint; she saw the flash of gladness quickly veiled. It warmed her heart a little, even as it deepened her wariness.

She was on perilous ground here: as dangerous in its way as the Field of the Binding. She steadied herself inside and out, made sure both magic and courage were near at hand and ventured through the door that the guards had opened.

THE OPPRESSION THAT weighed down the rest of the city lay somewhat lighter here. And yet Averil could not be glad of that. The smell of sickness caught at her throat. Her father might be alive, but he was not well.

Duke Urien lay on a couch in his study. A fire burned hot and strong in the hearth, but it barely managed to lift the chill. He had been reading: there was a book in his blanketed lap. His eyes were closed, his gaunt face turned toward the fire.

The Knight Commander Bernardin sat beside him, erect as if at attention, likewise focused on the flames. Neither chose to acknowledge Father Gamelin. It was prisoners' defiance, but it had its satisfactions.

Averil and Gereint were another matter. Bernardin rose. The duke was too weak, but he stretched out his hands. "Daughter. Oh, by the saints and Paladins. Daughter, what are you doing?"

She took those thin, cold hands and let them draw her into a trembling embrace. "I had to come back," she said. "I couldn't leave you to die alone."

"This is a pit of snakes," he said. "You would have been safer anywhere else than here."

"This is where I belong." She knelt by his couch with his hands still folded in hers. "Father, has he been torturing you?"

"Not at all," the duke said. "Rather the opposite, in fact. He ignores us fairly completely."

"That will stop," she said. Her glance flashed toward Gamelin. "Now."

The priest was watching with interest. Averil hoped he saw enough to satisfy him.

"You can tell the king," she said to her father, but also to Gamelin, "that there's no need for him to stay longer. Your heir has come back from the exile you enforced upon her. Paternal fondness and fear for her safety made you command her servant to wear the glamour of her face and die in her name. That's over. We'll live by the truth now. I trust we'll not die by it."

"Daughter," her father said. "Averil. I should never have summoned you here. Such a plan as I had—so clever, I thought, but it was an old man's folly. Can you forgive me?"

"There's nothing to forgive," she said. "All of this was meant to be. It may even come to good in the end."

"Pray God it will," he said. He raised a trembling hand to stroke her hair. "It is good to see you, even with the fear I have for you. I can't be glad you came back, but I can be glad to look on your face again."

Averil bent to kiss his forehead. His skin was cold. He was clinging to life by a thread.

She fed him as much strength as she could, not caring that the sorcerer watched, but it was a grudging trickle. After too short a while, it stopped.

Her father's eyes stared into hers. She did not want to understand what they were saying. He was dying; he had accepted that. She could not force him back to life again.

Now that she was here in spite of all his objections, he could let go. There was an heir of the blood to rule in Fontevrai.

He would not die tonight. That much comfort she could take to her cold rooms and her unfamiliar bed. She made sure he was at ease when she left, with a warm posset in him and his Lord Protector standing guard over him.

Bernardin would speak with her later—but not until she had rid herself of the king's spy. She hoped that was possible; that a lady's bower and her professed indisposition therein would be enough.

She need not have troubled herself. Outside the door of the duke's chambers, Gamelin bowed over her hand. "I see, lady, that you are who you claim to be. I shall assure the king of this. He'll rejoice to know that his sister's daughter still lives."

Averil bent her head. She knew better than to believe that the false priest was as easily satisfied as that. He must have decided to play the game through to its end.

So had she. She did not trust any words she might have said; she judged it best to resort to regal silence.

Then at last he took himself away. Half of his soldiers followed. Half, she was unsurprised to see, did not. Nor did they respond to her dismissal.

She could have enforced it, but that would give away too much. She had no choice but to suffer them and hope that in her own rooms as in her father's, they would take station outside and not follow her in.

39

The king's slave-soldiers stayed on the far side of the door. Averil made sure that Gereint did not. Her rooms—the rooms Emma had lived in, that Averil had known only with a servant's eye—were clean and carefully kept but empty of living presence.

Whoever the servants were who had lit the fires and kept the floors swept and turned down the coverlet of the high carved bed, they had not stayed to bask in her approval. There was no maid to wait on her; no one was there to tell her where Jennet had gone.

Averil had done without a maid for most of her life; she hardly needed one now. But there were certain trappings expected of a duke's heir, and that was one of them. In the next day or two, with so much else, she would have to see to it.

Tonight the bed was wide and soft, and there was a warming pan inside it. She had meant to find a less ostentatious place to sleep, but this too was expected of her.

Gereint was not. There was no one to take exception to his presence in the room or tut disapproval when he retrieved a maid's cot from one of the smaller rooms and set it firmly across the door.

A bath was waiting, still magically warm, and food enough for both of them. Averil insisted that Gereint take his share of both—after her if he insisted, but there was plenty.

While he splashed in the bathing room, Averil sat by the fire, wrapped in a warm robe, combing out her hair. She lingered over the long strokes; her eyes took in the luxuries of this room that was meant to be hers.

There was glass everywhere. It was natural; the heirs of the blood had been mages from the beginning. And yet so much had been destroyed and so much corrupted that to see all this pure and unsullied magic was almost startling.

This was magic as it had been before the king's stroke fell. Sparks and glimmers of it ran all through those rooms, hanging from beams and gleaming in windows and climbing in bright figures up the doorposts and along the edges of the hearth. Mirrors shone on the walls, and intricate workings in glass and enamel ornamented shelves and tables and niches between the tapestries.

Averil turned slowly where she sat, taking it all in. She did not remember half of what was here; much of what she did, she had seen in her father's rooms or scattered through the palace.

It was all gathered in this one place within protections both strong and subtle. Much of the room's warmth sprang from it. So did the sense that she was safe; that nothing could touch her.

Magic had betrayed her kind too often before for her to rest secure in this. And yet her heart persisted in telling her that it was true. Her father and Bernardin had made this a haven—whether they foresaw that she would come back or because they did not think the king would look for such treasures in the kingdom of women.

As she contemplated what they had done, she began to feel oddly short of breath. There was too much glass; too much magic. Too much protection.

The urge to shatter it rose until it was nigh on overwhelming. She throttled it down before it erupted. That was the wild magic in her, twisting her mind, making her see the world all awry.

She hung in balance between the two halves of her. The many workings stirred and glimmered. Past the sense of oppression was one of . . . freedom?

There were layers on layers of magic in this room, so many that each time she thought she had seen them all, another came clear. The same was true of the magic in her. Wild magic and magic of the orders could not exist in the same place. And yet they did—in her.

Gereint emerged from the bathing room, damp and flushed,

with his hair standing on end. The robe he was wrapped in was too short and narrow, but somehow it did not look absurd. He sat at the table where their dinner still steamed gently and began to fill a plate.

Her stomach pinched tight. She was suddenly, ravenously hungry.

She sat across from him and reached for a bowl. She snatched mouthfuls while she filled it, until the edge was off her hunger. Then she ate more politely and drank the wine that had been watered and made pungent with spices.

They were strong spices, well measured, meant to clear the head and focus the mind. They did not encourage her to overindulge in the wine, but what she did drink had the effect that was intended—and maybe one that was not. The balance of magics within her wavered and then set strongly, two halves of a powerful whole.

Gereint was still eating, but more slowly. She watched him, content in ways that she did not want just then to examine. Whatever tomorrow brought, tonight he was here. He was safe, as she was, and he seemed at ease.

That was new in him: he was comfortable wherever he was. He had brought it back from the Wildlands.

She liked it. It gave him substance. She could see the man he was going to be and the Knight he could be, if he still chose that path.

He might not. There was much more to him than that one kind and order of magic. The Rose might be too small for him, its powers too constricted.

She thought of saying that aloud, but decided against it. If he saw it, he did not need to be told. If not, he had to learn for himself.

Her brows drew together. She did not know if what struck her was prescience, but it had the taste of certainty.

She would ponder it and what it meant. But not tonight.

He sopped the last plateful with the last of the bread. When he was done, he sat back and sighed. "I'll last till morning now, I think."

She felt the laughter bubbling up in her. It had no single

source, but it was wonderful; delicious. She let it out in a shout of mirth.

There was nothing ladylike about it. She could not force herself to care. He was grinning, rocked back in the chair, with the firelight on his face and catching gold lights in his hair.

She was powerfully tempted to kiss him. But there was the table between, and she did not want to take the edge off the brightness. Temptation, for now, was enough.

That was heresy; she could burn for it. She only laughed the harder for the thought.

SHE TOOK THE thought with her to her warm and luxurious bed. The lamps dimmed; the fire burned low. Gereint's breathing by the door was soft and even.

She could have slipped in beside him. There was room, if they pressed close. She almost did; almost yielded.

Maybe she should have. She would regret it in the morning—but she would have had the night.

She could never marry this man. It did not matter if she loved him or lusted after him or was the other half of him. The world she had chosen by coming here was no world that would allow them to be together. Even if she changed it, she could not change it that much. Not in time for them.

She could be angry or she could grieve. Or she could look the truth in the face.

What they had, they had. Someday it might be more—or it might never be. Whatever end they came to, they could make the most of it.

She started to rise, but sleep fell on her, strong and sudden. She was safe, her last thought murmured. Nothing could touch her here. That was why . . . that was how . . .

40

L ady."
   Averil did not recognize the voice or the face that went
with it. They belonged to a woman in a servant's gown. She
looked as if she had been weeping.

"Lady," the servant said, "the Lord Protector says please
come."

Averil struggled for coherence. There was light beyond the
shutters, but it was wan and grey. Rain pattered against the
glass.

It had been raining for three days. She was proud of herself
that she could count that far.

The servant was too well trained to dance with impatience,
but her voice was sharp. "Lady! Wake up, I beg you."

Averil dragged herself out of bed. Gereint was at the door,
up and dressed and so grim that her heart tried to stop.

She did not feel so safe now. The sense of suffocating
closeness, of protections gone beyond all need or comfort,
swelled up again.

It was not about her magic, either half of it. It was about deception; blindness. Letting herself be coddled in this so-safe
place while the world spun on without her.

She ran past them both, not caring that she wore nothing
but a loose robe.

DUKE URIEN LAY still and cold. There was no sign of murder, no blood or marks of struggle. He looked as if the life had
simply and softly slipped out of him.

Averil rounded on the lot of them: clerks and priests and servants, guards, a courtier or two who looked as if he had caroused the night through, Bernardin and Gereint and the archbishop of Fontevrai who swept in with cope and crozier and caught the full force of her fury.

He rocked back in the doorway. His soul was secure in his body; he was no more corrupt than a prince of the Church would naturally be.

She was far too angry to care. "This is murder! Who did it? Tell me!"

"Lady," said Bernardin, "he was exhausted; his strength was gone. Once you had come, he could rest."

She shook her head fiercely. "He was not dying last night. He was ill and old, but there was still life left in him. Something— or someone—drained it out of him. Look at him! Does he look as if he died a natural death?"

"This is how the dead look," said Bernardin. He rose stiffly and held out his hand. "Lady, I grieve with you. But there was no murder done here."

"You are blind," she said. She shook him off and glared down anyone else who might try to comfort her. "Send for the king. Be polite if you have to, but get him here."

"Lady—" That was the archbishop: Bernardin had set his lips together.

"Send for the king," Averil repeated, so quietly that they all flinched.

Better yet, one of the clerks obeyed her, turning and bolting in a flurry of frayed gown and angular limbs. She marked his face for later, to reward or punish as he deserved.

She was the duchess now. That thought was very clear. The king's dog Gamelin was witness to her name and lineage. Bernardin would testify to it.

The rest of them would accept it. They had no choice.

She sat beside her father's bed—his deathbed. Everything about him and it declared that Bernardin was right; Urien had died as old men do. Averil's delusion was born of her own exhaustion and her ordeal in exile. There was no foulness in her father's death.

Her heart insisted that was a lie. She was learning to trust that subtle voice.

The crowd of people watched her as if she had been a snake coiled to strike. When she did not move or speak, one by one they dared to move, going about the duties of a duke's deathbed.

The archbishop spoke the words of blessing and farewell to the soul that was already hours gone. The clerks recorded them; the servants stood by to wash the body and prepare it for burial.

Two of the servants were women, and they had brought clothes for her. For a long while she ignored them, but when the archbishop had performed his rite and the servants' waiting had become conspicuous, she let herself be taken to an inner room.

Gereint and Bernardin were still on guard over her father. Bernardin might not believe her and Gereint might not be sure, but they honored both Averil and the duke with loyalty.

It was better than nothing. She stood while the two servants dressed her, combed and plaited her hair and made her fit to receive a king. One was grim-faced and silent. The other wept softly as she worked, but her hands were steady.

The servants had loved Duke Urien. They did not know Averil at all. She could feel these two reserving judgment.

She would have to change that. She began by relaxing the tension inside her, letting the anger coil deep, out of sight. It was not appropriate to smile, but she thanked them kindly for their service.

The grim one grunted. The sorrowful one took no notice. But they would remember. Servants always did.

KING CLODOVEC TOOK only until noon to answer Averil's summons: proof of how much weight he granted it. He found the duke laid in state in his hall, clothed in royal garb under a pall of cloth of silver.

Averil sat at the dead man's feet. Her chair was one of the ducal chairs, lower than the throne on the dais behind her but unmistakable in its authority. Its wood was ebony inlaid with silver; jeweled spells glittered in the back and arms. The duke's coronet lay in her lap. It was a simple thing, a circlet of silver inset with a dark star sapphire as large as an infant's fist.

The heart of the duchy was enclosed within the stone, both its magic and its humanity. When she touched it, it was as warm as flesh but hard and smooth like the bones of earth.

The first Mass of the dead had been sung. The second would be sung at nightfall. The rites of mourning were begun. The choir that chanted over the duke's body had completed half the psalms of their office.

Even the king could not interrupt their prayers. He had to wait, standing in silence, through two more long hours and an hour of priestly blessings thereafter.

Averil enjoyed his discomfiture rather too much, even while her own body stiffened in its seat and hunger and less noble bodily functions niggled for attention. But those she could face. Her years on the Isle had taught her the art.

As the choir departed in procession, with acolytes ahead of it and priests behind and a cloud of incense to bear it away, she let her eyes come at last to rest on her mother's brother.

By ancient custom the kings of Lys cultivated the long hair and elaborately curled beard of their first ancestors. For some, tales said, that was merely an inconvenience. For others it was a matter of pride; and for a few, of fashion.

It seemed clear which of those this king had chosen. He affected a robe of extravagant silk in a style as antique as the rest of him, with sleeves so long they trailed to the floor, hemmed with golden bells that jingled as he moved. His hair and beard were oiled and perfumed; his cheeks were touched with rouge like a court lady's.

Beneath it all he was by no means ill to look at. His features were fine, his skin clear; his blue eyes were wide-set under level brows. He could have seemed as innocent as Gereint, except for the shadow of discontent that lurked deep in his eyes.

He was born with it, or so it was said. For all the beauty of his body and the strength of his magic, his heart had failed to grow as it should. It was a tiny and twisted thing.

Averil looked into her enemy's face. That he was the enemy, and that he was not at all the foppish fool he seemed, she was certain. Whoever acted in his name, whatever was done, it came back to him. Her father's death, the destruction of the Rose, the fall of every great lord and lady in the kingdom of Lys, lay at his door.

She had not risen to greet him. This was her domain; though Clodovec be king and liege lord, it was proper that he should stand and she should sit in the presence of the dead.

She held out her hand. He took it in a light cool clasp. She had half expected his hands to be clammy, but they were dry, as were the lips that brushed her skin.

The touch was like the flick of a snake's tongue: swift and surprisingly soft. She fought the urge to recoil. When he let her hand go, she reclaimed it with dignity. "My lord," she said.

"My lady," he said in a beautifully modulated voice. "I grieve with you."

That was the proper formula. It would have been proper for her to murmur thanks.

She chose not to be proper. She arched a brow. "Do you?"

"Lady," he said, "he was my kinsman. I honored him; he had my respect."

"That I believe," she said. "He was honored, I'm sure, by the presence of your army in his city. Now that I am back from the dead and he has taken my place there, we have no more need of your . . . protection. I shall be pleased to provide an escort for all of you tomorrow morning, out of my city and to the borders of my duchy."

"Ah, lady," said the king with no sign of offense, "your grief is strong; of course you would wish to nurture it in solitude. But this is not your Isle. Here, we proceed differently. It would dishonor your father's memory if I were to abandon him before his funeral rites are complete."

"On the contrary, my lord," Averil said, "it would honor him exceedingly if you were to remove your forces—all of them—from his demesne and bid him farewell from beyond his borders. Tomorrow, my lord. Today you may bid him farewell as we all do, with prayer and fasting."

"Is that the way of the Isle, then?" he asked.

She looked for signs of anger, but either he was a master of concealment or he felt none. She listened for the sound of evil, the slither of scales or the hint of a hiss, but there was nothing. There was, emphatically, nothing.

That shook her in spite of herself. She could not be blind now—she could not afford to. She struggled to answer his question coolly. "It is my way. I thank you for accommodating yourself to it."

"Suppose that I do," he said. "Between rulers there is always exchange. What do you offer in return?"

"My respect," she said.

"Ah," said the king. "That's a great gift. But I have five hundred men in your city and ten thousand outside your borders, and I am your liege lord. A proper exchange would require a fraction more."

"You have two thousand men within my borders," she said, "though only five hundred of them may wear your livery. All of them will go, my lord. In return . . ." She let her voice trail off.

He saw the game: it seemed to amuse him. "In return?" he asked.

"In return, when the full time of mourning is over, I will come to court to perform my duty, as a vassal must do."

"And so you should, lady," he said, "but that is a requirement, not a gift. In what do you believe that duty to consist?"

"My oath of fealty to you as liege lord," she said, "and my presence in your court and council as is mandated under the law."

He inclined his head. "So it is. But you forget one thing."

Her breath caught. She hoped he did not hear it. "And that is?"

"Why, lady," he said, "of course you might not recall it, since the Isle practices no such thing and since you are so newly come to this world of courts and princes. It is required, lady, that each ruling lady take a husband to rule at her side, command her armies and serve as the strong right hand of her demesne."

"Ah," said Averil, throttling down the rush of relief. "Yes. I am aware of that. But there is no requirement that I must choose a husband immediately—only that I do so in due time."

"Choose one now," said the king, "and I will go with all my men this very night."

She met his bland gaze. He was smiling faintly. That was impossible and he knew it.

"Suppose," she said, "that I give my father his full mourning—a year and a day, no more and no less. Then I shall consider the suitors whom you present."

His brows rose. "I may present them?"

"Or they may present themselves."

"That," he said after a moment, "is a gift."

"Yes," said Averil.

"In the year of your mourning," he said, "you will conduct yourself in all ways as a proper ruler of a demesne under the crown of Lys. When the year is past, I shall present suitors of my choosing."

"That is so," she said.

"I will choose well," he said, "for my sister's child."

"I'm sure," said Averil.

"Done, then," said the king. "Tonight we share the vigil over the dead. Tomorrow I take my leave, with honor and respect."

Averil met those mild blue eyes. There was no guile in them; no hint of serpent subtlety. And yet her skin was crawling. The pendant under her shift, Gereint's conspicuously unmagical gift, had grown strangely warm.

Something was whispering just out of hearing. It could not be the king: he was directly in front of her, smiling faintly and saying nothing. None of his followers showed any sign of speech.

But someone somewhere close was trying to work a spell. If she slid her eyes sidelong she could see the shape of it, twining tendrils to tangle a soul in.

No wonder the king had given way so easily. He thought he could make sure of her.

It was fascinating to watch the spell take shape around her. Too much so. It almost snared her with her own curiosity. But for the sudden, searing heat above her heart, she would have slipped and fallen into it.

She dared not let him think he had failed. She let her eyes lose focus, her smile grow vague. "Majesty," she said.

His smile deepened with satisfaction. Once more he bowed over her hand. "My lady," he said.

Maybe she imagined it, but she thought he laid the slightest hint of stress upon that *my*.

He could dream. She would encourage it. She sat with hard-fought placidity while he took station at the head of the bier.

There was a long ordeal ahead of her. She had to hope she was strong enough to survive it.

41

"C lever," said Bernardin. "Perhaps too much so."

The vigil was over, the dead entrusted to the priests and monks who would chant through the night. Averil was allowed a few hours' rest before she had to return to her post in the hall. She was exhausted almost beyond words, but she had to stay upright and face her Lord Protector.

Bernardin had followed her to her chambers, ostensibly as escort, but she could feel the emotions roiling beneath the surface. Such loss of control was rare in a Knight of any rank; it told her how sorely taxed he was, between grief and long endurance.

Once they were alone but for Gereint silent by the door, he said what he had come to say. "You bargained well, lady, but have you given away more than you can afford to give?"

She resisted the urge to snap at him; to rail at his blindness. "I haven't given a thing," she said. "I've promised to consider the suitors he'll present. I haven't agreed to marry any of them."

"He will say you have."

"That," she said, "is why I spoke with him in front of witnesses, over my father's body. My clerks have written it exactly as it was spoken. That's what we agreed to, and that's what both of us will have to abide by."

"If he stops to think about the words you spoke," said Bernardin, "or if he has another and deeper reason for letting them be spoken in that way, you've gained nothing, and maybe lost it all."

He was remarkably close to the truth, but Averil was not

inclined to tell him so. "Maybe that's so," she said, "but in the meantime I'm rid of him for a year, and all his slaves and servants with him. We'll pray that year will give me time to secure Quitaine against him."

"He thinks he has you," Bernardin said. "Does he?"

Averil met his dark stare. "Do I look as if he does?"

"Looks deceive," he said.

"So they do," said Averil. "Yes, he tried to enspell me. He thinks he succeeded. That will protect us for a while."

"Beware overconfidence," Bernardin said.

That startled a smile out of her, brief but warm. "Rest well, my Lord Protector. I'm as terrified as you could wish; but I'm not without defenses. By tomorrow night this duchy will be rid of the king and all his minions. We'll see to the rest once that's done."

"Be sure it is done," he said.

"Will you help me?"

"Of course."

He said it without hesitation. His back had straightened; the pall of age and sorrow that had lain on him had lifted a little. For all his objections, he had gained strength from her defiance.

That was what she had hoped for. "Tonight," she said, "rest as you can. Heal as much as you may. Tomorrow, see to it that when the king leaves, all of his servants leave with him. Do you understand? Can you recognize them?"

"The soulless ones," he said. "Yes. I'm not completely blind, lady. I knew what he was doing. I should have fought against him, but—"

"You did all you knew how to do," she said.

"That's the trouble, isn't it? With all my learning, my mastery, everything I was, I had nothing left once my order was broken. We had a glaring weakness; we never saw it until it destroyed us."

"That's past," Averil said. "My coming here was no accident and no mistake. Nor was my father's sending me away. Exactly where we went and what we did, I'll tell you when the air is clean again and the enemy is gone. I learned much;

I saw more that I'm only beginning to understand. We can pray it will show us the way."

Bernardin bowed low as to a queen. "I'll pray for that, lady, with all my heart."

AFTER BERNARDIN HAD gone, Averil waited for Gereint's remonstrance. But he said nothing. He drew his bed across the door as he had the night before and lay in it.

Averil should have let be. This might be her last night of peace and near-solitude before flocks of maids and servants came to attend her. She needed to rest above all, and to reflect; she needed to pray that her plan had succeeded, and that the king truly would leave as he had promised.

She stood over the bed and looked down on the apparently sleeping body. "Tell me what's wrong," she said.

He was going to ignore her, she could tell. But she let her presence press upon him until he began to wriggle, then to toss. Finally he sat up, glaring at her. "There's nothing wrong," he said, shaping each word with vicious care.

"Then why are you so angry?" she asked.

"I'm not—"

She folded her arms and let the moment stretch.

He was not strong enough to hold against that. His glare barely softened, but the edge was off his voice. "It's nothing. Really it's not."

"Tell me," she said.

He shrugged. He was so seldom sullen or withdrawn that it was striking to see. "Bernardin is right. You've won nothing. Maybe you fought off the spell he tried to weave in the hall, but he'll leave more spells and spies, too many for you to find or fight. Then when the year is up, you'll be forced to marry the man he chooses. He's playing with you as a snake plays with its prey, to make it warm and full of fear before he swallows it."

"Ah," said Averil in sudden understanding. "You're angry because I didn't tell you what I planned—and then I didn't ask for help."

"That's not what I—"

"I had to do it," she said. "I couldn't risk letting him discover what you are—what we are. I had to make him think I'm just like all the others of my kind."

"At any cost?"

"At the lowest cost I could," she said, "but these things always have a price."

"You can't do this alone," he said. "I thought that was the lesson you brought back with you. But you didn't learn a thing."

"I learned that there is more to magic than the orders can imagine, and that there is more hope than I might have thought. You are part of that hope. So is Bernardin, and this city that, even with the king in the heart of it, has kept its soul."

He shook his head stubbornly. "You still haven't learned to look outside yourself."

She drew a careful breath. "I'm sorry," she said, "that I didn't fight this out with you before I did it. Can you at least understand that I had to do it?"

"I understand that you think so," he said. "I don't think it's going to be as easy as it seems. Even with the spell he tried to cast on you, he hardly put up a fight. Which means he sees some advantage in letting you have your way, or at least no disadvantage."

"Of course he does," she said. "He can go on to his next target. I'm as safe here as if I were in prison. He may gamble with the chance that I find a way out of it, or that someone else disposes of him, or his own magic destroys him. A great deal can happen in a year."

"That's what I'm afraid of," said Gereint.

She set her hands on his shoulders. He was too solid to shake, but she could tighten her fingers until there was no way he could ignore her. "I promise you," she said, "I'll do nothing rashly. I'll let Bernardin protect me and depend on my guards and servants. I won't be alone."

He met her eyes steadily. The sullenness had gone out of him. In its place was unhappy conviction. "You haven't mentioned me at all."

Averil's heart twinged with guilt. Of course he had seen it, though she had concealed it as well as she knew how. "You're always in my mind," she said.

He shook that off with the brusqueness it deserved. "You're going to send me away."

"Not with the king," she said.

That did not trick a smile out of him. "You don't want me here. You don't think I'm safe. But *you* will stay."

"That's not true at all," she said. "I do want you to go— back to the Knights, to learn everything they have to teach. You shouldn't give it up for me."

"My magic is with you," he said. "You can teach me. You can—"

"I can't teach you to be a Knight," she said, "and a Knight is what I need most. Bernardin is old; he's strong, but he can't protect me forever. I need you to be here when he's no longer able to be Lord Protector."

That startled him speechless. She could not see why: it was perfectly logical. But he was taken aback. "I can't do that," he said. "I can't abandon you."

"You can go where it's laid on you to go," she said. "I'll stay where I'm fated to stay."

"I can't," he said. "I can't leave you."

"Yes," she said. "You can. Because you must." She laid her hand over the warmth that still rested against her heart. "A part of you is always with me and always will be, no matter where you go or how long you are gone. Believe that, dearest friend. Trust it."

The misery in his eyes told her he saw it as clearly as she, but he did not want to at all. It wrenched at her heart, too, but she could be hard and cold when necessity demanded. She had seen what she must do and how, and this was as vital a part of it as the king's dismissal.

"If I go," he said after a painful while, "will you promise me something?"

"If I can," she said.

"Promise you'll let the wildfolk in. When the enemy is

gone, when the duchy is safe, open the door. Keep your promise to them. They'll watch over you when I can't."

She shivered. After all she had seen and done, she still could not think of wild magic without that shudder in the skin. But she said, "I'll try."

"You'll do it," he said, "or I won't go. I'll live in the stables if I have to, or forage in the streets. I won't leave you unguarded."

"Bernardin—"

"Unguarded," he repeated, "by powers that can overcome whatever the enemy may raise against you."

She could not invoke the Knight against that, and he knew it. "I'll open the door," she said, "after the enemy goes. I'll make this palace a haven for them. But—"

His finger stopped her lips. "No buts. No excuses. You blinded the king to the truth, but I know you too well. You'll do exactly what you promise, or I won't be the only one to exact a price. The Mother is much older and less forgiving than I am."

Cold walked down her spine. Of all the bargains she had made, that was the most perilous. It could save them all—or it could destroy them. She doubted that the Mother cared which.

From the day she left the Isle, she had trapped herself in webs within webs. She could only do as she judged best and keep the promises she had made—even the most difficult of them.

Letting Gereint go was one of those. Letting the wild magic in . . . not so much. But difficult enough.

She would do it because she must. It was not she who had forced these changes in the order of the world. If every human creature was not to go the way of the king's slave soldiers, she had to do everything she could to stop him.

She could not focus on that for too long or it would overwhelm her. Step by step, day by day: so she had learned to wield her magic, and Gereint would learn to wield his.

He would come back. Alive or dead, Knight or servant, he

would find her again. She was as sure of that as she was of anything in this world.

Tonight she would sleep. Tomorrow she would make sure that the king kept his word—all of it. Whatever came after, she would face it as it came. She would be ready for it.

42

The king rode out of Fontevrai in the grey morning. He put on a brave show, dressed in golden armor that had a brassy gleam in that light, with his escort clattering around him and his banners flying. Their long column wound like a snake through the streets of the city to the northward gate.

Averil watched them go from the tower of the citadel, standing by the parapet with Gereint tall and silent behind her. From there she could see not only the king riding out but the rest of his army breaking camp beyond the walls. Row by row their tents fell; they drew up in ranks, shadowy in the fog.

Others marched to join them. Bernardin had seen to that, assisted by the handful of mages whom he still trusted. The slave soldiers had been stripped of whatever badges they wore, but none of the mages knew how to unmake the spell that was on them.

It grieved Averil to see them go, marching stiffly in unison, without life or soul to animate them. They were a horror and an abomination; more than any other act or working short of freeing the Serpent itself, they would damn the men who had made them.

She had deliberately chosen not to bid her uncle farewell. It was an insult to the royal majesty, but she did not care. She had given him as much of herself as she could.

There was a bit of cowardice in it, too, and more than a bit of caution. If she did not confront him again, he could not challenge the bargain they had made. He would not see that his spell had failed; that her mind and soul were her own.

He seemed to have expected the slight. He neither came to her nor sent a messenger. Nor did he look back as he rode, to catch sight of her high above him.

She wanted to say that he slunk out, but he rode in pride as a king should. Outside the gate he paused. His trumpeters raised their instruments to their lips and blew a fanfare. The brazen voices mocked her with a torrent of echoes.

That, she had expected—but she did not have to suffer it in silence. She had brought her own weapon with her: the choir of the duke's chapel. At her nod, they raised supernally sweet voices in a psalm of thanksgiving. It drowned out the trumpets, soaring over the towers and spires and up toward heaven.

It was more than a prayer; it was a spell of healing. It spread outward from her tower and pursued the king down the long road to the northern border. It cleansed the land behind him and scoured away the stain of his presence.

It was a mighty working. Once begun, it took on a life of its own, drawing power from the earth and from the hearts of the people who lived in the towns and villages. It wove itself into a protection so strong and yet so airily light that Averil contemplated it in awe.

There was wild magic in it. Even though a psalm of the new order had begun it, other, older Powers had joined it. They had been waiting, sleeping in the earth until one came who could wake them.

The door had opened before she knew what she had done. Her presence here and Gereint's with her, and all that she had done and said and promised, came together in this hour, under this sky, on this earth for which she had been born. Her father's body below, and his soul secure from any devouring spell, made it all the stronger.

She reached behind her to the familiar warmth that was Gereint. His fingers laced with hers. It would be a tearing pain to let him go; but it had to be.

He was here for a few days yet: until her father was laid in his tomb and the king was gone from the duchy. She would make the most of what time they had.

The wild magic approved of that: it rose up around her in swirls and gusts of sudden wind, plucking at her skirts and tugging her hair out of its regal coils, sending it tumbling down her back.

The choir's voices rang bell-clear around her. Voices even clearer, high and inhuman, echoed and reechoed above them.

The air was full of wings. Wings of doves; wings of eagles. Great shining creatures rent the clouds asunder and cast them away.

Her choristers stared upward in astonishment too pure for fear. One or two voices faltered, but the great ones bore them up until they found their strength again. Their awe washed over her, tinged with delight. This they would never forget, though they lived a hundred years: that they had sung with angels, and heaven itself had smiled upon Quitaine.

A shaft of sunlight struck Averil full in the face, enfolding her in splendor. She felt as clear as glass, as transparent as water. All magics were contained in her.

She was the heart of this land; its soul was in her care. Gereint was her anchor, her strength and her protection. That would always be there through the bond that they shared, even when he was far away, safe from the king and his sorceries, learning to be the Knight that he was meant to be.

That knowledge comforted her beyond measure. She truly belonged here; this country was her destiny. Yet Gereint was the other half of her.

She turned toward him, not caring who saw, and kissed the hand that enfolded hers. There was a long war ahead, and perhaps a bitter ending. But they would fight with all the strength that was in them.

The light filled them both. She could not see defeat there, nor doubt or fear or any other dark thing. The Rose would rise again and stand against the Serpent as it had from the old time.

And then, who knew? It was a new world she saw ahead of her, with wonders and terrors that beggared imagination. They frightened her—but she could not find it in her to run away from them.

Either she was brave or she was mad. Just then, it did not matter. Quitaine was free—for a while—and so was she. The good God and the old Powers together would look after the rest.

⌒

Here ends the first book of the War of the Rose.
Deis gratias.

Turn the page for a preview of

Golden

Rose

KATHLEEN BRYAN

Coming in March 2008

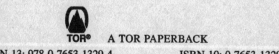

TOR®   A TOR PAPERBACK

ISBN-13: 978-0-7653-1329-4   ISBN-10: 0-7653-1329-4

The ladies smiled. They might have been three faces of the same woman, young and middle-aged and old. Averil had no doubt they were kin—as she was herself. They were all children of Paladins.

Mathilde was not so very much older than she. Next in age was Darienne, and eldest of them all was Richildis. Each was the wife of a high lord, a duke or a count, and high in the king's court.

Averil vaguely remembered their faces. They had done nothing to draw her attention, but clearly they had been watching her.

The Duchess Richildis held out a hand as smooth and pale as ivory. "Come, lady," she said. "Sit by me."

There was room beside her on the stone bench, not too uncomfortably close but familiar enough. Averil sat stiffly upright and folded her hands in her lap as she had done so often before the Lady of the Isle.

This lady recognized the posture: her brows rose slightly, and the corner of her mouth curved upward. "We're all equals here," she said. "All well schooled, none initiate, brought home to marry as the law decrees."

That was true, but Averil doubted it was the whole of the truth. There was too much power here, so quiet it might have seemed nothing at all, but her bones felt the force of it.

This place, she realized with a shiver down the spine, was perfectly warded. The shape and color of each bed of flowers mirrored exactly one of the panels of the roundel above

Richildis' head. Any magic that entered here would be perfectly contained.

The Serpent's prison could be such a place. All that twisted magic would coil on itself within such rigid order and be altogether powerless.

Magic of the orders belonged here. The three ladies bloomed like the roses trained in perfect lines and corners upon the lattice of a trellis.

Averil should have been as much at home as they. She caught herself wishing for a mob of wildfolk, no two of them alike, leaping and tumbling through the too-clear air.

She was corrupted. She looked into those clear eyes and those exquisitely well-bred faces. They were so like her own, and yet, within, so profoundly different.

Or were they different? What did she know of her own kind, after all? The Isle had been home all her life. This world she had been forced into was stranger with every breath she drew. She had been raised to work magic, not to be a courtier.

So too with these. It was not Mathilde in whom she found that answer. It was the one neither young nor old: Darienne. She had neither Mathilde's native warmth nor Richildis' wisdom, but something in her called to Averil.

Averil met eyes that at first seemed dark but in truth were deepest blue. She was not moved to smile, but her heart had eased.

"Tell me," she said out of that newborn quiet. "Why have you brought me here?"

"You brought yourself," said Richildis. "We merely offered the possibility."

"Why?"

"Because," Mathilde said, "every one of us has come to this place as you have, lost and ill prepared, while the wolves close in and the huntsmen watch and wait. We all found husbands, some sooner than others, and so will you. But more important than that, we found friendship."

"The three of you?" asked Averil.

"And more," said Richildis.

Averil nodded. That was logical. Courtiers, children of warriors that they were, liked to send outriders ahead of the army. Why should these be any different?

"If you would like," Mathilde said, "there is a gathering this morning. It's nothing dangerous, no meeting of conspirators: only a coming together of friends. Will you come?"

Neither of Averil's guardians appeared to object. It would not have mattered to her if they had, but she found it interesting. It was all interesting, and slightly disconcerting.

"I'll come," she said after not too significant a pause.

ONCE AVERIL HAD agreed to the adventure, Richildis rose and walked through the wall. Averil knew an instant's astonishment before the pattern of light flowed around her. It was cool, like a breath of wind; there was a faint singing in it.

The singing faded. Averil stepped out of the jeweled light into a sunlit hall. It was high and airy, with a breathless swoop of vaulting; the windows that marched around the circle of it were alive with many-colored magic.

It put her in mind of the Ladies' Chapel on the Isle, but this was much younger and brighter and more exuberant. It was like laughter given shape, or the taste of wine raised up in glass and stone.

Averil was gawping like a yokel at a fair. She lowered her eyes from the splendor of the vaulting to the human faces that watched her with interest and, here and there, a glimmer of mistrust.

They were all women, all ages, but all alike: they had the air of the Isle. Averil had never expected to see so many. There must have been a score of them, sitting on chairs or benches or standing at ease while a young woman played on a lute and a somewhat older one sang a sweet, sad song.

It could have been any lady's solar in this kingdom, though grander than most—except for the magic that shimmered all about it. Something, some taste of the air, told her that she was still in Lutèce and still in the cathedral: in the chapter house, perhaps, or what would be the chapter house when the ladies had no need of it. For the moment, no one could come here who was not shown the way.

Every woman here was a mage, and trained in the way of the Isle. Their presence together was power, strong enough to set Averil's bones humming.

Averil's guides found places in the circle, drawing her with them as the song wound slowly into silence. When it was done, Averil tensed, ready for the interrogation that she was sure would come. But after those first glances, whether curious or suspicious, they seemed to have forgotten her.

The singer withdrew into the circle. The player on the lute went on, weaving an intricate melody.

The circle flowed apart into smaller circles. A soft murmur of voices rose to the vaulting. Such snatches as Averil caught seemed harmless enough: bits of gossip, inquiries after husbands and children, daily commonplaces that seemed peculiarly exotic in this wonder of a hall.

Averil's guides had left her to her own·devices. She indulged in a moment's resentment, but she was too well trained after all: she saw what she had to do. She gathered her wits and her charm and such courtly arts as she had, and began the dance she had been brought here to perform.

It was not so difficult to be a courtier here. Averil was being shown how to move, how to speak, what to say. It was not obvious, but her senses were heightened, her awareness honed to a keen edge.

As she moved from circle to circle, she followed the signs: the lift of a brow, the tilt of a head, the slant of a word. Each face had a name, and each name belonged to a great lord of the realm, as did the lady who held it.

These were not chattel. There was power here, and not all of it was magic. While the men met in the king's council, their ladies met with much less fanfare.

"If there were a queen," Averil said, "she would be here. Wouldn't she?"